BEHIND THE SHATTERED GLASS

TASHA ALEXANDER

ISIS
LARGE
PRINT

First published in Great Britain 2016
by
Constable
an imprint of Little, Brown Book Group

First Isis Edition
published 2016
by arrangement with
Little, Brown Book Group
An Hachette UK Company

A catalogue record for this book is available
from the British Library.

ISBN 978–1–78541–243–1 (hb)
ISBN 978–1–78541–249–3 (pb)

Published by
F. A. Thorpe (Publishing)
Anstey, Leicestershire

Set by Words & Graphics Ltd.
Anstey, Leicestershire
Printed and bound in Great Britain by
T. J. International Ltd., Padstow, Cornwall

This book is printed on acid-free paper

33408793

For Jane, the sister I always wanted

Acknowledgements

Myriad thanks to . . .

Charlie Spicer, Andy Martin, Sarah Melnyk, April Osborn, India Cooper, Tom Robinson, and Anne Hawkins. You guys are the best in publishing.

Kate Dyson, Englishwoman extraordinaire, who gave Anglemore Park its name.

Ashley T. Hoffman, for the idea to have Eleutheria inscribed above the entrance to Anglemore.

Charles Cumming, for insider knowledge of all things Etonian.

Sarah Mackenzie, winner of the contest to name a character in this book. She was so good at it she wound up with two: Constance Sturdevant and Alice.

As always, my writer pals and dear friends, without whom this would be a lonely world: Brett Battles, Rob Browne, Bill Cameron, Christina Chen, Jon Clinch, Kristy Kiernan, Elizabeth Letts, Carrie Medders, Missy Rightley, Renee Rosen, and Lauren Willig.

Xander Tyska, who proves to be a more able research assistant with every passing year.

My parents, who are a constant inspiration.

Andrew, my everything.

I dared to rest, or wander, — like a rest
Made sweeter for the step upon the grass, —
And view the ground's most gentle dimplement,
(As if God's finger touched but did not press
In making England!) such an up and down
Of verdure, — nothing too much up or down,
A ripple of land; such little hills, the sky
Can stoop to tenderly and the wheatfields climb;
Such nooks of valleys, lined with orchises,
Fed full of noises by invisible streams;
And open pastures, where you scarcely tell
White daisies from white dew, — at intervals
The mythic oaks and elm-trees standing out
Self-poised upon their prodigy of shade, —
I thought my father's land was worthy too
Of being my Shakespeare's.

Elizabeth Barrett Browning, *Aurora Leigh*

CHAPTER
ONE

"This, Emily, goes beyond bad manners." Lady Catherine Bromley squared her shoulders, shook her head without displacing a single silver hair, and glowered at me, her only daughter. "One cannot have gentlemen falling down dead in the library, especially on an eighteenth-century Axminster carpet! It is entirely ruined; there is no possibility that bloodstain will come out. Such a thing would never be tolerated at Darnley House. What would your father say? I thank heaven that estate business took him home before he could see this."

"The dead are notoriously unreliable when it comes to standards of behavior," I said. "Particularly murder victims. They have no sense of decorum at all."

Another evening *en famille* at Anglemore Park.

Anglemore, prettily situated in Derbyshire in the midst of the Peak District, had been the seat of the Hargreaves family since Henry V's victory at Agincourt, after which the land had been given by the grateful king to one of my husband's ancestors for bravery in battle. During the reign of Henry VIII, the grounds, through a royal grant, expanded to include a nearby abbey, defunct after the Reformation and all but destroyed by Cromwell's men. Its ruins, perched near a large lake, were some of the most picturesque in all of England, as if the structure had crumbled with deliberately artistic intent. The main house, originally built in the fifteenth century, had been added to and altered over the years, leaving it now with an Elizabethan exterior replete with rows of the most charming bay windows, giving nearly every room a perfect nook for reading and none of the museum-like feel of so many great estates.

Anglemore was a house that was loved, a house that had sheltered the same family for more than four centuries. Generations of Hargreaves children (all born on the estate — no other location would be tolerated, even today) had carved their initials in the wooden bannister on the back stairs leading to the nursery. The family was rooted here, passionate about the land, deeply connected to their tenants, and confident beyond doubt that there was no better place to serve as one's anchor. Most of the family married in the chapel, and all of them were buried on the grounds in a towering mausoleum built in the late seventeenth century by a Hargreaves gentleman who, horrified by the Great Plague, determined he must make every effort to see his mortal remains well placed. In a letter written during the height of the epidemic, his wife, angry with him for spending what she viewed as too much time hunting, had threatened him with plague pits.

Today, despite tens of thousands of acres of land, a sizable house, and enough outbuildings to hold several villages, the estate felt nothing but crowded. Crowded by my visiting mother, the Countess Catherine

Bromley, whose inflexible views on child rearing, wholly at odds with my own, had not contributed to a state one could describe as domestic bliss. She had come to Anglemore months ago, following the birth of our twins, but had not stayed long, informing us she would return once the London Season had finished and after she had hosted at least two shooting parties. Only then, she said, would she have the presence of mind and clarity of concentration to ensure the children were being looked after properly. Now we were bearing the full brunt of this mission. Her visit had weeks ago taken on the feeling of an endless tour through one of Dante's less pleasant circles of hell.

The evening had started badly, with her complaining bitterly about each course at dinner. She had found fault with the game dish in particular, objecting to pheasant stuffed with foie gras for reasons wholly indecipherable to me. Afterward, we had retired to the library, where our second houseguest, Simon Lancaster, Earl Flyte, offered his apologies and went to bed after having been interrogated by her on the subject of politics. One could hardly blame the poor man. Unhappy with his views, she had hounded him, all but following him to his room when he at last excused himself. My husband, Colin Hargreaves, buried himself in James's *The Portrait of a Lady*, ignoring with deft skill my mother's litany of questions about his views on how our boys ought to be raised. She had, it seemed, either grown fatigued of political discussion or realized she would be incapable of besting him on the subject. Eventually forced to accept that she was quite unable to penetrate his wall, she turned her attention to reprimanding a housemaid for not having tended adequately to the fire — a fire I was not convinced we needed on such a fine night.

"There are infants in the house," my mother said. "I shall not allow Henry or Richard to catch a chill."

"Or Tom, Mother," I said. "You mustn't forget Tom." It was the presence of this third child, our ward, that caused my mother considerable agitation. "They are all two floors and one wing removed from us, not to mention in the care of an exceptionally capable nanny and her staff. I shouldn't worry if I were you. Furthermore, it is an unusually warm evening. They are more likely to be overheated than cold." To demonstrate the point, I crossed the room and flung open all six sets of French doors overlooking the neatly manicured terrace, its beds full of bright dahlias, chrysanthemums, and late asters. Autumn was at its best, a perfect September night. The sun had disappeared while we were in the dining room, leaving only a few streaks of gold in the inky sky. I pulled something to read down from the shelf without glancing at the title and installed myself in an overstuffed chair as far from the fireplace as possible. Nothing, I vowed silently, would distract me from this book.

Should it have become necessary, honoring this promise would have proved exceedingly difficult. The volume I had so carelessly chosen, a treatise on advanced mathematical theorems, had no hope of holding my attention for long, but it did not need to. No sooner had I soldiered through the introductory pages than the previously mentioned gentleman, tall and broad in his evening kit, staggered through one of the French doors. He braced himself on the frame, looked at Colin, took one step in his direction, and collapsed facedown on the floor.

My mother shrieked in a fashion so decidedly unladylike she would have been horrified to hear it. She swayed, unsteady on her feet, and appeared on the verge of fainting. I dashed to her side, took her firmly by the shoulders, and turned her to face me.

"Now is not the time, Mother," I said. "Do try to remember there are no smelling salts allowed in this house. Perish any thought you had of fainting."

The words — and, no doubt, my tone — shocked her into compliance, just as I had hoped. The color did not return to her visage, but she steeled herself, pulled her back straight, and looked away from the scene developing before us. There was no time to comfort her. We needed to focus on the injured man.

My husband, a trusted agent of the Crown and, hence, no stranger to trauma, disruption, and brutality, motioned for me to stay back while he knelt beside the prostrate stranger.

"His heart is not beating," Colin said, "and he is not breathing." His lips firm in a tight line, he closed the man's eyes. "I am afraid there is nothing to be done." I moved closer, standing behind him, watching as he carefully inspected the corpse for injuries.

"He is dead?" My mother's voice was rising to a screech. She pressed with trembling hands a linen handkerchief to her face. "This is too dreadful. I cannot bear it."

"Do try to be calm, Lady Bromley," Colin said. "Hysteria will help no one."

"There's a fierce scratch on his left hand," I said, ignoring my mother, who had started to sway again. This time I was willing to let her faint, although I doubted she would bother when the odds of anyone catching her were so low.

"He may have been fighting." Colin lifted the man's head to reveal a deep gash splitting the skull, blood congealing on the carpet beneath it.

"Have you any idea who he is?" I asked. "He is wholly unfamiliar to me."

"None," Colin said.

This admission revived my mother. She took a step towards us, made a point of forcing herself to look at the unfortunate corpse, and spoke, her voice loaded with a mixture of disgust and condescension. "That is Archibald Scolfield, the new Marquess of Montagu. He arrived from London yesterday. You ought to have known that, Emily, given that he's to be your nearest — and titled — neighbor. His cousin Matilda was hosting a party for him this evening. A party I believe you didn't bother to attend."

"No, I sent her our regrets," I said, noticing that my mother's face had gone an alarming shade of gray as she approached the body. She, unlike me, was not used to violent death. I had initially become close to Colin while trying to solve the murder of my first husband, Philip, Viscount Ashton. While embroiled in the case, I discovered I possessed a certain aptitude for the work, and had subsequently contributed to the arrests of six more violent criminals, earning for myself a reputation as a solid investigator. Colin and I, now married, made an excellent team, as even the Queen herself had been forced to admit on more than one occasion.

I stepped to the marble fireplace, over which hung a fragment of a Roman fresco depicting a joyful scene of marriage, and rang the bell next to it. "We ought to summon the authorities."

"The authorities?" The color rushed back into my mother's face. "Don't be absurd. Lord Montagu fell and hit his head, probably on a rock. Why on earth would you involve the police or sheriff or whatever unseemly sort of *authority* is to be found? Send for your personal physician and insist he sign a death certificate at once and be done with the dreadful business. Gentlemen ought not to be so cavalier about wandering around the countryside after dark."

"Nothing about this situation suggests an accident," Colin said. "I'm afraid we've no choice but to summon the police, Lady Bromley."

"Do you want a scandal?" she asked. "On your own estate?"

"Surely, Mother, you are not questioning my husband's judgment?" I asked. "I can assure you he —"

"It is quite all right, Emily," Colin said. "Your mother has nothing but the best of intentions. However, Lady Bromley, given my position, it is essential I report this incident with no delay. To do otherwise would be less than honorable. Perhaps you would like to retire upstairs for a bit? It will give you a chance to recover from the

7

shock of what has transpired. I shall send for you when the police are ready to speak to you."

"Speak to me?" My mother's eyes bugged. "Speak to me? As if I would be involved in such a thing."

"You saw Lord Montagu take his last breaths and collapse," I said. "The police will need to hear your description of what happened."

"I do not know why you are still standing here, Emily," she said. "If you believe there is some sort of criminal on the loose in the neighborhood who is going about murdering people, you ought to be ensuring the safety of your boys rather than embroiling yourself in an unsavory debacle utterly inappropriate for a lady. Children are always a mother's primary duty."

I took a deep breath and paused before replying. First and foremost, I knew I need not worry about the boys because they were in the hands of a most trustworthy nanny. Second, the idea that my mother, who had limited her involvement with her children up to the age of twelve to formal visits made once daily for not more than a quarter of an hour, would condemn me for relying on said nanny struck me as not a little hypocritical. I had always forgiven her neglect because she and my father had lost so many of their offspring to illness. I, the youngest, was the only one of seven to survive to adulthood. My mother had recovered from the death from influenza of my twin brothers, the only of my siblings I had ever known, by distancing herself even further from me until it was time to mold me into a sparkling debutante. "Perhaps you could take care of that for me. Nanny should be put on alert."

"I shall see to it at once," my mother said. "Heaven knows someone in this household ought to be concerned about what matters, rather than getting distracted by the details of some ridiculous alleged crime." She marched out, slamming the door behind her.

"I can't think of less propitious circumstances in which to find ourselves. She could impede an investigation before having her first cup of tea in the morning." I sighed. "One of us should go to Montagu and inform Matilda of what has happened."

"Would you be so kind as to handle that?" Colin asked. "You are better acquainted with her than I. I shall have Flyte come down and inquire whether he heard anything and then deal with the police when they arrive."

I nodded. "Of course. The police will doubtless respond better to you than to me. As for Matilda, I know all too well there is no good way to have this sort of conversation."

Matilda and I were not close friends, but our political beliefs, particularly those regarding suffrage, had thrown us together at meetings of the Women's Liberal Federation. We had worked to educate and enlighten the women in the district about their rights — that is, the rights we both believed they should have — and had organized several rallies on our estates. Our success could only be described as limited. While the women were captivated and energized, their husbands reacted to the issues with somewhat less enthusiasm. Through it all, our interaction had not escalated much beyond that of two business acquaintances. Nonetheless, it was appropriate that I, not my husband, speak to her about her cousin.

"Shall I bring her back here?" I asked. "She has a house full of guests whom I imagine the police will want to interview. It might be nicer for her to be in somewhat quieter surroundings."

"Quite," Colin said. "She may also wish to see Scolfield."

I shuddered. Colin gave me a quick kiss, and I set off, dread consuming me. I would never grow comfortable with the task of informing someone of the violent death of a loved one.

Matilda Scolfield's grandfather, the previous Marquess of Montagu, had outlived Matilda's father, making her cousin Archibald next in line for the title. The old man had not seen fit to settle upon his heir the significant fortune he had amassed during his lifetime. Instead, he left his money, a house in London, two in Scotland, and a seaside cottage on the southern coast to his favorite granddaughter. The only part of his estate entailed was Montagu Manor itself, and that was all Archibald got. This had proved no hardship to him, as he stood to inherit a sizable sum from his parents and was already the recipient of a generous allowance. He was a capable young man, cheerful and eager, who had distinguished himself well enough at Oxford (knowing himself incapable of getting a first, he avoided the dreaded second and secured the third that perfectly reflected his academic ambitions) and now devoted much of his time to sport, earning a reputation as a fine rower. *Had devoted much of his time.* I reminded myself it was now necessary to use the past tense when referring to Archibald Scolfield.

A festive atmosphere still filled Montagu Manor when I arrived, no one inside knowing yet of its owner's demise. I asked the butler to take me somewhere where I could speak privately to Matilda, and I informed her of the tragedy in the gentlest way I could. Her countenance did not change as I spoke, but a slight gasp escaped her lips. Maintaining her composure in the manner of the best Englishwomen, she went to the drawing room, explained to her guests what had happened, and asked for their patience when the police arrived. I bundled her into my carriage, and we returned to Anglemore, where Cook sent up a tisane for her. She sipped it slowly and did not speak, still shocked by my horrendous news.

Eventually Colin, returned from his dealings with the police, sent for me. I left Matilda in a drawing room and went to his study, where he had placed a carefully wrapped bundle on his desk. He opened it and showed me a heavy chunk of carved stone that I recognized as having come from the ruins of the old abbey near the lake on our estate. A sticky mass of blood and hair clinging to the object told me it was the instrument of Archibald Scolfield's demise.

"The ground is soft enough after all this week's rain for him to have left footprints," Colin said, "but even without them I wouldn't doubt the abbey is where the murder occurred."

"Were there any signs of a struggle there?" I asked.

"Not particularly, but you know what the place is like. There are bits and bobs of stonework all over. It always looks a mess. I have contacted Scotland Yard and told them I will handle the investigation. Where is Matilda?"

"I've put her in the cinnamon drawing room," I said. "She's rather stunned, but quite upset beneath the surface."

That particular drawing room, hung with cinnamon silk after some long-ago resident of Anglemore had returned from a trip to India, was decorated with family portraits and Eastern artifacts and filled with a suite of Chippendale furniture upholstered in cream silk embroidered with small gold flowers. When we entered, Matilda was standing in front of one of the long windows, where she had pulled back a curtain to reveal bluish darkness lit by an enormous full moon.

"This ruins everything, you know," she said, not turning to us. "Nothing will ever be the same."

"I am so terribly sorry," Colin said. "It is a dreadful loss. Emily tells me you and your cousin were close."

"We grew up together," she said, her voice trembling. "It is a crushing blow to lose him. He was so good, like a beacon of light. Montagu won't be the same without him."

"But he did not live at Montagu?" Colin asked.

"No," Matilda said. "He came to shoot every year and at Christmas. There were no better times." Her hazel eyes pooled with tears, but her face was like stone. "I suppose my guests have all been tormented with questions?"

"No more than necessary, I assure you." Colin sat her on one of four delicate chairs surrounding three sides of a small rectangular table and took the seat beside her.

"Should I be pleased by that?" she asked.

"Tell me about tonight's party," I said, sitting perpendicular to her. "You threw it in your cousin's honor?"

"Yes," she said.

"Why did he wait so long to take possession of the estate?" Colin asked. "Your grandfather's death was —"

"Nearly a year ago, yes," Matilda interrupted. "My cousin has always preferred London, while I have always loved it here. I could not bear the thought of living anywhere else, so Archie agreed to let me stay on at Montagu and manage the estate for him. In exchange, he was living in my London house. It was quite convenient, as his parents did not much like him insisting on them keeping their house in town open year-round."

"So this was a pleasant arrangement for you both?" I asked.

"Quite."

"And who will inherit now?" Colin asked.

Matilda lowered her eyes. "Archie was supposed to live long enough to have a surplus of sons."

"Does he have any brothers?" I asked.

"Five sisters."

"Do any of them have sons?" Colin asked.

"None," Matilda said. "Which I suppose leaves me next in line. There are no more males, you see, and when there are none, the title goes to the first female."

"That's considerably more fair than letting the line die out," I said. "Although what would be even more fair would be to let females inherit in the first place."

"Better yet, halt the archaic practice altogether and let people earn what they can through their own merits," Colin said.

I stopped him before he could set off on an anti-aristocracy tirade. Right or wrong, his views on the subject would not be helpful in the present situation. "Had Lord Montagu any difficulties this evening, Matilda? Any arguments?"

She shrugged. "Not that I saw. He was as amiable a man as you could ever hope to meet. Altercations did not come naturally to him." The new Marchioness of Montagu shifted her weight with an awkward movement. "Do you need anything further from me at the moment? I must confess to being rather exhausted. It has been a trying night. I should like very much to return home."

"Of course," Colin said, rising. "I shall send for the carriage at once."

He offered to accompany her home, but she refused, insisting that what she needed now was solitude. We respected her wishes, and stood and watched as the carriage pulled away. "A peeress in her own right," I said. "Imagine that."

"Her grandfather would no doubt be pleased," Colin said. "If he'd had any faith in young Archibald he would have left him the fortune."

"Perhaps," I said. "Everything seems to have worked out very nicely for Matilda, don't you think?"

"Already focusing on who benefits from the murder, my dear?"

"Naturally."

"You suspect your friend?" he asked.

"We have never been much more than acquaintances, and even if we were, it wouldn't keep me from considering her motives. I've learned through experience the dangers of overlooking suspects I trust."

"Matilda did not leave the party all night," Colin said. "There was never a time when any of her guests reported not seeing her."

"I never suggested a lady of her means would deign to sully her own hands in such a matter."

"Would she have cared so much about a mere title? She already had the money, and she was going to be able to continue to live in the house she loves."

"Not everyone, Colin, shares your disdain for the aristocracy," I said. "Understand that or it could prove your undoing. Matilda may have wanted the title very much. It would be a mistake to underestimate the desire most people have to rise in the ranks of society. You are far too well-educated to need me to remind you of all the wars fought over the subject."

He glowered and raised an eyebrow. "I shan't argue with you now," he said. "But do not expect me to remain silent on the subject forever."

Downstairs

i

Lily was applying herself to her work that morning with more vigor than usual. Always a conscientious girl, she valued her position as a housemaid to the Hargreaveses. They were a generous and fair family, not expecting their servants to hide themselves from sight, and they hosted regular servants' balls every month. Furthermore, unlike so many other employers, they allowed their staff to marry instead of giving notice to a maid at the first hint of her having a follower. Not that they would tolerate indiscretions, of course. Nothing like that. They were reasonable, and Lily respected them for it. What she liked the most about her position, however, was the way her labors showed immediate results. Feathers swept away dust, leaving gleaming wood. A crisply made bed pulled together an entire room. Blacking and polishing a fireplace revealed a shine that was like nothing else. Lily felt that, in a way, it was she who kept the day moving along for the family. She opened their shutters in the morning and closed them at night. She prepared their dressing rooms so that everything was ready when it was time to make one of their frequent changes of clothing. She lit fires before sunrise and tended to the coals after the family had gone up to bed. The routine suited her, as she liked rules and order. They gave rise to a feeling of ritual, and that was something Lily had craved from the time she was a tiny girl.

Last night, though, a man had died in the library. Work was more than just satisfying today, it was also a welcome and necessary distraction. She scrubbed hard, blacking the fireplace, but it was not enough to remove thoughts of the poor dead man from her head, so she began to sing, softly, "Ave Maria," a favorite hymn that transported her from Derbyshire to the Welsh parish church of her childhood, where she had sung in the choir. Father Michael had always said her voice was like an angel's, but her Irish mother only frowned, reminding her daughter of the evils of pride. The simple melody calmed Lily's nerves a little, and she let her voice grow just a bit louder until it filled the room.

The sound drew the attention of a guest of Mr Hargreaves's. Lord Flyte knew breakfast wouldn't be laid for some hours, but he made a practice of rising early as he enjoyed the quiet time when the rest of the house was asleep. The habit had started when he was a young boy and would accompany his father — a much-admired eccentric — on his morning inspection of his Yorkshire estate. The old Earl Flyte had never liked London so stayed in the country, where his tenants swore he was the best landlord England had ever seen. His son emulated his father in every way but one. He did go to London, but only to sit in the Lords, feeling a deep obligation to contribute whatever he could to the parliamentary process. He considered it an extension of looking after his tenants.

He followed the sound of the song coming from the drawing room and stood in the doorway, watching the wisp of a girl from whom it came. She was a housemaid, but her luminous beauty would have been more fitting in a London ballroom or on a Sargent canvas. Her skin, smooth and pale, glowed as her cheeks colored at the realization she was no longer alone.

"Lovely morning," Lord Flyte said, smiling at her. "I do hope I haven't disturbed you."

"Of course not, sir," she said. "I shall be out of your way in just a moment."

"No need to rush," he said and walked to the window. The view was a striking one, over the gardens with the peaks in the distance. "It would be difficult to find a house more pleasantly situated than this one, wouldn't it?"

"Yes, sir." Her voice was soft and husky, not ringing with the clarity it had when she was singing.

"Have you worked here long?"

"I came with Lady Emily," she said. "I'd been with her in London before she married Mr Hargreaves."

"So you are used to being spoken to instead of being ignored?"

This drew a smile from the girl. Her mistress was notorious for talking to her staff. Just last week Lady Bromley had stormed into the servants' hall and demanded that they stop replying to her daughter when

18

she tried to engage them in conversation. Mr Davis, the butler, had handled her well, letting her think her request would be honored, but making sure, once she had gone back upstairs, it was clear that they all were to obey their mistress, not her mother. "Quite right, sir."

"And singing is tolerated in the house?" He grinned but then saw the wave of panic cross her face. "I am certain it is. Lady Emily may not be particularly musical herself, but she admires the talent in others, and you have that in spades. I apologize if I alarmed you."

"Not at all, sir."

"Do you sing often?"

"I suppose I do, sir," Lily said. "Nobody's ever minded, and it does pass the time ever so pleasantly."

"You have an enchanting voice. There's something almost ethereal about it." He paused, wondering if she knew the word. "Ethereal is heavenly or —"

"Yes, ethereal," she said. "I've always thought it a beautiful word. It sounds like it means, doesn't it?"

"Yes, it does," he said. "What is your name?"

"Lily, sir."

"It is a pleasure to make your acquaintance, Lily."

Lily watched him. He had moved away from the window and was standing near her, smiling. She couldn't decide if it was unnerving or a compliment to be paid such attention. She nodded her head in acknowledgment of his words and turned back to her work, feeling heat flush her cheeks. She narrowed her eyes, scrutinizing the room, making sure she had left not a single speck of the fireplace short of gleaming.

"I am Simon Lancaster, Earl Flyte."

He was still hovering over her. Having not the slightest idea what to do, she gave him a small smile, unwilling to meet his stare.

"You've lovely eyes, Lily." He was quite taken aback, in fact, to find such a stunning girl hard at work. It seemed wrong, an offense against beauty itself.

Her whole body stiffened and she looked away, attacking a small dull spot on the fireplace with renewed vigor.

"I don't mean to alarm you," he said. "It was an inappropriate comment. Can you forgive me?"

"Of course." Her voice was barely audible.

"You will find I am even worse than your mistress when it comes to chatting with the staff. I rarely entertain at home, and my servants are more like friends than employees."

"That's very odd, sir." Lily bit her tongue, worried that she'd overstepped her bounds. But Lord Flyte laughed.

"I am quite aware of it," he said, a warm smile on his narrow face. "Fortunately for me, one benefit of being an aristocrat is that everyone around you is forced to accept your eccentricities. Do you like these early morning hours?"

"I do, sir, I do," Lily said. "It's almost like magic opening the shutters and watching the light pour in. Lovely is what it is. It's like waking up the world." She clamped her mouth shut. She hadn't meant to say so much.

"Good girl. I shall leave you to your work. I'm off for a constitutional. Best way to start the morning."

"Yes, sir." She smiled at him as he retreated from view. A nice-looking man, she thought. Not like the master, but then no one was as handsome as him. Lord Flyte was shorter, and thin, but he carried himself with dignity despite a slight limp. Lily admired dignity. Lost in thought, she let her brush clatter to the floor just as Alice pushed the door open.

"Cook's having a go at that useless kitchen maid again. Don't know why she bothers. Pru will never amount to anything."

"I heard she went upstairs last night," Lily said, pushing the image of Lord Flyte out of her head.

"She did. Wanted to see the dead body. Morbid thing." Alice flashed a wicked smile. She had been self-conscious about her crooked teeth when she first came to the house, but had started to let herself smile once Lily had convinced her no one else noticed anything but her contagious sense of fun. Alice organized every amusement for the staff and was the only one of them who had ever spotted a ghost at Anglemore. It was a nun, she had told the rest of the junior servants, murdered by one of Cromwell's men when they'd overrun the old abbey. Lily had always thought that she, a devout Catholic, would be more likely to encounter the ill-treated sister who had shared her faith, and half suspected Alice of inventing her stories wholesale, but they were so entertaining she wouldn't say anything that might make her stop telling them.

Lily's eyes widened. "Did she see it?"

"Heavens, no. Mr Hargreaves marched her straight back downstairs. Cook near thrashed her, and I can't say I would have regretted it if she had."

"Flirting with Johnny again, is she?" Lily asked. Alice had been sweet on him, one of the grooms, for months.

"I suppose you could call it that."

"He's not worth it if he lets her," Lily said. "A gentleman should stay true to his lady."

"Johnny's no gentleman any more than I'm a lady," Alice said. "Which is just as it ought to be. But that girl had better keep her distance unless she wants there to be a second murder in the house."

"What are they saying upstairs about last night?" Lily asked. "Do they know what happened?"

"Lady Matilda could've been in on it, that's what I hear. Lady Emily said near as much. But I don't see how a lady like her could whack someone the size of that corpse and leave much of a mark."

"She's not so little," Lily said. "Her shoulders are as broad as a boy's. Still, I wouldn't think she could kill a man."

"Anger makes for strange strength," Alice said. "If he trifled with her —"

"Ladies like that don't get trifled with," Lily said, rubbing the last bit of blacking off the now gleaming fireplace. "It's girls like us who do, if they're not careful."

"I know, I know. Don't start lecturing on that count again. I must admit I could do with a bit of trifling just now. That would show Johnny a thing or two."

"That is not something to joke about. I'll tell you — watch Lord Flyte. He's up too early every morning for a gentleman, and he has far too much to say to a housemaid."

"Was he bothering you?" Alice asked.

"I don't let myself be bothered, and you shouldn't either."

"Lord Flyte doesn't seem like a bad bloke. Can I do the fireplaces tomorrow? I wouldn't mind a chat."

"Alice!" Lily flushed. "How can you say such a thing?"

"I'm only half serious," she said. "Though I do know a girl who worked with someone who married a son of the house. A younger son, mind you, but a son nonetheless. She's a proper lady now."

"Things like that only happen in fairy tales, Alice, if they even do there. In real life, the endings are much worse."

Alice rolled her eyes. "Dismissed without a character."

"Keep that in mind next time you're tempted to talk to Lord Flyte."

"So far as I can tell, you're the only one he's talked to, Lily. Maybe you're the one who should take care."

CHAPTER
TWO

After breakfast the following morning, I made my way through wide, painting-lined corridors and up two flights of stairs to the nursery, eager to kiss the babies before I set off for Montagu Manor with Colin. Henry and Richard, our twins, were sleeping, their round faces rosy and cherubic. Tom, six months older than they, was awake, sitting in the middle of a braided rug, banging a rattle against a wooden block, laughter bubbling from his small mouth. I picked him up, gave him a cuddle, and frowned when I noticed the sullen nursery maid in the corner of the room paying not the slightest attention to the child.

"Fetch Nanny for me at once," I said. She obeyed without responding or looking at me.

Finding capable employees to assist Nanny had proven challenging, which was nothing more than Colin and I had expected. We had taken in Tom as soon as he was born at the request of his mother, Donata, a friend I had made in Venice while working on our last case. Unfortunately, she had befriended me not out of a desire for companionship, but in an attempt to hide from us her guilt. It was she who had killed the man whose murder we were investigating and therefore she who had taught me not to overlook friends as suspects. The revelation had been devastating. When Donata begged me to come to see her in prison, I had known she was expecting but had no idea that she would ask Colin and me to raise her child. In the end, we found we could not deny the request. Tom's father took no responsibility for him — he refused even to see his son — and we could not bear the thought of leaving an infant to be a ward of the state when we had ample resources to care for him.

My husband, magnificent as always, agreed with enthusiasm when I insisted that we look after the boy as if he were our own, and he loved little Tomaso as fiercely as he did the twins. Tom was easy to adore, all chubby cheeks and smiles, with the sweetest temper a baby could have. His nurses should have been grateful to have him as their charge. Yet one after another had let us down, put off by the knowledge that his mother was a murderer. This latest in a disappointing series had assured us she did not care in the least, but seeing her attitude this morning towards the boy alarmed me.

Waiting for Nanny, I tickled Tom's little feet. He laughed, delighted, and as he kicked, his gown pulled up, revealing pudgy legs. My smile faded.

"Nanny!" I shouted.

"Very nearly there, Lady Emily," came a small voice from the doorway. So far as I could tell, Nanny had been with the Hargreaves family since the first house at Anglemore Park had been built in the fifteenth century, but she had the vigor (if not the speed) of a much younger woman, and Colin would never have allowed anyone else the oversight of the nursery. Nanny had, after all, raised him. Given the spectacular result, who was I to argue?

I crossed to her, holding little Tom out in front of me. "Look at his legs. Red marks all over them. She's been pinching him." I glared at the maid. Nanny peered down, investigating the evidence.

"Stupid girl," she said and soundly slapped her across the face. The maid scowled and raised her hand to her cheek but said nothing.

"You will remove yourself from this house at once," I said. "And you will receive no character."

"Wouldn't want one, madam," she said. "Not from anyone who harbors murderers."

"You felt somewhat differently when you accepted the position," I said. "We were straightforward with you about Tom's mother from the start."

"Didn't know then what it would be like," she said. "Evil breeds evil. It was his presence what brought that murdered man to the house last night, and mark me words it won't be the last time you face such violence and horror."

"Get out." I could not tolerate the sight of her for another moment. "You would be fortunate to ever find yourself with the charge of a baby half so good as he." She slunk out of the room and down the servants' narrow stairs.

"Glad to see the back of her," Nanny said, taking Tom from me and planting a wet kiss on his fat cheek.

"Nanny, you must alert me at once of any problems like this. We cannot have the boys harmed."

"She hid it well from me, Lady Emily. You can be sure of that. I would never have stood for an ounce of nonsense from her. I think she just decided she didn't like the job."

I pressed my palm against my forehead. "Will he be all right?"

"Right as rain, madam," Nanny said. "Don't worry your pretty head about our Tom. He's a good, fine boy."

I gave him a kiss and then went back to the twins, who were still sleeping.

"Lady Bromley came up last night, insisting Tom should have separate quarters," Nanny said.

"My mother is only slightly less in need of a slap than that maid," I said, although I knew I shouldn't have. "Ignore her. If she gives you any trouble, send for me."

Nanny stifled a laugh. "Madam, if you were one of my charges I should remind you of the necessity of honoring one's parents. As you are not, I can tell you my true feelings, and they are that our Colin did well to find you."

"Thank you, Nanny. I take that as the highest compliment. I'll be back to see the boys this afternoon."

"Very good, Lady Emily."

"Mr Hargreaves said to be sure to take them outside. It is a fine day, and he wants them to look at the horses."

"Only our Colin could think a baby would benefit from being around horses, but I'll do as he asks." She smiled. I had known within five minutes of first making her acquaintance that she viewed my husband as something only slightly short of a god. He was her greatest accomplishment, she always said. I kissed Henry and Richard, careful not to wake them, breathing in their clean, warm, buttery smell. I heard footsteps in the corridor, and then a shrill voice. My mother. "I'm off, Nanny, and going down the back, if you don't mind."

Having seen to the boys, I met Colin in front of the house, where he was waiting with our horses and talking to Simon, Earl Flyte, one of his dearest friends and now the twins' godfather. Around them, Colin's pack of foxhounds milled, sniffing the air and looking ready to run in hot pursuit of any small creature that might catch their notice. He had named them after the Argonauts — Acastus, Iphitos, Bellerophon, Leitus, Pollux, and Telamon — and they viewed him as their leader, just as their namesakes had done Jason. None of them made a move in his presence without first looking for his approval. Now that I consider the matter, I imagine the Argonauts were much more unruly.

Colin and Simon had met on their first day at Eton. A pack of older boys were teasing Simon about the limp he'd had since childhood, when he had fallen from a tree and broken his leg. Simon had fought back with such vigor and energy against hopeless odds that Colin, seeing his plight, stepped in and offered his fists in assistance. They were both soundly trounced by the others and put on the Bill by a Beak who spotted them from across the street. The sharp words he had for them paled next to the Head Man's ire when they stood before him, but the incident had sealed their friendship. They were inseparable through all their days at school. Simon did not visit us often. It was difficult to pry him away from his own estate, but once he'd been persuaded to come, he was a delightful guest. He loved our grounds and woke before sunrise to take full advantage of his surroundings. A good constitutional, he had told me time and time again, helped him focus and relax so that he might better face whatever challenges the day threw at him. No doubt today he had already walked six miles by the time I saw him, or perhaps eight, given the distress on his face when Colin had called for him to come down to the library last night and see what had become of Archibald Scolfield.

"Simon, dear, I am so sorry your visit has been marred by all this," I said.

"No apology necessary, Emily," he said. "I know enough about Colin's work to expect nothing less. Fiascos follow him."

I smiled, tugging at the bottom of my riding habit's double-breasted jacket to pull it straight. "Do you think he attracts them?"

"I don't see any other explanation," Simon said. "I understand that he goes where he must in the service of the Crown, but when murder follows him to his own estate, what else is one to think?"

"Enough of this nonsense," Colin said, grinning. "Simon, chess when I'm back?"

"If you are ready to face inevitable defeat." He gave a jaunty wave and turned to go inside, taking Pollux with him as Colin and I climbed onto our horses and set off for Montagu Manor. The ride took us through vast meadows and rolling hills. The panorama we saw when we reached the top of a slope confirmed my already steadfast belief that no part of England could compete with the Peak District for natural beauty. From dark forest to almost yellow chartreuse, it was as if every shade of green imaginable fit together in perfect puzzle pieces throughout the valley, with no sign yet that soon the leaves would turn rich with autumn's gold and crimson. Trees bordered fields, forming them into perfect rectangles, and sheep dotted the centers white. Clouds that looked as if they had been fashioned from spun sugar hung in a bright sky but did not threaten rain. It was a spectacular day. At least it would have been spectacular had our minds not been full of the grievous events of the night before.

"Did the Yard agree to give us charge of the investigation?" I asked.

"They did," Colin said. "Although they hesitated, as the incident occurred on our grounds."

"They trust you to be impartial."

"They know that I would gladly hand over even you to the authorities if necessary."

"Heartless beast," I said. "Only imagine the life of crime I could have if I weren't saddled with you." He shot me a look that was half wicked, half irresistible. I wished we could go home at once.

"The police and I interviewed the guests at Matilda's party last night as well as the staff," he said. "No one stood out as an obvious suspect."

"Let's see what we can turn up today. If, that is, you can catch me." I dug my heels into my horse

Bucephalus, named after Alexander the Great's famous steed, and pulled ahead. Colin had a fine seat, but I was fearless in the saddle and had yet to meet a rider who could reliably catch me. As a result Montagu Manor loomed before me long before it did him. He claimed he was being a gentleman and had let me pull away, but the sparkle in his eyes told me he knew this was far from the case.

Montagu was a new house, the construction finished not more than thirty years ago, when Matilda's grandfather had pulled down the Tudor monstrosity previously on the site and used the proceeds of his many excellent investments to build a castlelike structure in its place. His late wife had been fond of the old house, but Lord Montagu had always found the Tudors revolting and fancied himself a feudal lord. While Anglemore Park was a medieval home improved over the centuries, Montagu was the Middle Ages reimagined. The great hall, dominated by a hammer-beam ceiling and an enormous stone fireplace, stood in the center of the building, every inch of its walls covered in re-creations of medieval murals. It was here, at a table beneath an image of a monk bent over the page he was illuminating, that Matilda received Colin and me.

She looked strained; her eyes were red-rimmed, her face pasty, any shock that had numbed her the previous evening having given way to raw grief. She was back in the mourning dress she'd only recently stopped wearing for her grandfather. Her hands shook as she poured tea for us before we started our search of Archibald's rooms, wanting to scrutinize them more than Colin and the police had been able to the previous night. Some things are better tended to in daylight, particularly as Matilda's grandfather had forbidden the use of gaslights on the premise. They were not medieval enough for him. I could well imagine his opinion of electricity.

Archibald had taken over his grandfather's rooms, a suite on the first floor whose decoration was so ornate it started to give me a headache. Mirrors, gilt, religious statues, and elaborate paneling assaulted the senses. The old man's belongings had long since been cleared away, but Archibald had added very little of his own to replace them. In fact, he had made virtually no mark on the house. The wardrobe contained a few suits, changes of shirts, and other ordinary items of clothing, but beyond garments and toiletries, there was not much to be found. There were no books on the shelves, no letters in the desk, no personal stationery, no abandoned newspapers. Nothing about the space revealed the slightest hint of Archibald Scolfield's personality.

I rang for a servant. A few moments later a petite maid entered the room and greeted us with a smart bow.

"Milady?" she asked.

"How long did Lord Montague plan to stay at the house?"

"I couldn't rightly say, milady. We expected the rooms to remain his for as long as he wanted them."

"Lady Matilda didn't plan to use them?" I asked.

"Oh no, madam. She's happy where she is. Always has been. She's in the same rooms she moved into when she left the nursery, you know."

"Did you serve the new Lord Montagu while he was here?"

"Enough to know he was the finest gentleman to be found," she said. "It was a pleasure to tidy up for him."

"It doesn't appear there was much to tidy," Colin said. "Is his valet still here?"

"He went back to London this morning. Is there a problem?"

"No. I spoke to him last night and asked that Lord Montagu's things be left here. Can you tell us anything more about him?"

"Lord Montagu?" she asked.

"Please," Colin said.

"No." There was something in her voice, the slightest hesitation.

"Colin, darling, could we have a moment?" I asked. He raised his eyebrows but acquiesced, pulling the door shut behind him.

"Have I done something wrong, milady?" the maid asked, nervously tugging at her hands.

"Not in the least," I said. "I was not acquainted with Lord Montagu, but I have heard it said he was a most handsome and affable gentleman." She flushed as I said the words, and I suspected she was exhibiting the signs of a maid enamored with her employer.

"Oh, he was, madam. So kind and polite."

"And handsome?"

She blushed darker red. "Very."

Now I was certain my suspicions had been correct when she had hesitated in front of Colin. "Was he . . . close . . . with any of the staff?"

"No, madam, he was not." She was shaking her head and speaking quickly now, in passionate defense of the gentleman. "He wasn't like that, I'm sure of it. None of us maids have a complaint against him, if I understand your meaning."

I smiled. "I believe you do."

"To be right honest, madam, there were some who were a tad put off that he wouldn't, well, pay any of us meaningful attention."

"He always behaved honorably?" I asked.

"He did, madam, and his valet told us he gives his staff the most wonderful presents at Christmas. Not things that are useful, like cloth to make uniforms. Things that a person might actually want."

"I have always thought it a perfectly horrid custom to pretend uniforms are a gift," I said, remembering the sadness I felt as a girl when each Christmas it was my duty to pass out the extremely disappointing but ever so practical presents my mother had selected for our servants.

"So I've heard, madam. Everyone knows —" she stopped. "I don't mean to speak out of turn."

"It is quite all right. Do go ahead."

"We're all of us at Montagu envious of your servants' balls. A dance every month! It must be like heaven in your house."

"Mr Hargreaves and I do hope the staff are happy," I said.

"We all talk, you know." She pursed her lips. "And I'm saying too much again."

34

"It's perfectly fine. Is there anything else you can tell me about Lord Montagu?" I asked. "Did you see him last night after the party had started?"

"No, madam. I was busy with work. Last I saw him was in the afternoon when I brought tea for him and Lady Matilda."

"What was the atmosphere like in the room?"

"Atmosphere?"

I should have chosen a different word. "Did they seem happy and relaxed?"

"They did, indeed. Nothing was out of the ordinary in the slightest."

There was a sharp rap on the door. I opened it to find my husband.

"These were just delivered," he said, handing me two letters addressed to Archibald. "Rather interesting reading."

Downstairs

ii

An enlightened architect who believed in natural light, high ceilings, and pleasant workspaces had designed the facilities below stairs at Anglemore. There were no dingy rooms, dimly lit corridors, or cramped quarters to be found. The servants' hall with its high ceiling was so tall it reached above the ground, and it had large windows, a smooth stone floor, and a fireplace with clean lines and the ability to kick out an enormous amount of heat. Mr Hargreaves had ordered electric lights installed through the whole house the previous year, so it was always bright no matter what the time or the weather. The new lights had caused an awful upheaval, and Cook still wasn't convinced of their safety. She was always telling tales about people blinded by them, but even she had to admit they worked like magic.

"I don't care what the lot of you think, she shouldn't have been let go like that." Pru had only worked as a kitchen maid in the house for a handful of months, but she had always been free with her opinions. She had not been close with this latest in the string of ill-fated nursery maids — the nursery staff kept to themselves for the most part — but like the nursery maid, Pru had been horrified that a murderer's baby lived under the same roof as all of them. It wasn't decent.

"You have no right to speak that way," Lily said. They — the lower five, all of the junior servants on staff, called that regardless of their actual number — were sitting around the large, smooth table in the servants' hall, having just finished eating, "We're lucky to be in a household like this."

Pru snorted. "Maybe you can think so. I can't. Being a kitchen maid doesn't allow me the lazy lifestyle of you housemaids."

"If you don't like your position, you're welcome to work hard enough to get moved to something better," Cook said, poking her head into the hall. "Just don't look to me for a hand up. Not after I've seen the way you tried to get by without polishing the copper pots all the way last week."

"Mr Davis would have something different to say," Pru said.

"Mr Davis would throw you out of the house if he got wind of your rotten attitude," Alice said. "That nurse wasn't careful with the babies, and she deserved just what she got."

"That's enough from the lot of you," Cook said. "Come now, useless girl. We've six sauces to prepare for the family's dinner tonight."

"How many sauces will we be having tonight?" Pru asked.

No one replied to her. Lily silently recited a Hail Mary to herself, hoping it would bring her patience, and before long Pru flounced out of the room. The mood lightened considerably with her absence.

"That girl is the worst sort of —" Alice clamped her mouth shut when she saw Mr Davis, the butler, coming through the door.

"Good day, everyone," he said. "I know we have discussed the events of last night already, but I wanted to say again how pleased I am with the way you have all managed to uphold your high standards of work in the midst of such unpleasant circumstances."

"It's our pleasure, sir." Alice grinned.

"Mr Hargreaves spoke to me this morning and asked me to pass his and Lady Emily's compliments along. He also wanted me to assure you that the servants' ball will take place as scheduled at the end of the month. He hopes there will be no further disruptions in the household."

"That's excellent news," Alice said, and several of the footmen murmured approval.

"I'll leave you to it, then," Mr Davis said. "I believe you all have work to do? And, Lily, if I could have a quick word?"

"Of course, sir," she said and followed him into his room, a small parlor next to the housekeeper's.

"Meg tells me Lady Emily's dressing room was not prepared on time last night."

"I'm sorry, sir." Lily looked down, unable to meet his eyes. "It is my fault entirely. I fell behind in my duties and know full well that for that there is no excuse."

"The unfortunate incident made things difficult for all of us last night. I understand that. Please, however, do not let it happen again."

"No, sir, it won't."

"We will not mention this to Mrs Elliott."

"Thank you, sir." Lily sighed relief. The housekeeper would not have been so generous with her.

"Meg made a point of coming to me about it rather than her. You might thank her for that." There was no lady's maid more gracious than Meg. It was no wonder Lady Emily said over and over that she could not do without her.

"Yes, sir." She nodded with great enthusiasm to the butler and scurried upstairs, eager to get back to work, vowing never again to make so careless a mistake and wondering what she might do by way of thanking Meg for her much-appreciated kindness.

CHAPTER
THREE

Colin and I sat next to each other on the monstrous fifteenth-century canopied bed that dominated Lord Montagu's room at Montagu Manor, its heavy red curtains held back with golden tasseled ties. We read through the letters that had arrived for Archibald Scolfield three times before we went downstairs to confront Matilda, who had abandoned the great hall for a smaller sitting room. Like much of the rest of the house, it was wood paneled, but here two-thirds of the walls were covered with embroidered hangings. Delicate flowers dotted wide horizontal backgrounds of alternating burgundy and cream. The windows were leaded glass in a diamond pattern, with bits of colored glass used to accent the design. Matilda was sitting at a writing table, papers strewn around her. She tensed when she saw us, knitting her eyebrows together and turning down the corners of her mouth.

"Were you aware of Archibald's plans to renovate Montagu Manor?" I asked. "It seems odd no one has mentioned them to us."

"Archie? Renovate?" Matilda gave a strained laugh. "How ridiculous. The house is practically new."

"Was he planning to live here?" I asked. She had never mentioned any such scheme. Quite the contrary.

"No, that wasn't the agreement." She frowned. "I already told you that."

"Yes, you did, but this seems to suggest he planned something else altogether." Colin passed her an envelope and waited while Matilda read its contents.

"He promised me," she said and pursed her lips. "He would never go back on his word."

I studied her face. Nothing in her expression suggested surprise, only anger. "This letter is from an architect who discusses very specific plans for revamping the house," I said, "and mentions dates by which your cousin was planning to move in. Clearly, he did go back on his word. Are we to believe he did so without informing you?"

"He may have decided to renovate without discussing the project with me. He would be perfectly entitled to." Matilda sat up very straight and squared her shoulders. "And he may well have planned to keep a set of apartments here for his own use. I see nothing wrong with that."

"The second letter suggests something rather different," Colin said. "It is from Lord Montagu's fiancée."

"Fiancée?" Matilda blinked. "I know nothing about this."

"Which is strange considering the young lady in question believes she was to be married next Christmas and would be living in this house," I said. Matilda grabbed the letter from Colin.

"I swear to you I knew nothing about this," she said.

"I hope that is true," I said. "If it is not, it gives you a powerful motive to want your cousin dead."

"I wouldn't kill him over a house, not even this one." Her eyes flashed and she scowled, anger consuming her for just a moment before she regained her composure. "Archie and I were always close."

"So close that he never mentioned his engagement to you?" Colin asked.

She lowered her eyes. "We'd had something of a falling-out a few months ago."

"Explain." Colin folded his arms across his chest.

"This young *lady*, as you call her, is nothing of the sort. All she wants is this house and to be marchioness. She's a vile American, you understand. Constance Sturdevant, she's called, and I understand she had her heart set on royalty. Unfortunately for her, the princes of Europe had the good taste to ignore her untoward advances. Unfortunately for us, my cousin was not so strong. Archie and I argued more times than I can count about his growing affection for her."

Many Englishwomen, my mother leading their charge, violently opposed what she described as "the unseemly exportation of heiresses from the States." The wealthy — extremely wealthy — daughters of American businessmen had stormed London society, making an especially favorable impression on unmarried gentlemen. American heiresses had not been trained, as their English counterparts had, to avoid eye contact, to refrain from stating strong opinions, or to refuse to discuss controversial subjects in public. The American contingent was, for the most part, better educated and studied subjects far broader than those my governess had dared address. While I had more than made up for the inadequacies of the system on my own, learning ancient Greek so that I could read Homer and becoming something of an expert on ancient art, many English girls had no opportunity to follow my lead. Their parents would never have stood for it. As a result, the Americans were like beautiful, exotic birds, irresistible to gentlemen tired of vapid society girls capable of little more than riding with the hounds and making insipid comments about the weather. It did not surprise me in the least that Archibald would have fallen for someone more invigorating.

"I am not acquainted with Miss Sturdevant," I said. "Do you know her well?"

"Not precisely," Matilda said.

"I do remember hearing about her in London last year. Is she the girl who caused a scene by swimming in the Serpentine on an unusually warm July afternoon?"

"The very one. You can see why I object."

Quite the contrary. Miss Sturdevant's action had endeared her to me. While I always liked to find ladies of spirit, I thought it best to refrain from saying so to Matilda. "What was the result of these arguments with your cousin?" I asked.

"He told me he would wait a year before proposing to her. If he still loved her and had found no significant flaws in her character, I was to accept the match."

"Would you have?" I asked.

"It would never have lasted a whole year," she said.

"It appears he disregarded your advice and proposed," Colin said.

"And was going to punish me by forcing me out of my home?" Matilda asked, her eyes flashing. "If that's the case, he deserved to die. Do let me know when you've identified the murderer. I should like to send him a thank-you note." She flounced out of the room without another word.

"Can we prove she knew about this?" I asked my husband.

"We can try," he said. "I'll wire the Yard and arrange to search Montagu's house in London."

"Matilda's house, you mean."

"Right." He started to pace. "I don't have a good feeling about this. Matilda is a suspect, but she's too obvious, and something isn't quite right."

"Perhaps it is time to delve further into Lord Montagu's life," I said. "You interviewed the guests at last night's party, and we could claim that each of them had opportunity. Motive, I would argue, has a greater role in murder. Who benefited from his death? Other than Matilda, that is."

The rail journey to London passed quickly, and a man from Scotland Yard met us at St Pancras, ready to drive us to Archibald's house in Mayfair. As Lord Montagu did not care for country life and kept only one house, the full staff were in residence, and not a single one of them had a negative word to say about their master. Archibald's inheritance had made little difference to his lifestyle beyond him having moved from his parents' town house to the one technically owned by his cousin. His allowance was the same, and his patterns appeared to be the same. He belonged to the Turf Club, lunched weekly with friends he'd met at Oxford, and rowed on the river every day. His possessions suggested he wasn't a man of high intellect. There were very few books in his library and none at all in any other room of the house. Nothing, however, impugned his character.

"He would bore me, I'm afraid," I said, reading through the correspondence in his study. There were piles of letters, bills (all paid in a timely fashion), and scores of invitations to shooting parties. He seemed a perfectly ordinary gentleman, dull, even.

"Anything from his fiancée?" Colin asked.

"Nothing yet." I made my way through the rest of the stack and turned my attention to his desk drawers.

"The man doesn't own a chess set." Colin had finished going through a cabinet filled with files. "But his records are meticulous. It appears he saved every receipt from every item he purchased."

"Can you trust a man who doesn't play chess?"

"Absolutely not."

"Can you trust a man who receives passionate letters from a lady of possibly dubious reputation?"

"This sounds promising." He came to me and sat on the edge of the desk.

"A whole box of letters," I said. "All from a Miss Cora Fitzgerald who lives in Melton Carbury."

"Melton Carbury?"

"That's right. Not five miles from Montagu Manor."

"Are we acquainted with her?"

"Not so far as I can remember, but then we don't spend much time in Melton Carbury, do we? I can't think when I was last there. I'm sure Matilda goes for church, but that's simply because her grandfather wanted a Roman Catholic chapel in the new house."

"Despite the fact that he was Church of England."

"He was interested in authenticity, my dear, so the family worships in the village, and the chapel is a lovely museum. It need not concern us at the moment. Listen to this." I read from the letter in my hand. "'*I cannot bear another day away from you, my dearest love.*' They all seem to be in similar vein. The explicit nature of some of them is what makes me suspect the authoress is a woman of dubious reputation."

"When are they dated?"

"Going back two and a half years, the most recent sent last week."

"And not a single word from his fiancée?" Colin asked.

"Not any he considered worth saving, so far as I can tell."

"Two more rooms here and we'll head back north," Colin said. "I, for one, am greatly looking forward to making Miss Fitzgerald's acquaintance."

"Not quite yet, I think." I held up Archibald's diary. "His Oxford chums were scheduled to lunch together at the Turf Club today. You could check there and see if any of them is still around. I'd be more than happy to assist, but I wouldn't be allowed over the threshold."

"I do remember a time, long ago, when you barged into the Reform Club," he said.

"Looking for you." I smiled. "These circumstances are altogether different."

He took my face in his hands and gave me a most delicious kiss. "Were you then still operating under the delusion that I'd murdered your first husband?"

"I'd rather not think about it, if you don't mind." It was a tad embarrassing now to remember that I had once suspected Colin of having a hand in Philip's death. Such were the follies of youth.

"You were full of fire that day. I can recall it with absolute clarity. Your eyes ablaze —"

"You should not have been noticing such things then."

"I was already in love with you."

"And I had no idea how lucky I was." I squeezed his hand. Our eyes met and I wished there was no work to be done.

London was empty at this time of year, only a handful of gentlemen around, most of them staying at their clubs while in town to tend to matters of business. Society had retreated to the country in time for the Glorious Twelfth, the day grouse season opened, and would not return until the social season started back up the following spring. Archibald having chosen to keep his primary residence in town was decidedly unusual, especially after he had inherited his grandfather's title. No doubt his influence among his friends was what enabled him to draw them in every week at such an unusual time of year. It suggested he was a good friend, a man respected by his peers.

I had only rarely been in London in the autumn, but found it quite pleasant in its semi-abandoned state. There were no dowagers to contend with, no rules to follow, and, best of all, no calls to make, so I took the opportunity to browse the British Museum while waiting for my husband to finish at the Turf Club. I started in the gallery that housed my favorite object in the museum: a Greek vase depicting the judgment of Paris. My first husband had donated it from his collection years ago, and it was one of the pieces that had catalyzed my interest in classics and my study of Greek. From there, I made my way past the Parthenon friezes and paused in front of the Rosetta Stone, wishing I could touch the carved ancient letters that had revealed the secrets of Egyptian hieroglyphs. I had been studying the Greek language for more than five years now and agreed passionately with the words of the Duke of Buckingham: *Read Homer once, and you can read no more; / For all books else appear so mean, so poor, / Verse will seem prose; but still persist to read, / And Homer will be all the books you need.* Much as I adored Greek, perhaps it was time to take on Egyptian as well. Expanding one's knowledge is always a noble pursuit. Wanting to further consider taking on another culture, I spent the remainder of the time I had in the Egyptian galleries, feeling as if a whole new part of the world were opening to me. Too soon, it was time to meet Colin back at St Pancras for our train to Anglemore.

"I can categorically guarantee Archibald Scolfield never played chess," Colin said as we took our seats in a private compartment. "That is not to say he was a man of bad character. His friends assure me he was dependable and loyal, a true gentleman."

"And?" I could tell by his tone there was more.

"And he had requested that none of them breathe a word of his engagement."

"He had informed them he was engaged?"

"They toasted him not two weeks ago."

"Did they know why he required secrecy?" I asked.

"He felt strongly that the news would distress another lady, and he wanted to spare her feelings for as long as possible."

"Matilda?"

"Cora Fitzgerald."

"Miss Fitzgerald." I had not suspected this. "What, precisely, do they know about her?"

"They were vague at best, wanting to protect their friend's reputation," Colin said. "It was, however, quite clear they thought Scolfield was bound to have a difficult time giving her up."

"After his marriage to the American?"

"Yes. They feared Miss Fitzgerald's upbringing would prevent her from being, shall we say, Continental about the situation. One of them made mention of the 'bastions of middle-class propriety'."

"Did they know Miss Fitzgerald expected to marry him?"

"They made no mention of any understanding, but I would not have expected them to," he said.

"I think it is best I stop thinking about Archibald Scolfield for a few moments. My opinion of him is becoming entirely unladylike."

"Perhaps I ought to come up with a way to distract you. I can't bear the thought of you becoming unladylike."

"That is hard to believe," I said. "I have been convinced since the first days of our marriage that you preferred me unladylike. Heaven forbid that ever changes."

Downstairs

iii

Lily was singing again, this time a rousing chorus of "Jerusalem," and so taken with the music that she was not paying close attention when she turned the corner from Lady Emily's room, where she had just finished tidying and changing the linens. She was moving so quickly she came close to slamming into Lord Flyte, who was heading down the corridor, his nose buried in a book. "Sir! I'm so sorry," she said, blushing and bending down to retrieve the dirty bedclothes she had dropped.

"No damage done, Lily. I can stand up to much more, I assure you." He was dressed in tweeds and carrying a pipe that filled the air with the warm and comforting scent of tobacco and spice. "I should have been alerted by 'Jerusalem'."

"Yes, sir."

"I believe this fell out of your apron pocket," he said, handing her the sketchbook she always carried with her. "Are you an artist?"

"No sir, not at all," she said. "I do like to draw, but I have no real talent for it and no training. It's just a lark, really."

"May I?" He nodded at the book, and she passed it back to him. He opened it and flipped through the pages, which were filled with portraits of the household staff, rendered with exceptional skill, the images so realistic, so lifelike, they were reminiscent of photographs. "These are quite remarkable, Lily. You do indeed have real talent."

"Thank you, sir." She squirmed a bit, feeling uncomfortable. "I would never sketch while I'm supposed to be working."

"I would have expected nothing less," he said. "You're an admirable girl. I am most impressed." He returned the book to her.

"I'm much obliged, sir." She bobbed a curtsy and continued along her way.

"Lily!" Lord Flyte called after her. "During my walk this morning I noticed a particularly fine vista from a hill overlooking the lake near that charming folly the Temple of the Muses to the east. Do you know it?"

"I don't, sir."

"I should love for you to see it. I think your artist's eyes would appreciate it."

Lily tried to keep her eyes on the floor but wanted nothing more than to look up at him. "I'll do my best to do so on my free afternoon next week, sir. Thank you for the suggestion."

"My pleasure entirely." His smile warmed her to her feet, and while the feeling wasn't entirely welcome to her, Lily's step was lighter as she went back to her work. His tobacco reminded her of her grandfather, and she found herself trusting him more than was likely wise. Gentlemen in the house should be treated with civil courtesy, but not noticed by the female staff beyond that. She thought about what Mrs Elliott would say should word get back to her about a housemaid conversing with Lord Flyte. That brought Lily back to earth.

Alice was waiting in Mr Hargreaves's room with a bundle of clean linen to be put on the bed. The bedclothes were changed regularly, although the master never slept in the room. He was always in Lady Emily's. His was a pleasant space, very manly, Alice had always thought, all done up in a deep claret color with old paintings on the walls. Lily told her one of them was very famous, by some Italian bloke, Leonardo something or other, but Alice didn't know anything about that. Lily was the one who knew about art. "You're bright today," she said, noticing the color in Lily's cheeks. "Been arguing with someone, or have more pleasant things improved your complexion?"

"More pleasant, if you must know, and I've nothing further to say on the matter."

"If I didn't have such gossip I'd pry more out of you," Alice said. "But I heard Pru talking to Mr Davis. She says she saw someone coming across the grounds to the servants' entrance last night after the murder. Thing is, none of us should've been out then."

"Did she see the person enter the house?"

"No, but she heard the door open and close."

"What makes her think it was one of the staff?" Lily asked. "It could have been someone else entirely."

"As if Mr Hargreaves would be using the servants' entrance to his own house." Alice snorted. "I don't think so."

"What did Mr Davis say?"

"Only that he would speak to Mr Hargreaves when he returns."

"I imagine we'll all be interviewed again," Lily said.

"That's the trouble with murder," Alice said. "It doesn't go away. You don't think there's any truth to that nonsense the nursery maid was always spouting, do you? That having a murderer's child in the house will bring evil?"

"Utter rubbish," Lily said. "You know, Alice, I thought I saw someone that night when I was up here getting the dressing rooms ready after dinner. I don't know what time it was, but I'm sure it was a man, and he was near our entrance to the house."

"Could it have been the same person Pru saw?"

"It's possible. I hadn't really remembered it till now." Lily crinkled her brow. "I suppose it must have been. Surely there weren't two people marauding in the night?"

"You'd better tell Mr Hargreaves."

Lily nodded and took a deep breath. "I must indeed."

"Let's get this finished, then," Alice said. "Won't get easier for being put off. And that way you can get straight to the master. Lucky girl. Wish I had an excuse to talk to him."

They both giggled, then made quick work of the room, quicker than Lily would have liked. Mr

Hargreaves was faultlessly kind, but she didn't like the idea of talking about murder to anyone, even him.

CHAPTER
FOUR

Colin and I agreed it would be preferable for me to call on Miss Fitzgerald without him, both of us aware that gentlemen don't often bring out candor in young ladies with indelicate romantic connections. I stopped at Anglemore only to get my pony trap to drive into Melton Carbury, neatly avoiding my mother, who was taking tea in one of the sitting rooms in the west wing. Melton Carbury was picturesque, pleasantly situated near a stream over which stood a mill so quaint one could hardly believe it functioned in any way but to add to the charm of the village. I asked the first person I saw to direct me to the Fitzgeralds', and was surprised to learn they lived in the vicarage, a living that was part of the Montagu estate.

I had not figured Cora for a vicar's daughter.

Letting myself indulge in a flight of fancy for just a moment, I imagined Cora to be a particularly fetching housemaid, but then I remembered her letters, as well as Archibald's friends' statements about her middle-class background. An educated — and daring — lady had written them.

A dour-looking middle-aged housekeeper opened the door, ushered me inside, and seated me in a cozy drawing room decorated modestly and with a sense of decorum appropriate to a vicarage. A few moments later, a slim girl in an uninspired black dress joined me. Her hair, blond and wispy, was pulled into a low bun. Neither her appearance nor the pained expression on her face could detract from her beauty. Her delicate features, rose-colored lips, and emerald eyes were beguiling, even as she pulled an unpleasant face. It was easy to see why she had inspired romantic passions in Archibald Scolfield.

"Do forgive me," she said. "I was not expecting visitors."

"The fault is entirely mine," I said and introduced myself. "I am here on behalf of the Marquess of Montagu."

"That seems unlikely, Lady Emily. Lord Montagu is dead." Her voice trembled.

"You heard about the unfortunate event?"

"His cousin, Lady Matilda, sent for my father this morning. She was in need of religious consolation."

"Of course," I said. "I understand you were well acquainted with Lord Montagu?"

"Archibald? I was going to marry him." A small sob caught in her throat, but she retained her composure. The cost of this was visible in the deep lines on her brow and the tears pooling in her large eyes.

I counted to ten, silently and in Greek, and then drew a deep breath before speaking. Another erstwhile fiancée? "Forgive my impertinence, but was your engagement official?"

"He had not yet spoken to my father, if that is what you mean," Cora said. "As a result, we had made no announcement."

"But your father was aware of your understanding?"

"Not as such." She lifted a black-bordered handkerchief to her eye, catching the tears before they could fall. "We thought it best to exercise a certain amount of discretion."

"Why was that?"

"The very idea of planning a wedding while Archibald's family was in mourning was distasteful. They all adored his grandfather."

"So you had not made any firm plans for the wedding?"

"Archibald had arranged with Lady Matilda to swap that hideous nouveau medieval heap for her house in London. We were going to live there."

"You are not fond of Montagu Manor?"

"Lady Emily, I have spent almost my entire life holed up in the country. I realize Melton Carbury is lovely, but I despise it. There's such limited society and so little to do. What would I accomplish by moving from this house five miles up the road to a pile of stones made up to be a castle? I want to be in London, to go to the theater, to parties and balls."

"So you would be married from this house and move to town?" I asked.

"Archibald thought it would be much more romantic if we eloped." She pressed her lips together and looked down. "Forgive me, it is difficult to talk about such things now that they can never happen."

"I am truly sorry for your loss," I said, "and I would not press you to speak on the subject if I did not believe it to be of grave importance. The more we know about Lord Montagu's life, the more likely we are to find his killer."

"I understand." Her voice shook in what in other circumstances would have been considered a most ladylike and attractive way. She was the picture of frail beauty waiting to be rescued and looked after with the tender care that might only be provided by one of the empire's finest gentlemen. "Eloping, he insisted, would best capture the . . ." Her voice trailed off, and she looked away from me. "Would capture the passion of his love for me."

Archibald, I thought, had very little shame. "What would your father say?"

"He would hardly notice. He's the least sentimental man alive. So long as I was married and respectable, he wouldn't care about the details of the arrangements. You'd think a man who was devoted to missionary work in his younger years and spent so much time in exotic locales would have little patience for country life, but that has proven not to be the case. Father is barely aware of what I do, so long as I refrain from embarrassing him. It has taught me well the art of discretion. Archibald noticed my skills in that area straightaway."

I felt a deep dislike for the Marquess of Montagu brewing in the depths of my soul. Archibald's attempt at romance did not sound like something a gentleman would suggest. Quite the contrary. More likely, it was a disgraceful attempt to seduce a respectable young lady.

"I understand there was frequent correspondence between the two of you."

"That is true."

"Would it be possible to see the letters he wrote you?"

"I burned them after I read them. I could not risk my father stumbling upon them."

"Is that because his were like yours?" I asked.

"I do not understand your meaning."

"Yours were rather explicit."

"Archibald had a great appreciation for my epistolary talents," she said, "and I knew what to write to ensure he would not forget me in the face of London's myriad temptations."

The unabashed way she admitted this came as a shock, and I wondered if, in the absence of her mother, anyone had cautioned her against behaving in such a reckless fashion. Her letters had reeked of confidence and sophistication, but Archibald's treatment of her suggested he was doing little more than taking advantage of a young lady not wholly aware of what she was doing.

"When did you accept his proposal?" I asked.

"He never made a formal proposal, Lady Emily," she said. "It merely became evident to us both that marriage was the only way forward given the deep passion we shared."

"So you would marry and then move to London. Did Lord Montagu have many friends there?" I asked.

"A few, I'm sure, but most of them live abroad, so we would not entertain much at home. We planned to travel as often as we could."

"What about his chums from Oxford?" I asked.

"He did not remain close with any of them," she said with a little sigh. "It was difficult for him to connect with people there. They did not understand him."

"So you have not met any of his friends?"

"No. As I said, he doesn't often invite them to England."

"I see." I took a moment to compose myself and to attempt to be open to the possibility that there was an honorable explanation for Archibald's devious behavior. I strongly suspected he had no intention of ever marrying Miss Fitzgerald. He would move her to London and live with her — perhaps even stage a false wedding — all the while going forth with plans to take the wealthy Miss Sturdevant as his bride. "Were you at home last night?"

"No. I was assisting the widow of a local farmer. She has seven children, very little income, and fever sweeping through the house."

"I am sorry to hear that." I knew all too well the difficulties faced by tenants, particularly those in these past decades, when agriculture had become a tenuous way of life. I did everything I could for my own, making sure they were never in need and sending our own physician to treat them when they were ill. Colin ensured none of them lived in a condition he considered unacceptable. We both loathed poverty and did whatever was in our power to help those less fortunate than ourselves.

Landholders had responsibility for their tenants, and we condemned in the strongest terms those families that did not take adequate care of the people living on their estates. "Might I offer any assistance?"

"I am sure she would be grateful, but you really ought to leave it to Lady Matilda. They're her tenants."

"I suppose," I said. "Although I would imagine the more help, the better, and Lady Matilda is unlikely to have much spare time while dealing with the aftermath of her cousin's death."

"That would have to be up to Lady Matilda." Her curt tone left no doubt as to her feelings on the matter. "I shall be sure to pass the information along to her. If there's nothing else, I must beg your leave, Lady Emily. Losing Archibald is a blow I am not sure I can withstand. I want nothing more than to sit in the church and pray for his soul."

Her tone, measured and calm, did not reflect the tightening around her eyes or the tension in her clenched jaw. I did believe she was mourning her loss, but there had been too many complications in her relationship with Archibald. There was something nervous about her manner, revealed by hands that couldn't seem to remain still and eyes that flitted too quickly. I did not doubt Cora Fitzgerald would pray for the soul of her dead fiancé, but I wondered if she needed to pray for her own as well.

Colin and Simon were playing billiards when I returned home. This came as no surprise. Chess was Colin's first love, but billiards came a close second. Simon might joke about trouncing Colin in chess, but my husband was difficult to beat, and Simon was something of an expert when it came to the precise shots necessary to urge small, hard balls across a felt table and into a distant hole. It was a skill I certainly had never mastered. The billiard room was on the upper floor of the front of the house, opposite the nursery wing. The dark wood paneling on the walls, deep green velvet curtains hanging over the windows, and the thick, rich carpet made it a cozy retreat. It was an exceedingly comfortable space, particularly for gentlemen. The air had a permanent scent of cigar smoke, and all the best whisky in the house was consumed here. Due to my hopelessness when it came to the game, I tended to avoid the room in favor of the gallery that ran the length of the back of the house on the same floor, where we displayed our large collection of antiquities, and often sketched there while my husband played. This habit had led me to associate the click of billiard balls with Roman frescoes and Greek sculpture.

I entered the room, avoiding Simon's cue stick as he lined up a shot, and sat on the leather sofa that hugged one of the room's long walls. Telamon, the smallest of the foxhounds, slunk over to my feet, and I reached down to pet him. "Cora Fitzgerald has left me questioning everything I have ever believed about vicars' daughters." I leaned against the stiff back of the sofa, brushed a dog hair from the blue wool of my bolero bodice, and recounted for them our meeting. "I'm not sure what to think about her. Half of me thinks she's the naive victim of a cad, the other half that she's very good at whatever game's afoot. It is as if she is part innocent young lady and part sophisticated woman of the world."

"What makes you doubt her?" Colin asked.

"Her unwillingness to let me help the widow. I felt she was trying to keep me from speaking to the woman, perhaps because Miss Fitzgerald invented the entire incident. I am not convinced she was at the farmhouse when Archibald was murdered."

"What of this mysterious American set to marry Montagu, Hargreaves?" Simon asked. "Could Miss Sturdevant have killed her faithless fiancé?"

"Unlikely, as she's been in New York for the past two months," Colin said. "Before that, she was in Paris for the better part of six months. Much of their relationship transpired via letters."

"I am not personally acquainted with Miss Sturdevant," I said, "but the only criticisms I have heard of her are the sort that lead me to believe I would like her very much."

"A spirited girl who bucks convention?" Colin asked.

I raised an eyebrow. "Quite."

"I wonder that you didn't take her under your wing," Simon said. He dropped two balls into a side pocket with a single shot.

"I might have had I known more about her when she was in London last," I said.

"So Montagu likes his girls a bit wild," Simon said.

"Even when he's proposing to the daughter of the local vicar," I said. "I wonder how many other potential brides Archibald had accumulated."

64

"I am not sure you're being entirely fair, Emily. We don't know that he was trifling with Cora. He may have never talked about marriage with her. We only have her word on the subject."

"You saw her letters — they were having a torrid affair," I said. "At least one of words."

"A gentleman rarely has a torrid affair with a lady he would consider marrying. It could impugn her reputation." He leaned over the table, lining up his shot.

"Colin!"

"It's true, Emily," Simon said. "Cora Fitzgerald, no matter what she claims now, could have had very little hope of marrying a marquess."

"And you think that is acceptable?" I asked.

"I am not offering judgment on the situation," Simon said. "I merely confirm your always-brilliant husband's observations. You know how I feel about the separation of classes. It is poison."

"Cora Fitzgerald is a vicar's daughter," I said. "She is hardly the sort of girl who would seem obvious prey to a man of loose morals."

"How quickly Archibald has fallen in your esteem!"

"Simon, do not tease me."

"Let us stay focused on what matters," Colin said, sinking his last ball and winning the game. Without comment, he began to rack the balls so they could start again. "Archibald didn't spend much time at Montagu, so he couldn't have seen Miss Fitzgerald often. The affair, such as it was, would have been conducted primarily via letters."

"Much like his relationship with his so-called fiancée," I said. I found myself liking Archibald Scolfield less and less the more I learned about him.

"It would have been simple for him to keep the two relationships separate," Colin said.

"Until he was discovered," I said, finishing for him. "Thereby giving both ladies ample motive to want him dead."

"The two of you frighten me," Simon said. "Sometimes I think you share your thoughts without having to say them aloud. It is unnerving."

The door to the room opened. Lily, a pretty girl of no more than eighteen who had worked for me for several years, stepped inside quietly, tended to the fire, and started to leave. Simon stopped her.

"Wait, please, if you would, Lily." He put down his cue and disappeared from the room, returning a few moments later with a piece of heavy watercolor paper that had been rolled into a scroll. "The vista I told you about," he said. "I painted it for you so you won't have to wait until next week."

Lily's face flushed, and she looked at me, fear in her eyes. "It's all right, Lily," I said. "Lord Flyte is perfectly harmless. Although one might expect a gentleman to be more considerate about putting young women in awkward situations."

"Thank you, madam." She turned to Simon. "And, sir, I —"

"There's no need, Lily. I do hope you enjoy it. I've not your talent, but I do hope the work brings you some pleasure."

66

"It's the loveliest thing I've ever seen," she said. "You are a master. The way you've painted the water it's as if it's really rippling."

"That is a very kind compliment. You are familiar with watercolors?"

She studied the painting, seeming almost lost in it. "I've never painted myself, of course. I only have pencils. I've never tried anything else."

"Lily is quite talented," I said. "Her sketches seem almost real."

"Thank you, madam," Lily said, her cheeks coloring.

"I have seen them," Simon said, "and have already told her she is in possession of a not inconsiderable talent."

Lily murmured more thanks, carefully rolled the watercolor, and then held it behind her back, her gaze fixed to the floor. "Will there be anything else, madam?"

"No, that is all," I said.

She bobbed a curtsy and left us.

"Do I need to worry about my staff?" Colin asked. "Please tell me you're not harassing the maids."

"Of course I'm not," Simon said. "I was taken with a view on your magnificent grounds. I mentioned it to her. She said she would take a look at it the next time she had an afternoon free. It struck me as terribly sad that she'd have no opportunity for almost a week, so, knowing she has an interest in art, I painted it for her. Is that wrong?"

"Not as such," Colin said. "So long as she doesn't feel pestered."

"What a life it must be. Time to yourself only once a week. Can you imagine?" Simon asked.

"I cannot," Colin said, "but then my work sometimes occupies me for months at a time with no break. None of us has unlimited leisure, Flyte."

"Spoken like a gentleman," I said. "Most ladies are forbidden to have anything but leisure, no matter what we would like."

"Lily might find that appealing," Colin said, turning back to his game and lining up his cue for his next shot. The ball bounced off the felt side of the table, missing the hole.

"I don't think so," I said. "It is deadly dull to have no useful purpose, particularly when you have no choice about it."

Simon looked wistful and paused before taking his next shot. "Sometimes I think I should move to America, where every man can make himself into whatever he wants."

"You will never leave Yorkshire," I said.

"Truer words were never spoken, Emily," Colin said. "I am still amazed we persuaded him to come as far as Derbyshire."

"I thought it would be unreasonable to ask that you have the twins baptized at my chapel," Simon said, "but do not expect me to make a habit of traveling. I'm far too comfortable in my home."

Davis cracked open the door and popped his head into the room.

"Lady Matilda Scolfield for you, madam," he said. "I surmised from her appearance that things have gone rather pear-shaped for her, so I put her in the library and will bring up port at once."

"Thank you, Davis. What would I ever do without you?" I gave him a quick smile and started for the door.

"This from a lady who scolds me for taking liberties with the staff?" Simon asked.

"Nothing will ever come between her and Davis," Colin said. I stopped, returned to my husband, and gave him a kiss.

"Nothing at all," I said.

Davis had been the butler in my first husband's household, and soon after Philip's death had become indispensable to me. He understood my passion for port, anticipated the times I would require it, and did his best to keep me away from cigars. It was a battle he frequently lost, but I appreciated his vain efforts to protect my reputation. Colin understood long before our marriage that he would have to take Davis along with me, and soon after, he realized Davis was at least as necessary to him. Few things in life can compete with a good butler.

The instant I went downstairs and saw Matilda, I knew Davis had judged the situation with a keen accuracy. Red eyes told me she had been crying, but now she looked to be heading at a terrifying pace to rage. Her hair, escaping from its pins, formed a deranged sort of halo around her face, and mud covered the bottom six inches of her skirt. It was as if she had run the entire way from Montagu. She had all but collapsed when I entered the room.

"It's over now," she said, dissolving into angry sobs. "Every bit of it."

"Every bit of what?" I asked, sitting down and pulling her next to me.

"My life. Everything." She spat the words, flailing her arms as she spoke. "I don't even know where I shall go. I'm practically homeless."

"You own no fewer than four houses, so I doubt you've nowhere to go, whatever the circumstance," I said. "What has happened?"

"I am not Archie's heir. There is someone else claiming the title, and unless you help me expose him for the charlatan he is, there will be no reason for me to go on living."

Davis entered the room discreetly and placed a silver tray with two glasses and a decanter filled with port on the table nearest to me. He poured, although standard practice would have one serve port to oneself. I had not known that — what lady could? — when I first became fond of the libation. Davis, a consummate professional, had not corrected my error, and I found I rather liked him pouring for me and had decided to disregard convention and instead do as I pleased.

"Take a sip, then a deep breath, and then tell me exactly what has put you in this state," I said once the butler had left as quietly as he had come.

Fortunately for me, Matilda followed directions. The port had its usual soothing effect, and soon she was calm enough to talk rationally.

"A solicitor came from London. Unannounced. Very bad manners." She took another slug from her glass.

"He sat me down and informed me that I am not the Montagu heir. That role goes to some far-distant cousin called Rodney Scolfield who sounds like an absolute reprobate."

"Do you know him?"

"I have never heard mention of him until today. He is some sort of fortune hunter, currently en route from South America or Mexico or California or some equally dreadful place where he's been searching for the lost gold of Cortés."

"Cortés?" I asked. "Fascinating. How exactly is he related to Archibald?"

"The genealogy doesn't matter because it is all fabricated. Of that I am certain."

"Why?"

"Because I have never even heard anyone in the family refer to him! Don't you think someone would have mentioned him?"

"How distant a cousin is he?" It was not unusual in the least for entailed estates to go to relatives heretofore unknown. Primogeniture ensured such situations would arise with frequency, and the widows and daughters (or in this case granddaughters) forced out of their ancestral home had little reason to rejoice at being displaced so that the family name could continue, unbroken, through the male line.

"I can't remember the details. Not that it matters. What I need now is for you to help me prove that he is a fraud."

"When do you expect Mr Scolfield to arrive at Montagu? I suppose I should call him Lord Montagu."

"Do not dare call him any such thing, no matter what he claims," she said. "I've not the slightest idea when to expect him. Who could say how long it takes to extract oneself from the godless jungle? If, that is, he is still in the godless jungle."

"Did the solicitor give you any proof of the relation?"

"Yes, but I didn't bring it with me. Do you need to see it?"

"It couldn't hurt," I said. "I suppose for the moment it would make sense to take as a foregone conclusion that his claim is legitimate."

"Absolutely not, Emily. How can you suggest such a thing?"

"Whatever evidence there is satisfied Archibald's solicitors, correct?" I asked. Matilda nodded. "So why do you think the solicitor is wrong?"

"Though I have never heard his name, I do know that entire line of the family is illegitimate."

"Is that so?" I asked.

"I have never been more sure of anything," she said. "My nanny told me the story when I was a girl."

"But you've never heard of this branch of the family before?"

"Well, I knew of them in theory." She scowled. "I just didn't remember the particulars."

"And your nanny's story is the extent of your knowledge of the situation?"

"Nanny was the most honest person I've ever known." Matilda sounded like an obedient schoolgirl.

"I take it she is no longer with us?"

"She died six years ago."

"A pity," I said. "Do tell me the story."

"It's the usual sort of thing — broken hearts, forbidden love. A long-ago Montagu fell in love with a servant. The servant wasn't trifled with, mind you, this was love, real and true. But the baby born to the unlucky couple was passed off as a legitimate heir and never knew the true story of his birth. I admit to having only a tenuous grasp of the details."

"I am afraid, Matilda, we shall need more than a nursery bedtime story."

"I cannot deal with this on my own." Desperation filled her voice. "Will you help me?"

"Of course. I promise to do whatever I can, but you must be realistic about your expectations. Just because you want Mr Scolfield to be illegitimate does not mean he will turn out to be."

"I will do anything necessary to keep Montagu Manor out of the hands of this professional treasure hunter. Grandfather would be spinning in his grave."

"I shall come to you in the morning, and we can go over whatever family records we can find."

"Thank you, Emily."

"You must promise me, Matilda, that you will not cling to false hope."

"I'll promise anything you want, so long as it keeps Rodney Scolfield as far away from me as possible."

Downstairs

iv

Lily had never seen anything outside of a museum quite so lovely as Lord Flyte's watercolor. She had always loved drawing and spent whatever she could afford on pencils and paper. When she had worked for Lady Emily in London, she had used her afternoons off to visit the National Gallery and sketch her favorite canvases, but she never dreamed of being able to paint. She could hardly imagine being able to afford the materials. An earl could, of course, and she was so very flattered that Lord Flyte had chosen to share his talent with her. She wondered if she could somehow manage to go to the lake sooner than next week, but it didn't seem possible. There was too much work to be done. She rolled the painting back up and slid it into one of her dresser drawers.

"Have you finished with the State Rooms?" Mrs Elliott asked, standing in the doorway to the bedroom Lily shared with Alice. The State Rooms were rarely used, but the wood, with its elaborate carving done when Elizabeth had been Queen — or maybe when her father reigned, or was it the Scottish bloke who came later? Lily couldn't remember. At any rate, it still needed frequent polishing. The present Queen had never visited Anglemore Park, but Lady Emily was acquainted with her, so it made sense to keep the rooms at the ready. Mrs Elliott always said one never could predict the whims of royalty.

"Yes," Lily said. "The tea leaves worked wonders for getting the dust out of the carpets."

"Very good." This was as close to high praise as one could expect from Mrs Elliott. She ran a tight household and was convinced kindness could lead to idleness. "Mr Hargreaves has asked to see you. You can find him in his study. I do hope there's nothing for me to worry about?"

"No, no, of course not, Mrs Elliott." Lily smoothed her crisp apron. "I'll go down right away." Mrs Elliott reached up and adjusted Lily's lace-trimmed cap.

"You should be more careful to present yourself well. A sloppy maid is a lazy maid. Go now, and be sure not to get behind in the rest of your work. Mr Hargreaves would not appreciate it."

The master of the house frequently retreated to his study during the afternoon, when his wife went for a ride. Lily wondered if Lord Flyte would be with him, and then caught herself thinking about the latter gentleman in a rather undignified and decidedly dreamy manner. She wondered about the origin of his limp. Had he been injured in battle? Or defending someone's honor? Or perhaps hunting elephants in Africa? She shook her head, scolded herself silently, and marched to Mr Hargreaves's study.

"Thank you for coming so quickly, Lily," Mr Hargreaves said, motioning for her to sit on one of the two stiff leather chairs across from his desk. As she sat, he stood up, came around the desk, and took the other seat. "Davis has informed me that Prudence, the kitchen maid, saw someone coming into the house through the servants' entrance shortly after the time the Marquess of Montagu was murdered."

"Yes, sir. I have heard that."

"He also tells me that you informed him of having seen someone, too?"

"Yes, sir. I believe I saw the same man."

"You are quite certain it was a man?"

"Oh, yes, sir." Lily was sitting bolt upright. "It was definitely a man. That's the one thing I'm sure of."

"Could you see his face?"

"No, but he was too big and bulky to have been a woman."

"Was it a servant?"

"I couldn't rightly say, sir. It was dark except for the moon."

"Where exactly were you standing?" Mr Hargreaves asked.

"I was in the gallery on the first floor. I can't say for sure where he was going. He was below the terrace, coming around the side, like he was headed for the servants' entrance. I'd just finished putting fresh water in the bedroom ewers, sir. The moon was bright, and I stopped at the window. I didn't stay for long. I know I was a bit late getting things done that evening, but I wasn't shirking my duties."

"No one suspects you of that, Lily."

"Am I suspected of something else?" There was fear in her voice.

"No." He smiled kindly. "I am glad you spotted the moon and took a moment to appreciate it. A harvest moon like that deserves notice."

"Yes, sir."

"Do you think you could describe any bit of the man's clothing?"

Lily tensed, trying as hard as she could to think clearly. She shook her head. "I'm afraid not, sir. He might have been wearing a cloak of some sort, but I can't be sure. He was really just a big, dark mass. I'm sorry if that's not enough help."

"You've done wonderfully. I shan't keep you from your work any longer." He flashed her another of his devastatingly charming smiles — she would have to remember to tell Alice — and rose again to standing. "Thank you, Lily."

As she left the room, Lily became aware that her heart was pounding and her mouth was dry. It was silly to have been nervous, she thought, but how could one avoid it? Murder's ugly head would let no one in the house have peace.

CHAPTER
FIVE

I suspect, when it came to the matter of Rodney Scolfield's legitimacy, I initially proved something of a disappointment to Matilda. I was already used to this, as our previous acquaintance had similar results. While we both believed passionately that women ought to have the vote, she wanted a much more radical and violent fight than I. I preferred a more subtle approach, convincing, for example, members of Parliament, one by one, to reconsider their views on suffrage. Matilda would rather fling rocks through their windows until they were battered into submission. Now, when it came to the unexpected heir to Montagu, she wanted immediate and extreme results, but that was not to be. After studying the documents supplied by Archibald's solicitor, I saw no reason to doubt Mr Scolfield's claim to the Montagu title. This enraged Matilda, and I did my best to pacify her, but to little result. In the end, I decided there was no harm in indulging in a bit of genealogical research while we waited for Scolfield's arrival from, as Matilda so aptly described it, the godless jungle. Colin had ventured to Oxford so that he might dig into Archibald's academic career, and he then planned to conduct further interviews with the man's closest friends. I was glad to have something of my own to do and knew that if there were some irregularity to be found in the family records, it could, perhaps, have a significant impact on the murder investigation.

The actual genealogy of the Montagu line was underwhelming. Mr Scolfield was related in a distant but direct manner, and I could find nothing that even remotely suggested an illegitimacy that could undo him. I decided it would be best to turn to a more general sort of family history. Odds were we wouldn't uncover anything damning, but it might at least keep Matilda from coming unhinged while she waited for her unwelcome long-lost cousin.

First, we read her father's personal papers, which proved dry, dull, and utterly uninformative. He had been strangely obsessed with geese and had named and taken extensive notes about the habits of the ones that summered at Montagu. It was little wonder Matilda's grandfather had felt relief at outliving his son. Estate management, other than waterfowl preservation, would no doubt have suffered had he ever inherited the title.

"Why did your grandfather leave his fortune to you instead of Archibald?" I asked, as we gathered the old man's notebooks and journals. "The estate may not have been entailed, but most peers would have wanted to guarantee there was enough money in the hands of the heir to keep up the house, if nothing else."

"Grandfather knew Archibald had money of his own, and he had a special affection for me. He knew I would manage the finances well, and he knew that I would never let Montagu Manor fall into disrepair, even if it meant taking the burden of expenses onto myself."

"Despite the fact that the house didn't belong to you?"

"Yes."

"Did he trust Archibald?"

She looked thoughtful for a moment before answering. "He liked Archie well enough — everyone did — but Archie might not have proven the best landlord, and Grandfather felt the whole estate would be better served if I had control of the money."

"You are very rich, Matilda," I said, "and entirely in control of your life. Do you wish to marry?" This might not seem an obvious question. What young lady of our day and age did not want a husband? I, as I suspected Matilda might, knew well the value of being wholly in charge of one's life. There was a time, after my first husband had died, during which I believed fervently that I would never again marry. For ladies, marriage meant a loss of independence, and I could well believe love mattered far less to Matilda than her freedom.

"Never. Grandfather knew that, too, and no doubt it contributed to his wanting to look after me. He took care to arrange things so that I would never require a husband to maintain my lifestyle." Matilda did not have the elegant figure currently favored in society. She was strong and sturdy, with broad shoulders and long limbs, more warrior queen than fairy princess, an image cemented by her passion for fencing, an activity in which most ladies would never consider partaking. Her features were even, her eyes perhaps a bit small, but the overall effect was attractive, albeit in an unusual fashion.

"Would you have settled your own fortune on Archibald's children, had he survived to have some?"

"Not necessarily," she said. "My plan has always been to set up a trust to maintain Montagu Manor. I love this house and I love the land. Nothing matters more to me."

We took a break from our work around noon to have a cold luncheon in the cavernous dining room. Spears, swords, and shields hung from the walls between rich modern tapestries whose bright colors were most likely a fair re-creation of their medieval counterparts before the ravages of time had faded them.

"This was one of my grandfather's favorite parts of the house," Matilda said. "He insisted that the table be placed like this, up on a dais, with more narrow ones below, just as it would have been in the Middle Ages. My grandmother refused to let him scatter reeds on the floor, no matter how authentic he claimed it would be."

I smiled and examined the ornate gold saltcellar in the center of the long table at which we sat. "We are above the salt."

"But of course." Matilda smiled. "Grandfather would tolerate nothing less. I think it disappointed him greatly that salt is no longer the commodity it was in the Middle Ages. His guests never fully appreciated the honor of being seated above it."

"Matilda, does it really matter if Rodney Scolfield inherits?" I asked. "Do not get angry with me. You and Archibald had a comfortable understanding of how the estate would be managed. Why couldn't you have the same with Rodney?"

"I don't know the man at all. How on earth could I trust him?"

"You could set up a trust for the estate, just as you had planned. He would have no cause to object to that."

"Perhaps," Matilda said, "but what are the odds that he would let an unknown relative stay in the house? Even if he did agree to my staying, I don't harbor the slightest interest in living with a total stranger."

"You might find that you like him."

"That, Emily, is utterly impossible. Nothing could be more certain."

I smiled and pushed my plate away. "Then I suppose our only option is to continue our work in the hope it offers some escape from what seems an unavoidable fate."

We returned to our research. It quickly became clear that Matilda was very much enjoying reading her grandfather's papers. It was also clear that he had nothing to say that would impugn Mr Scolfield. So I left my friend to the reams of papers surrounding her and focused my attention on the earlier Montagu peers. The seventh marquess, Matilda's great-grandfather, had distinguished himself in the Napoleonic Wars. The third had been born in London during the Great Fire. But the one who most took my fancy was the sixth, not a marquess, but a marchioness, Charlotte, a peer in her own right, just as Matilda might have been had Rodney Scolfield not materialized.

Charlotte had been born in 1758 and inherited when she was twenty-two years old, only a few months before she gave birth to her son, who became the seventh marquess upon the death of his mother in 1805. The marchioness's portrait hung in a sitting room at Montagu and showed her to be a proud, handsome woman with strong features not unlike Matilda's. She posed seated on a fallen tree branch, in what I recognized as the grounds at Montagu Manor, wearing a jaunty riding habit and a tall powdered wig that would have given Marie Antoinette pangs of envy. One of the few outbuildings Matilda's grandfather had left standing, an orangery in the classical style, was visible behind her. Far in the background, a man in livery stood with a horse, holding its reins and looking wistfully at the lady who must have been his employer.

I asked for any family stories about Charlotte, but Matilda knew nothing of her, except that she had inherited the title. "I might have been more taken with her had I, too, been marchioness," she said. "There doesn't seem much point now."

"You're surrendering to Rodney Scolfield?" I asked.

"No." Her voice was not so strong as it had been when previously discussing the new Lord Montagu. "Although I shall have to accept him if we cannot find anything of use."

"Did your nanny ever tell you when the line went illegitimate?"

"It might have been during the Restoration," she said. "I can't really remember. Grandfather kept the mementos of the family in a room upstairs. We can root through them if you would like."

"Where did they come from?"

"When he decided to pull down the old house, he knew he should keep bits of the family history. He didn't want to reinvent everything, only the space in which he lived. When the staff were emptying the contents before demolition began, my grandfather put aside everything he thought important and then sorted it by person. Each marquess, and the solitary marchioness, has a dedicated trunk."

"Let's take a look," I said. "I do not mean to frustrate you further, Matilda, but the genealogy is so solid it is unlikely that anything in these trunks could change the current situation. Even if there is some sort of irregularity, Mr Scolfield's ancestors were accepted as legitimate. If someone came forward today and could prove that George III was, in fact, a bastard, it would not threaten the current Queen's reign."

"I will cling to any tenuous hope," Matilda said, setting her jaw in fierce determination. "Let us not forget our medieval ancestors who felt no compunction at usurping the throne."

"A strategy that did not work well in the long run for Richard III," I said, "although it might have if the throne had not been usurped from him as well."

"I blame Henry Tudor altogether," Matilda said.

"Agreed. Wretched man."

The trunks were neatly stacked in a sunlit room on the second floor of the house. Going through them was a delight, a tactile history of England. I held the seventh marquess's saber, touched the ermine trim on a robe worn to Charles II's coronation, and gently cupped in my hands a collection of fragile dried rose petals Charlotte had saved in a dark violet velvet bag. A pale pink drawstring of fine satin closed the container, and attached to it was a slip of paper that read *Keep these always.* Nothing else in her trunk referred to the petals, but no decent person could have ignored the girlish handwriting on the tag and tossed them out.

The remainder of the afternoon disappeared in a shot; treasure hunting is a pleasant pastime if not always a productive one. Diverted though we were, nothing turned up to cast even the slightest aspersion on Rodney Scolfield's background. We returned downstairs and called for a pot of tea. Matilda sifted through her mail while I munched on a small cake and wondered what on earth I could do next to keep her occupied and even-tempered.

Even-tempered was not an expression that could be used to describe Matilda after she had opened one particular envelope. She frowned as she read and flung the papers on the floor.

"It has already begun," she said, her neck and cheeks colored a deep, angry red. "He has hired architects to destroy Montagu. Already. Can you imagine? Setting this in motion before he has taken possession of the house?"

"Who?" I asked.

"Mr Scolfield, of course."

"He has never even seen the house," I said. "How could he know he wants to change it?"

"Not the house. The grounds. The fool has set in motion plans to construct a faux medieval village on the east side of the property. Have you ever heard of anything so ridiculous?"

"How very Marie Antoinette of him." I tried to imagine a jungle explorer flitting about the queen's Petit Trianon and Hamlet.

"I will not allow this."

"Not allow what?" The voice came from just beyond the door. "Surely you are not already disparaging my plans. I am going to turn Montagu into the medieval fantasy it was meant to be. The house is off to a good start, that much is clear, but there is more to be done."

A tall, lanky man strolled into the room. Rodney Scolfield, I presumed. His accent was strange, Oxbridge English with just a touch of American, as if he'd spent too much time in New York. Or, given what we knew about his penchant for exploration, the Wild West. His face was deeply tanned and his brown hair streaked from the sun. He carried a well-worn satchel fashioned from the same leather as his boots and held in his right hand what I believe would be called a cowboy hat.

"My dear cousin Mattie!" A wide grin split his face, revealing white, even teeth. "What a pleasure to make your acquaintance at last. I'm Rodney Scolfield, but you must call me Rodney. Never did like ceremony, no matter what title is foisted on me."

Matilda said nothing. She pursed her lips and looked away. Rodney was undaunted.

"I am well aware that I make a certain impression, and it is not always considered to be a good one. You shall get used to me, though. I understand from the family solicitors you would like to keep living here, is that correct?"

Still not a word from Matilda, but there was thunder brewing in her eyes. I felt just a bit sorry for Mr Scolfield. Or, I corrected myself, Lord Montagu.

"You arrived much sooner than we had expected," I said. "I am Lady Emily Hargreaves, a friend of your cousin's. Have ships started crossing the Atlantic at a new record speed?"

"No, no," he said, taking a seat before one had been offered. "I was already halfway to New York when I heard the news about Archibald and hopped on the first ship I could. Terribly sad death. I was more affected by it than I would have thought, given that I never knew the bloke. Still, he was family, and —"

"More likely you were terribly delighted to hear you had come into such a valuable property, Mr Scolfield." Matilda's emphasis on the "Mr" left no doubt as to her opinion of her cousin's new status.

"That is not true at all, Mattie." He looked sincere.

"My name is Matilda."

"I prefer Mattie."

"I was named after Matilda the empress, daughter of Henry I. You are unlikely to be familiar with her." Matilda's face hardly moved as she spoke, but the anger clouding her eyes was evident and growing.

"She married the Holy Roman Emperor," the new Lord Montagu said. "Henry V. I studied history at the Sorbonne."

"Should I be impressed?" Matilda asked. "You are aware, I hope, that he was not the Henry V who emerged victorious from the field of Agincourt?"

I had not thought about it previously, but Matilda's name was apt. She, like her namesake, was fighting for what she thought was her birthright. Of course, the Empress Matilda had better resources, not to mention an army.

Lord Montagu studied her face and narrowed his eyes. "Boudica."

"Pardon?" Matilda scowled.

"Boudica seems a more appropriate name for you. A warrior queen. I shall call you Boudica."

"I shan't answer."

"We'll see about that," he said.

Matilda crossed her arms and looked away from him. I suppressed a smile. "Boudica" was a quite decent nickname for her. Boudica, whom Tacitus described driving a chariot and rallying her troops before a battle against the Romans. Boudica, who killed those who had not fled from Londinium and mutilated their corpses before skewering them. Boudica, who took poison after facing defeat. I all but shuddered. Matilda would never be quite *that* extreme, but I had no difficulty picturing her in command of a chariot.

"Hargreaves . . ." Lord Montagu paused and turned to me. "You are a neighbor, is that correct?"

"Yes. My husband and I live at Anglemore Park."

"The coachman pointed it out on our way. Lovely grounds."

"Thank you."

"I shall have to meet your husband. Does he like whisky?"

"He does," I said, feeling something of a traitor to Matilda for conversing with him.

"Tell him I'll bring him a bottle of my best this evening if that's convenient."

Matilda winced, no doubt cringing at the thought that the whisky to which he referred had, only a few days ago, belonged to her. Or at least so she had thought.

"He's away at the moment, but I expect him back tomorrow."

"Capital. I shall make up the welcoming party."

"I take it, Mr Scolfield, your quest to find Cortés's lost treasure was less than successful?" Matilda asked.

He laughed. "I never expected to find the gold. That's bound to be long gone, but I am awfully keen to learn whatever I can about Chicomoztoc, the Aztecs' lost ancestral city. Do you know about the Aztecs, Boudica?"

"My name is Matilda. You may call me Lady Matilda."

"How about Empress instead?"

Matilda looked as if she were about to explode. She jumped up from her chair, stomped her foot, and looked — for the first time — directly at her visitor. "You needn't bother to call me anything. I shall not stay in this house with you any longer than strictly necessary and shall arrange to have my things sent to London at once. Now if you will excuse me, it is time for my fencing practice."

With that, she tore out of the room, losing several hairpins along the way. All in all, a most impressive exit.

Downstairs

V

Ordinarily, the staff took their meals at regular times, scheduled so as to best avoid interfering with the family's needs. Today, however, the servants' luncheon was later than usual. Mr Hargreaves had wired to say he would be arriving home sooner than expected and had thrown off Cook's plans for dinner. She had been a right terror, ordering everyone around in a furious tone. Pru had offered to prepare the servants' luncheon, but Cook had only rolled her eyes and snorted in response. This set Pru off on a tear, but there were fewer people on whom she could take out her anger than Cook could. When at last the staff sat down to eat, Pru shot wicked glances at Lily all through the meal, until at last Lily could take it no more.

"Have I done something to offend you, Prudence?"

"Prudence? Prudence?" The kitchen maid scoffed. "What sort of airs are you putting on now, missy? One gift from an earl and you think you're better than the rest of us?"

Lily was not pleased the others knew about Lord Flyte's painting. Alice must have told them. Much though this chagrined her, she knew her friend would have done it out of excitement and pride rather than envy. She could never be mad with Alice. Alice was closer to her than anyone else in the world, and she knew she could trust her endlessly. If she had asked Alice to keep the painting a secret, she would have. How she wished she had done! "'Prudence' was how Mr Hargreaves referred to you when I was speaking with him. I thought I would extend you the same courtesy."

"Putting on airs." Pru shook her head.

"Why have you been throwing the evil eye at me all day?" Lily asked.

"Only because of what you told Mr Hargreaves during your famous conversation," Pru said.

"I don't understand your meaning."

"You told him you saw a man after the murder. How could that be?"

"What on earth do you mean?" Lily blanched and her stomach turned. "I told him what I saw."

"How do you know the murderer was a man?"

"I have no idea if the person I saw was involved in the crime."

"But you're sure it was a man?"

"Yes, I am." Confidence came back into Lily's voice.

"That's funny. Real funny." Pru sopped up the stew in her bowl with a piece of bread. "Because I could've sworn I saw a woman."

"It might not have been the same person," Lily said. "We don't even know if it was the same time."

Pru shrugged. "Maybe you're right. Or maybe you're lying."

"Why would you say such a thing?" Lily asked.

"Because I don't trust you," Pru said. "You're striving to go above your station, and I don't like it. Like I said, it isn't seemly. I'm watching you, Lily, and you'd better take care."

"Leave her alone," Alice said. "What did she ever do to you?"

"I don't have to listen to you, Alice," Pru said.

"You do have to listen to me." None of them had noticed Mr Davis standing in the doorway. "I will not tolerate strife among the staff. You will not want me to have to address you on this topic again. Pull yourselves together and get back to work."

Mrs Elliott came in almost as soon as Mr Davis had left. "Lily, I want you to help polish all of Mr Hargreaves's boots and shoes tonight. They will need to be done before you can go to bed."

That was a footman's job. Lily was being punished. It wasn't fair, she knew, but there was no point speaking out. Pru had soundly defeated her in this round.

CHAPTER
SIX

I made what I thought was a neat escape from the drama unfolding between Matilda and the new marquess at Montagu Manor. How happy I was to see Anglemore's facade looming before me! I had come to appreciate the concept of home more and more, especially since the birth of the twins. Anglemore might not be the height of fashionable elegance, but I loved it for that. I approached its off-center entrance, the sort favored by the Elizabethans, who preferred amusement to symmetry and liked guests to have to make a series of turns before entering the hall of a house. Davis opened the door before I had come all the way to it, a wire in his hand. Colin would be back in only a few hours, sooner than expected. I went down to the kitchen to give new instructions to Cook for dinner and had just settled into the library with W. M. Flinders Petrie's *The Pyramids and Temples of Giza* when my peace was interrupted.

"The Marquess of Montagu to see you, madam?" There was a hint of question in Davis's voice.

"The new marquess, yes," I said. "What do you think of him?"

"Madam, I would never comment on the appearance of a gentleman."

"Davis." I raised an eyebrow.

"He looks like I have always imagined the red savages in America do."

"Only slightly less red," I said.

Davis very nearly cracked a smile. "Only slightly."

"Send him in, and bring Mr Hargreaves's cigars." I suspected Davis would ignore anything I said about the cigars but thought it worth a try. Our visitor might have ruffled him enough to throw him off center.

"I must warn you, madam, that Lord Montagu has come with a large stack of luggage."

"Luggage?" I asked. "Oh dear. This will be an interesting evening. Tell Cook to expect another for dinner."

Davis did not return with Colin's cigars, only with Lord Montagu. I gave our guest, who had not abandoned his cowboy hat, my hand to kiss and invited him to sit before he did so of his own accord. I was as yet undecided as to whether his casual enthusiasm was charming or off-putting.

"I am a cad to descend upon you like this," Lord Montagu said, "but I didn't know where else to go. I do hope you can find it in your heart to forgive me. I cannot drive Boudica out of the only home she's ever known. Any chance you might have room for a spare peer until I can get this matter settled?"

"Of course, Lord Montagu —"

"You really must call me Rodney. I can't tolerate all this Lord this, Lord that."

"Rodney, then."

"Thank you."

Simon opened the door. He was too much of a gentleman to show even a hint of curiosity as to the identity of my visitor, and, without missing a beat, he poured whisky for all three of us, dropped onto a chair, propped his legs on the nearest table, and asked Rodney how his travels had brought him to Anglemore Park.

"What makes you think I've been traveling?" Rodney asked.

"One could never get that much sun in England," Simon said.

"Fair point," Rodney said. His skin was the color of chestnuts. "I've been abroad for some time."

"Rodney is an explorer," I said.

"An explorer?" Simon asked, his voice rich with amusement. I did my best not to meet his eyes, as I feared I might laugh. Simon had a way of drawing inappropriate reactions from me.

"More like an amateur archaeologist," Rodney said.

"Or a treasure hunter," I said.

"What sort of treasure?" Simon asked.

"Most recently the lost Aztec city Cortés described," Rodney said.

"Streets paved in gold?" Simon asked.

"The very one."

"And before that?" Simon asked.

"I spent three years in California." Rodney did not seem eager, or prepared, to volunteer more information. I wondered if he had something to hide.

"Looking for more gold?" I asked.

"I would not have objected to finding any," Rodney said, "but it never was my primary object."

"What was?" Simon asked.

"I was making a study of the religious missions in the state. Fascinating architecture."

I was far from convinced. Gold had to hold more appeal to a man like Rodney than mission architecture.

"So now you're the prodigal heir returned, ready to collect his inheritance?" Simon drained his glass.

"Something of the sort," Rodney said. "If only I can figure out what to do about Boudica."

"He means Matilda," I said.

"Who else?" Simon smiled, tipping his empty glass back and forth in his hands.

"I'm curious, Lord — Rodney," I said. "Had you ever met the late Lord Montagu?"

"Lord Montagu as in Archibald or his grandfather?"

"Either of them."

"No. I never met any of that side of the family. Grew up abroad, you see. I was only nine when my parents abandoned England and settled in the south of France. They sent me back to Harrow for school, and then I studied at the Sorbonne before setting off to explore the Americas. Archibald's path would never have crossed mine. As far as the old lord goes, he wasn't likely to seek me out in California, was he? But I find myself quite taken with him now. I greatly admire what he accomplished with Montagu Manor."

"You like medieval architecture as well as mission?" I asked.

"Not especially," he said, "but I admire his passion and his devotion to his ideals. He wanted to be a feudal lord, and he did everything his fortune would allow to make it so he could live like one. Most blokes would sit around their London clubs complaining that life isn't what it used to be. Montagu took action. I respect that."

"I understand that you have already hired an architect to implement more changes to the estate," I said.

"Yes, and I am afraid the move has made me even more unpopular with Boudica. I should like to think her grandfather would have approved. My idea is to re-create a medieval village, only with better plumbing and no serfs. It would suit the manor."

"Will you play peasant there?" I asked, finding I could picture with little difficulty Rodney wielding a scythe in a tall field of grain.

"I thought some of the tenants might like living there. The houses will be new and well built."

"So you turn to the ancient to improve your tenants' lives?" Simon asked.

"I hope it improves their lives."

"Do you plan to live at Montagu?" I asked.

He leaned back in his chair and stretched out his legs. "All my time abroad has left me missing England, even if it is the England of a schoolboy's memory and probably far less romantic than I imagine. But I have never lived someplace I considered a real home, and I think perhaps the time has come to change that.

Assuming, of course, Boudica can't prove I'm the illegitimate relative of heaven-knows-who."

"She told you her scheme?" I asked. This came as a surprise. I thought Matilda would have kept her plans close, not wanting to reveal any strategy to the gentleman she viewed as her enemy. How had Rodney wriggled it out of her? I studied his face. He was handsome enough, in a rugged sort of way, and I could see the appeal of a man bent on adventure. He cut a dashing figure. Yet surely Matilda did not see him that way?

He nodded. "Admirable girl. Isn't taking the news sitting down. A chap cannot fault her for that. I do hope that somehow we can come to a reasonable understanding. As I said, I have no interest in driving her from her home."

Davis opened the door. "Lord Montagu, your bath is ready." Acastus and Leitus had slipped into the room and started sniffing around Rodney's shoes. Rodney gave them each a pat, leapt to his feet, and headed out of the room, clapping Davis on the back as he passed him.

"Thanks, old boy. It was a long and dusty trip."

Davis stood, unmoving, and made no reply, waiting for Rodney to leave. Once my visitor had gone, Davis turned to me.

"I thought it best to go ahead and draw the bath, madam," he said. "There seemed no point in arguing, and I did not think you would object."

"Very good, Davis."

"I do hope, madam, there will be no more unexpected guests demanding baths."

"You know as much as I do," I said, "and generally much sooner." I could see Simon doing his best not to laugh. "Thank you, Davis."

"I see I was right not to bring the cigars."

"This time, perhaps," I said. "I do not, however, want this particular incident to set a precedent for the future."

"Of course not, madam." He made a neat bow and left the room.

"What do you make of Rodney Scolfield?" Simon asked.

"I have not had time to form much of an opinion," I said. "You?"

"What, you think I've had time enough?"

"You might be cleverer than I."

"I don't trust him at all," Simon said. "There's something of the charlatan about him."

"What makes you say that?" I asked.

"He's too free with himself and everyone around him. In the matter of a few minutes he has insinuated himself into your household completely uninvited. He's wild. Unkempt."

"It could just be from the journey."

"It rained all night, Emily. And he claims the trip was dusty?"

"Metaphorically speaking, perhaps?"

"Heavens, you aren't suggesting you like him, are you?" Simon asked.

"No," I said, "but I don't dislike him yet either. He does seem to appreciate Montagu Manor, and he's at least trying to be sensitive to Matilda's feelings. It's awfully convenient, though, that he was able to arrive so quickly after learning of his inheritance. It seems a bit like a setup."

"Rodney Scolfield was supposedly deep in some jungle on the other side of the world, is that right?"

"So we thought," I said. "I do believe Rodney Scolfield is Archibald's legitimate heir, but how do we know the man presenting himself to us is who he claims to be? He could be anyone."

Davis came back into the room. "Lord Montagu's valet has arrived, madam. He is a Red Indian. Nothing slight about it."

"Very well, Davis," I said. "Have you somewhere to put him in the servants' quarters?"

"I offered him a room upstairs. It appears he has brought with him some sort of tent and would prefer to occupy that, if you do not object."

"My," I said, "how wonderfully exotic. Do tell him to make himself comfortable. Perhaps one of the gardeners could help him find a spot suitable to his accommodations?"

"As you wish, madam."

Simon made no attempt to contain his laughter. "I may never leave Anglemore, Emily. Your household is too diverting."

"I should give anything to be below stairs right now," I said. "Can you imagine the state in which the servants must be?"

"Managed pandemonium, I should think," he said. "What will Hargreaves say?"

Colin was able to answer the question himself, as he entered the room soon thereafter. "A bit too much mirth for a murder investigation," he said. Simon poured him a whisky, and I brought him up to date on all that had happened.

"I'm half inclined to go back to Oxford at once," he said. "Is it safe to remain here among all this upheaval?"

"Was your work a success?" I asked.

"Archibald Scolfield's career at Oxford was not so blemish-free as we were led to believe. Yes, he was an excellent oarsman, and well liked in college, but he was embroiled in a cheating scandal during his second year that resulted in another student, Cedric Porter, being sent down from university."

"What was Archibald's role?" I asked.

"He came forward and accused Porter of stealing an essay he'd written and turning it in as his own. Trouble is, Porter insisted Montagu had stolen the essay from him. One gentleman's word against another's."

"And Montagu came out on top?" Simon asked.

"In spades."

"Where is Mr Porter now?" I asked.

"He was forced to turn to trade and had operated a tailor's shop in London until six weeks ago, when he relocated to a small village approximately twenty miles from Montagu Manor."

"Archibald's past catches up with him," I said. "When do we go see Mr Porter? First thing in the morning, I hope."

We were interrupted again, this time by my mother, who had come down from the nursery in a fit of vapors. At first, it looked as if she might faint. She wobbled on her feet, staggered a bit, and then, remembering she ought to be graceful, lowered herself with studied elegance into Colin's arms. He led her to a settee, where she recovered with remarkable speed and no smelling salts. She had no choice but to reconcile herself to doing without the latter, as I forbade them in my house. I never could tolerate ladies with a tendency to faint on command whenever faced with something difficult.

"Mr Hargreaves, I simply cannot allow you to continue to keep that child of a murderess in such close proximity to my grandbabies."

"Lady Bromley." Colin's voice was smooth and calm. "Let me assure you I would never put Henry or Richard in harm's way. Tom is a sweet boy, and you must accept that he, too, is ours. I have just arrived home from a strenuous trip to find my house invaded by an unwelcome guest and I am doing my best to catch a murderer whom I would prefer not to have on the loose so near my family."

"What unwelcome guest?" my mother asked. "Do tell me it is not one of those wretched Women's Liberal Federation people. You must stop associating with them, Emily. It is not seemly, particularly now that you are a mother."

"Do try to remember, Mother, that my mother-in-law is also a member of the Women's Liberal Federation," I said. In fact, it was Mrs Hargreaves who had first introduced me to the group. Our intellectual and political views were an excellent match, but she and I could not be described as close. We had clashed frightfully when we first met, and I was convinced (rightly) that she considered me a grave disappointment. Colin, who had always been the favorite of her two sons, was devoted to her, but he had made it clear that I would always take priority in his life, as a wife should. The transition was, for her, difficult, but we eventually managed to come to a tenuous understanding as to who took precedence in her eldest son's life and now corresponded regularly, having come to appreciate each other. Over time a deep respect had grown between us. She had lived in France since her husband's death years ago, but was now in the process of setting up a household in England, wanting to have better access to her grandchildren.

"The new Marquess of Montagu," I said.

"Well!" This brought a smile to her face. "Why did you not tell me? I would have been on hand to receive him. This is an honor, Emily, that he should call so soon after arriving in the neighborhood." She was nodding her head with such vigor I worried her neck might snap. "Where is he now? I must be introduced at once."

"He is not paying a call, Mother. He is staying here, as Matilda won't tolerate him at Montagu. You can find him in the bath, if you think it would be appropriate to disturb him there in order to make an introduction."

"There is no need to be rude, Emily."

"I think, Lady Bromley, you will be most interested in Lord Montagu's valet. He has brought him from America," Simon said. I did adore the wicked man.

"Is that so? How interesting. Did he steal him from the Astors, do you think?" Much as my mother despised Americans, she was fascinated by the wealth they accumulated. They might be vulgar and reprehensible, but so far as she was concerned their fortunes could not be ignored.

"Highly unlikely," I said.

"Have you given Cook new instructions for dinner?" my mother asked.

"I have. It was the second alteration today, and she is most displeased."

"Is the menu suitable for a marquess, Emily? I know how little you pay attention to propriety. It is so important to treat nobility in the proper way. Given that your father is an earl, I should not have to explain this to you."

I smiled. "It would be a great help to me if you were to go downstairs and speak to Cook yourself. That way none of us will have to worry that we might offend Lord Montagu's delicate sensibilities."

My mother pulled herself up taller and looked quite well pleased. "Why, thank you, Emily. This is an excellent idea. I was planning to return to Darnley at the end of the week, but I should perhaps consider staying on longer. You have so many demands on your time now with the boys, and your father can do without me a little longer."

"That would be delightful," I said. I hoped she did not notice my clenched teeth. My father would no doubt rejoice for an extension of his solitude. I could only envy him.

Downstairs

vi

Lily could not help feeling a sense of smug satisfaction when she passed the kitchen and heard Lady Bromley in the midst of a rampage of criticism against Pru's evidently substandard work. It sounded, too, like the countess was requesting more changes for dinner. Cook would not be pleased, and Lily felt bad about that, but not bad enough to change her opinion about the barrage being hurled at Pru. Lily smiled and went upstairs to dust and tidy the rooms on the ground floor. She started in the white drawing room, an airy space with bay windows and heaps of paintings that Lady Emily loved but Lily couldn't understand. To her they looked like bad sketches with blurry lines. She preferred the collection in Mr Hargreaves's rooms. They vibrated with mastery, the work of artists whose talent allowed them to re-create the world with precision. Lily would be embarrassed to paint like this Monet or Renoir did. Still, they did make a lovely use of color, blues especially, she thought, and she started to sing "Land of Hope and Glory" as she ran her feather duster over one of Mr Monet's landscapes. It was just then that Lord Flyte interrupted her.

"Lily, what a pleasant surprise to see you here," he said. She smiled at him. "Your song reminds me of my school days. Will it distract you if I speak to you while you're working?"

"Have I done something wrong, sir?"

"Not in the least. I find I enjoy your company. You've a most pleasant character. Tell me about yourself. How did you come to be in service?"

"I was just a girl when I started," she said. "Lady Emily hired me, although I was a bit young to go straight to being a housemaid. She told me I deserved a chance."

"She is a very kind lady."

"I'd wanted to be a lady's maid, you see," Lily said, gently dusting a Greek vase displayed on the mantel. "I thought if I could stay in school, I might be able to learn French. Real lady's maids speak French, you know."

"Do they?"

"Oh, yes." She was nodding her head vigorously. "It's quite important, although I'm not entirely sure why."

"And did you stay in school?"

"I couldn't, sir. My mother fell ill and we needed the income, so I started with Lady Emily in London and now find myself most happy here. I like the countryside."

"Why do you want to be a lady's maid?" Lord Flyte asked.

"I've always fancied seeing the world," Lily said. "Lady Emily travels everywhere, you know, and she takes Meg with her. Meg's been to Paris and Vienna and all kinds of places. Constantinople and Venice, too. And to the villa in Greece, of course. It's on an island called Santorini, I think it is. She told me there are views of the sea out every single window and that the house is built on a cliff so perilous she doesn't like to go outside at night."

"I see." Simon's eyes were warm and soft. Lily's innocence was the most charming thing he had ever known. He loved the excitement in her voice when she named each city, her pronunciation skewed deliberately to the exotic. It was more than endearing. He had never particularly craved travel but had done the requisite Grand Tour. Now, though, seeing her excitement, he started to reconsider the position he had more or less inherited from his father, who had never appreciated travel in any form. What would it be like to visit country after country with a person who possessed Lily's eagerness?

"I very much enjoyed visiting the National Gallery when I was working in London, and I'd so like to see the Louvre."

"As I have said, you are very talented."

"I don't know about that, sir, but I do enjoy drawing. A girl in my position can't travel on her own, of course, but if I could become a lady's maid . . ."

"You, too, could see the world."

"Yes, sir." Her smile brightened her face, and Simon found himself captivated by this eager girl. He wanted to give her the world she craved.

CHAPTER
SEVEN

I spotted Rodney's valet in the corridor on my way to breakfast the next morning and was deeply disappointed to see he looked essentially the same as any other valet, Red Indian or not, dressed in a coat and tie. He was not altogether ordinary, though. His face was strikingly handsome and his carriage more erect than that of a soldier. I was tempted to pull him aside and beg him to tell me about his people, about life on the vast American plains (I assumed he was from the plains), and about the thrill of seeing thousands of buffalo stampeding by.

Fortunately (or perhaps not, so far as he would have been concerned), I resisted the urge and continued on my way. Colin and I were to interview Mr Porter about his ill-fated experience with Archibald at Oxford, and we wanted to get started as early as possible. Mr Porter's tailor shop was on the high street of a medium-sized village north of Melton Carbury. It was well appointed, and the clothing samples he had on display beautifully made. He was expecting us, and we all went into the back room, where he poured tea after imploring us to sit down.

"I say, this is awkward." He pulled his spectacles from his face and wiped them with a handkerchief.

"You're here about Scolfield, of course, and I must tell you I never did quite understand what happened between us. We had started out mates. Met during our first term."

"You were in the same college?" Colin asked.

"No. He was a Christ Church man. I was at Merton. About a week after I'd arrived, I was run down by an errant bicycle rider. Scolfield was on hand and offered his assistance. We became fast friends after that."

"How close were you?" I asked.

"Close enough that I spent Christmas with his family during our first year and we traveled abroad together after that Trinity term."

"So what happened?" I asked.

"It all fell apart during Michaelmas term exams in our second year. I was summoned to Christ Church, where I was accused of having stolen Scolfield's essay for a history course."

"Had you stolen it?"

"Most certainly not," he said. "I had written it myself and turned it in at Merton. Best I can tell Scolfield copied the draft. I'd left it on my desk, and as often as he was in my rooms, he would have had a thousand opportunities to take it. I told the truth, but no one believed me. I'm not from a background like Scolfield's. My father is a gardener on an estate in Shropshire. The only reason I got an education was that our landlord took an interest in me while I worked assisting his steward when I was a boy. The steward thought I had an aptitude for learning, and his master agreed. He sponsored me at school, and I did well enough there to earn a spot at Oxford. My lack of

111

breeding made it easy enough for the dons at Christ Church to suspect the worst of me."

"Did you show them the draft you had written as evidence the work was yours?" Colin asked.

"I did, but they insisted it proved nothing. There was no way to confirm beyond doubt I hadn't copied it from something Scolfield had written."

"You were sent down?" Colin asked.

"Yes," he said. "Scolfield had gone to the master of the college and drawn his attention to the matter, and no one believed he would have done so had he been guilty, particularly as the essays had been turned in for different courses. If he hadn't spoken up, it is likely the duplication would have gone unnoticed."

"It sounds as if he were deliberately trying to sabotage you," I said.

"Yes." Mr Porter's shoulders slumped. "I never have been able to understand why."

"You must have been angry," Colin said.

"Of course I was," Mr Porter said. "Yet there was nothing to be done. It was difficult enough for me at Oxford — it was a miracle I had been accepted in the first place, really — and in the end I came to see it as not a terrible outcome. What difference would staying have made? I am not a gentleman, Mr Hargreaves, and never will be. I would have had to work for a living regardless of whether I had a university education."

"You would have had so many more opportunities, though," I said, feeling my hackles go up. "Beyond that, your life would be all the richer for having had more years of study. It is terribly unfair."

112

"Is it?" he asked. "You can say so, but my place is here. I enjoy my work, and I will always benefit from what education I did receive."

"You deserved more," I said. Colin shot me a cautioning look. "Why did you decide to leave London?"

"Not to make it easier to murder Archibald Scolfield, I assure you," Mr Porter said. "My sister lives in this village and has been very happy here for the better part of a decade, far happier than I ever was in London. I like being close to my nieces and nephews and find country life suits me well."

"Were you home the night he died?" Colin asked.

"Getting right to it, are we? I dined with my sister and her family and then returned home. They will be happy to vouch for me. Furthermore, I board my horse at a stable in the village. You can confirm with the owner that I did not take him out that night."

"Was there ever any strife between you and Scolfield before the incident at Oxford?" I asked.

"No," Mr Porter said. "I have gone over every minute we spent together more times than I can count and have found no explanation for what he did. I believed, and still do, we were the closest of friends."

"How long did you stay with his family at Christmas?" I asked.

"A fortnight."

"Did they like you?"

"Very much, or at least so I was led to believe. I was invited back for several weekends thereafter. I assure you, Lady Emily, nothing out of the ordinary happened."

"Did Scolfield visit you?"

"No, but we did stay with my aunt in Dover when we were making our way abroad. She is settled nicely, running a seaside inn. Treated us like kings while we were with her. Nothing so grand as what Scolfield was used to, mind you, but he found her charming nonetheless." He rose from his chair. "I am sorry to rush you out, but I've loads of work to do. I do wish I could be of more help. I have thought long about this, and the only insight I can offer is that a man who is capable of so completely turning on a friend is bound to have done it more than once. Maybe another time, Scolfield's victim wasn't so congenial as I."

I was not as yet convinced that Mr Porter was quite so congenial as he claimed.

"Did you ever hear from Scolfield again after you went down from Oxford?" Colin asked.

"No," Mr Porter said. "He excised me from his life altogether. Not that this should have surprised me, given what he had done."

"Regarding the essay?" I asked.

"Of course. There was never any other strife between us."

We thanked him and took our leave. "I should like very much to speak with Mr Porter's aunt in Dover," I said.

"Why her in particular?" Colin asked, taking my hand and helping me into our waiting carriage.

"Archibald found her charming. I want to know what she thought of him."

We drove to the stable, where Colin leapt out to confirm that Mr Porter's horse had not been taken out the night of the murder. Leaving him, I continued on to Mr Porter's sister's house, where I was welcomed with bright smiles, but both she and her husband seemed rather nervous. He stood behind her chair, clutching the back of it with a hard grip; she twisted a handkerchief in her hands. Their comfortable parlor reflected their modest means but was kept tidy and clean. A piano, its top covered with a collection of framed pressed flowers, stood in one corner, and a portrait of the Queen hung over the mantel. I heard the sound of children's voices coming from the back of the house, their laughter spilling through the rooms.

"We know why you are here, Lady Emily," Mr Porter's sister said. "Cedric was with us on that dreadful night until approximately half ten. He went home straightaway after he left us; I'm sure of that."

She couldn't possibly be sure, but I saw no need to torment her. "Did you ever meet Archibald Scolfield?" I asked.

"Never," she said, "but I have heard all about him. Cedric was mad about him while he was at Oxford."

"They stayed with your aunt in Dover, I believe?"

"Yes. Does that cause a problem?"

"No, but I am curious to know her opinion of her guest."

"She never said anything directly, but did mention, in a roundabout sort of way, that gentlemen aren't always gentlemen."

"What do you think she meant by that?" I asked.

"I couldn't rightly say, madam. I don't think she meant he was trying to take her silver."

Her husband grimaced. "Do you have more questions, Lady Emily, or are we done here? Anyone who has spent time with Cedric knows him to be incapable of murder. He is gentle and timid and so far as I know has never even been in a fight. He may have gone above his station at Oxford, but he knows his place now."

"That is quite true, Lady Emily, and my brother would never hurt anyone."

"I believe you," I said, "and won't trouble you further except for one thing. Would you please give me your aunt's address?"

Colin was waiting for me outside when I emerged from the house. He had walked from the stable. "The horse was in all night," he said.

"And Mr Porter's family corroborated his alibi."

"You believe them?"

"I have no reason not to," I said. "They seemed honest and respectable. However, he could have got a horse from elsewhere and ridden to Montagu after he had left them."

"Not if he was there until half ten. Montagu would have been dead before Porter could have reached him." We climbed back into the carriage. "The trouble is, even if the sister is honest, she may not have particularly noticed what time her brother left. Do you remember when we went up to bed last night?"

"Not precisely, but it was before eleven," I said. "The clock hadn't chimed."

"You're certain?"

I thought for a moment. "Yes."

"It was quarter past midnight when we went upstairs."

"You're certain?" I asked.

"Absolutely. I always check the time on the clock in the hall near the stairs."

"Either of us could be wrong."

"Emily." He clasped his hands around mine. "My darling girl, I am most certainly not wrong. The point, however, is as you implied. People are notoriously unreliable."

"So you would recommend that Mr Porter plan no trips abroad?"

"For the present, yes."

"I should like to speak with him again," I said.

"To warn him to stay home?" Colin asked. "I don't think he has the means to flee."

"No. For another reason altogether. I want to know every detail of the trip he took abroad with Scolfield."

It seemed obvious to me that there was something missing in the picture we had formed of Archibald Scolfield. Those close to him had nothing but compliments for him, but when one moved beyond his immediate circle, chinks started to appear in his character. A trip abroad would have given him ample opportunity to indulge himself without worrying about proper English manners or exposing himself to society gossip. He might have shown a more honest self on the Continent. So I returned to Mr Porter. When, three-quarters of an hour later, we took our leave and headed back to Anglemore, my husband was shaking his head. "What exactly do you plan to do, my dear? Re-create student travels abroad?"

"Don't be silly," I said. "Something happened when Mr Porter and Archibald were abroad. They were inseparable after the Christmas they spent together, but then they fell out during exams at the end of the term immediately following their trip. What changed?"

"It needn't have happened abroad," Colin said. "They might have argued in a pub outside either of their colleges about cricket."

"It's possible. How would you suggest we follow that particular lead?" I asked and held up the notebook in which I'd recorded everything Mr Porter had told us. "We now know exactly where they stayed on every leg of their trip to the Continent. Some of the time it was with friends of the Scolfield family, some of the time at various inns and hotels. Let's see if anyone noticed something awry."

"I am at your service." He sidled closer to me on the carriage bench. "Your active mind is most beguiling, my dear. I'd very much like to take you home and do extremely rude things to you." He kissed my neck.

"I shall remember that tonight when you and Simon threaten to play billiards until dawn." I pulled away from him and smiled. "Until then, you may have nothing but this." I gave him an extremely long kiss.

"I'm not sure I remember how to play billiards."

Back at home I locked myself in the Spanish room. Much though I loved the library, with its soaring shelves, stunning view, and cavernous fireplaces, sometimes I craved more intimacy. One of the things I had adored about Anglemore from the moment I first entered the house was the way books were such a presence throughout it. The library, obviously, had the most, and was furnished in the ordinary way libraries in country estates were, but other rooms — Colin's study, the cinnamon drawing room, all the bedrooms, and even the music room — held a respectable number of shelves. This smaller room, well situated to overlook a reflecting pool and formal garden, had originally been designed as a State Dressing Room, before the west wing was built during Elizabeth's reign and the State Rooms all moved there. Now called "Spanish" for the leather that covered the wall from the tops of the bookcases to the ceiling, it had intricately carved paneling from the time of James I and two doors disguised as bookcases. One led to my husband's study, the other to the servants' passage. The library served as my own study, such as it was.

I loved doing my work there, surrounded by books, and had installed a desk in front of a window. The Spanish room, however, I took as my private retreat. I stocked the shelves with favorite books, only ones I would happily read over and over, and decorated the room with my most precious antiquities. Everywhere I looked I saw something I loved, such as a bust of Apollo done in the manner of Praxiteles, black and red figure Greek vases, and an ivory triptych carved in the Middle Ages. My greatest treasure, a golden apple engraved with the words *tê kallistê* — "to the fairest' — I kept on a table next to my favorite chair. It was the first Christmas present given to me by Colin.

Ordinarily, I reserved my work for the library and pleasure for the Spanish room, but today, with both my mother and Rodney threatening my peace of mind, I sought the consolation of this warm and much-loved chamber instead. I had several letters to write, the first of which was to the housekeeper at Archibald's parents' estate. I had finished that and had begun to compose a series of wires to those who had hosted the boys abroad when I heard Davis clearing his throat outside the door. I unlocked it.

"Yes?" I asked.

"Miss Cora Fitzgerald to see you, madam. Shall I bring her here?"

"Take her to the library. I'll meet her there."

Miss Fitzgerald was even paler than when I'd first met her. Her face was drawn, her eyes dull. "Is it true?" she asked. "Was Archibald promised to someone else? My father tells me it is so."

"Dear Miss Fitzgerald." I hardly knew what to say. "It appears that there had been negotiations with an American family, the Sturdevants, and that he was promised to their daughter, Constance."

"You need not protect me, Lady Emily," she said. "I may not be the daughter of a railroad baron, but I am no fool. I want the truth."

"The young lady and her parents certainly believed there was an engagement, but it had not been formally announced. Lady Matilda did not approve of the match, and I believe that is why Lord Montagu was treating it as a delicate situation."

"Why didn't she approve?"

"She had numerous objections to the lady, not the least of which was her being American."

"I see." The skin around Miss Fitzgerald's eyes crinkled, and three deep lines appeared on her normally smooth brow.

"I am so very sorry, Miss Fitzgerald. This must be extremely painful."

She did not move a muscle.

"Is there anything I can do for you?" I asked. I heard the door open and, assuming it to be Davis, turned to ask him to bring port. Instead, I saw Rodney. Rodney, however, had no eyes for me.

"Cora? Little Cora Fitzgerald?" He rushed towards her, pulled her to her feet, and embraced her in a most inappropriate fashion. "What a surprise! I hardly know what to say — I certainly never expected to see you again."

Cora stepped away from him, her eyes wide, raised her hand, and slapped him soundly across the face.

"Not the welcome I would have hoped for from an old friend," Rodney said, "but I do seem to have a deleterious effect on people's manners.

Downstairs

vii

Pru was lingering outside near the stables when Lord Flyte returned from London that afternoon. She had started off looking for Johnny but had paused beneath a window to listen to two of the other grooms talking about Alice. Johnny had been sweet on Alice for a while, although Pru could never understand why, so Pru had done the only thing she could think of. She showed him what sweet really meant, and Johnny had never gone in search of Alice since then. But now the grooms were on about that wretched girl again. And why? She was an ugly thing, with her mousy hair and crooked teeth. It was as if they never noticed how bad she looked. All they cared about was that she made them laugh. As if they couldn't laugh by themselves. Pru felt her head starting to throb and wasn't sure she wanted to find Johnny anymore. Then she heard the carriage and saw Lord Flyte, who made her forget all about Johnny and his grooms. She liked the way he looked, tall but not too tall, nice eyes, and a straight nose. He was carrying a slim package and whistling one of those tunes Lily liked to sing. She watched him as he walked around in the direction of the folly near the lake. The Temple of the Muses, Lady Emily called it.

"I hear you was in London," she shouted after him. "Is it true?"

"It is," he said, pausing.

"I ain't never been there, me. Is it nice?"

"Very."

"I know you like to talk to Lily," she said. "I thought you might like to talk to me as well."

He stopped and took a few steps in her direction. "Do you work in the kitchen?"

"I do. Lowest job in the house, but I was made for better things."

"Then I do hope you get them," he said with a guarded smile.

"I think I will," she said. "I understand how things work, you see."

Lord Flyte glanced around, wondering where all the grooms had disappeared to. They'd made quick work of putting away the carriage that had picked him up at the train station. He was beginning to regret not having let them drop him at the front of the house. His penchant for long walks was getting him in trouble.

"I'm Prudence. That's what the master calls me. The others call me Pru, but I like Prudence better. It suits me, don't you think?"

"It is a pleasure to make your acquaintance, Prudence." He smiled at her and tipped his hat but stepped away. "Do enjoy the rest of your day. I am very much looking forward to dinner. Cook is bound to give us another masterpiece."

He hadn't been gone from her sight for more than a minute when Johnny stepped out of the stables. "Don't think you've got a chance there," he said. "Though he stopped you just in time to keep you from making a fool of yourself."

"I don't know what you're about," Pru said, suddenly self-conscious. "I was here waiting for you."

"Well, here I am." He grinned and put an arm around her waist. "How long before you have to be back?"

CHAPTER
EIGHT

After Cora Fitzgerald slapped Rodney, she pushed him away, almost flinging him into a pedestal holding a first-century bust purported to be Marc Antony. I would have been most distressed to see it damaged. "Forgive me," she said, ignoring both the precariously rocking bust and me. Her entire focus was on Rodney. "Forgive me. You are supposed to be dead." She smoothed her skirts and crossed to the opposite side of the room, not taking her suspicious eyes off him. There was a strange look on her face: half rapture, half paralysis. "Are you a ghost?"

"You know I'm not a ghost, Cora."

"I take it you two have already been introduced?" I asked.

"We met in India," Rodney said. "Years ago, when Cora's father was a missionary. He hosted me for a handful of days while I was in the midst of searching for a ruby that was lost in the fourteenth century. It was a bridal gift to a beautiful princess, who —"

"The details are not important," I said. "Why is Miss Fitzgerald laboring under the delusion that you are dead?"

"That, I'm afraid, is a question I cannot answer."

"My father told me you were," Miss Fitzgerald said. "He said I must stop waiting for you to come back, that he didn't like to be the messenger of heartbreak, but that he'd had news of your party having been accosted by wild tigers, and that you had all been killed." She stopped for a moment and then broke out laughing. "I never realized how silly his story was until now. I suppose he didn't know what else to tell me. I was too young to understand you had not formed a romantic attachment to a twelve-year-old over the course of a long weekend."

"You were waiting for me?" Rodney asked. He was walking towards her now, his hands clasped behind his back, a wide grin on his face.

"I looked for a letter every day and sat by the side of the road at sunset each evening. That was the time you had arrived on our doorstep on the day we met, and I was convinced you would return to me when the sky was streaked pink and gold."

"Oh dear. How could I have been so dreadful?" Rodney was laying on the charm. He was extremely good at it, all bright blue eyes, broad smile, and his easy drawl. I wondered how many ladies, east and west, had fallen for him. Fallen but not stayed, or he wouldn't be so well practiced. "I'd never seen a prettier little girl in my life," he continued. "I am sorry to have caused you any heartache, and I do heartily beg your forgiveness."

"It is yours. I shall always be grateful to you for awakening my romantic nature, even if you were unaware of how significant an experience it was for me," Miss Fitzgerald said, her face now bright with adoration. She looked almost like a little girl, and it was difficult to reconcile this image with the lady who had written such passionate and sophisticated letters to Archibald Scolfield. "But why are you at Anglemore Park? This is so unexpected I hardly know what to think."

"Rodney is the new Marquess of Montagu," I said, watching her reaction carefully. She was not, in my estimation, quite so surprised as she ought to have been. She raised her eyebrows slightly, and her eyes danced.

"How is this possible?" she asked. "No, don't explain. It is too much to bear. I was engaged to Archibald Scolfield, you see, so my feelings on the subject are rather complicated."

"You were to be married?" Rodney asked, sitting on the settee and pulling her down next to him. A little closer than necessary, I thought. "I am terribly sorry that you lost your fiancé in such unfortunate circumstances."

"It is even worse than it seems," she said in a tone that could only be described as conspiratorial. "I thought we had been engaged until my father informed me that Archibald's affections had been promised elsewhere."

"Cad!" Rodney was all sympathy. "You poor, poor girl."

"I don't know what I shall do now. The humiliation stings like nothing else." Her smile was too sweet. She was all vicar's daughter, hiding every sign of the sophisticated lover ready to elope at a moment's notice.

127

"Well, perhaps not so much as when I thought you'd been eaten by tigers."

"This is all quite the coincidence," I said. "Imagine finding each other here, now, at such an opportune time." *Far too convenient*, I thought.

"I couldn't agree more," Rodney said. "A wonder, truly. Cora, I must apologize for this rogue of a relative of mine. I do not like to hear that someone has toyed with your trusting nature. A girl who believes stories about treasure hunters and tigers ought to have her innocence preserved for as long as possible."

I coughed.

"You are too kind, Mr Scolfield — I mean, Lord Montagu," Cora said.

"You must call me Rodney."

She smiled up at him so sweetly my teeth started to ache. I had seen quite enough. "I shall leave the two of you to catch up," I said. "I wouldn't want to stand in the way of your reminiscing."

"Many thanks, Emily," Rodney said.

I exited the room at a most unladylike pace, my head spinning. I closed the door behind me and then leaned my ear against it, only for a moment. It was shameful to eavesdrop in my own house, and besides, I couldn't hear a word through the heavy oak door. I knew Colin had retired to his study and I decided to follow him there, but went through the great hall and the Spanish room, not wanting to go back into the library and interrupt the reunited couple.

Colin was bent over a notebook, so engrossed in his work he did not hear me enter the room. He was writing, his hand moving smoothly over the page without pause or hesitation. He never started to put his thoughts down on paper until he had first let his ideas form fully in his mind (usually while he was pacing) and he had a clear view not only of what he wanted to say, but how he wanted to say it. Despite his fluid motion, his shoulders betrayed the tension he was carrying, tension that would not disperse until he was satisfied he had done everything possible to serve the cause of justice in whatever case was currently consuming him.

I waited, not wanting to disturb him. Eventually, he put his hands together and stretched his arms out in front of him, and I knew the flow of words had stopped. I crossed to him, stood behind his chair, and wrapped my arms around him. He leaned against me. I was distracted beyond reason but forced myself to pry my arms away and describe for him the scene in the library.

"It was an absolute load of rubbish," I said after having finished. "What is the meaning of all this? I am heartily confused."

"This might be the time to try to get some evidence to corroborate Rodney's identity," Colin said.

"How do we do that?"

"I have a few ideas, none of them too outrageous. I think I'll start by taking him to London tomorrow. Rodney Scolfield is listed as a member at both the Travellers and the Alpine clubs. I should like to see if anyone at either recognizes him."

"Don't give him any warning," I said. "He'll plant someone inside."

"That's not so easily done, Emily. But I shall take your suggestion under advisement."

"How much do we know about the Fitzgeralds?" I asked. "I wonder if Rodney and Cora have plotted this all together. Consider this: What if Cora found out Archibald had no intention of marrying her? She reaches out to her old family friend, explains to him the situation, and together they hatch a plan. First, Cora has to find out who is Archibald's heir —"

"Stop right there," Colin said. "We do know there is a real Rodney Scolfield. Cora couldn't have planted the name with the Montagu solicitors."

"Perhaps the real Rodney Scolfield is dead."

"The solicitors would know."

I paused. "You're probably right."

"As is generally the case," he said. "This, Emily, is nothing more than a flight of fancy."

I decided to let him have his delusion of always being right. Marriage requires many such moments. Sometimes I would let Colin go on thinking he was right. In exchange, he would resist questioning my political beliefs, particularly when we discussed the details of suffrage. "Unless our Rodney knew the real Rodney. Perhaps they were both explorers, and the real Rodney perished deep in the Amazon jungle —"

"You truly have a flair for fiction, my dear."

"No, that wouldn't work," I said, hardly hearing him. I tapped a finger against my lip.

"Your fantasies would make for a fine sensational novel," Colin said.

I resisted the urge to throw something at him. "I am going to invite Matilda to dinner," I said. "I want to see her and Cora together."

"You expect Cora to still be here at dinner?"

"I would be astonished if Rodney has not already invited her."

"Far be it from me to stand in the way of any of your schemes."

"Thank you. Would you object to me working in here with you?" I asked. "I'm afraid to return to the library."

"I would be delighted," he said, "particularly if we both abandoned, just for a short while, any thoughts of work."

Heat consumed me, and I saw the same burning in his dark eyes. Truly, the man was irresistible.

We did eventually — too soon, really — return to our work, and by dinnertime I had sent a letter to the Scolfield family's housekeeper and a stack of wires elsewhere. Colin and I gathered our guests for drinks before going into the dining room. I had always found the white drawing room to be one of the most pleasant spaces in the house. The pale color and large Elizabethan bay windows made it bright and airy, a perfect place to display our collection of Impressionist paintings, done by a group of artists I both admired and was fortunate to consider dear friends. The furniture was eighteenth century, some of it Chippendale, and the gilded chimneypiece was the only thing in the room that could be considered ornate. We had some pieces of Roman glass on the mantel, but what I liked best in the room was the alcoves formed by the bays. I had put comfortable settees in each of them and liked to read there, surrounded by windows that looked out over the grounds stretching from the front door all the way to the stone medieval gatehouse at the entrance to the estate.

Tonight, Matilda was an exercise in incongruity, wearing full black mourning more appropriate for the death of a husband than that of a cousin and sipping champagne without taking her eyes off Rodney, who was beginning to look less and less comfortable having Cora attached to him.

"*Cora Fitzgerald* thought she was going to marry Archie?" Matilda asked, nodding in Cora's direction. "Whatever can she have been thinking?"

"I could not begin to tell you," I said. "You don't know her well?"

"Not particularly."

"It seems odd. Her father is your vicar."

"I have passed her in church more times than I can count, and she's been round to dinner with her father, but I can't say I would consider her more than a distant acquaintance. She was Grandfather's guest, not mine."

"You must have spoken with her if she was dining in your house."

Matilda made a motion reminiscent of someone shooing a fly. "I avoid all discussion of religion — which is why I get on so well with your husband — and the vicar talks of nothing else. Every time they came I

132

pleaded a headache and fled upstairs. Archie had abominable taste in women." She laughed and squeezed my arm. "Emily, I know I've been dreadful, and all the while you've been a saint. I'm so appreciative."

"There's no need, Matilda."

"I found something this afternoon that might amuse you," she said. "Charlotte's journals. The marchioness, you remember? I do hope you will come see me tomorrow and have a look."

"I would like that," I said. "Where were they? Not in her trunk, obviously."

"No," Matilda said. "In Grandfather's study. He had a shelf full of old notebooks."

"Have you read them?"

"I started to, but stopped, if you must know. There were too many words, and I couldn't bear to face them. It's all too dire. My life, that is. I don't know how I shall ever be rid of Rodney, and I hate the thought of going to London or, worse, Scotland. I despise porridge."

"Why don't you stay at Montagu?" I understood the difficulty of her situation, but if she loved the house so very much, surely being there would be preferable to self-imposed exile? "He does not want to make you leave."

"Would you want to live with him?" she asked.

I had no interest in trying even to imagine such a thing. I could easily understand that Matilda would not welcome disruption in the privacy to which she had grown accustomed, and of course there was the matter of the Red Indian. Despite myself, I laughed.

"Exactly," she said.

"May I be serious for a moment?" I asked.

"Of course."

"Can you remember anyone telling stories about Archibald misbehaving?"

"As a child?"

"No," I said. "I've chosen my words poorly. I know about what happened at Oxford. Was that the only time he was in trouble?"

"He was constantly in trouble at school, but I don't think that's what you mean. Are you asking about young ladies?"

"Yes." I felt my cheeks go hot. "It is awkward, but I need to know. He certainly trifled with Miss Fitzgerald."

"Unless he was trifling with the wretched American," Matilda said. "Maybe he planned to marry her, take her money, divorce her, and run off with Miss Fitzgerald." She nodded. "Yes, I like the idea of that very much. It would very nearly make me forgive him his appalling taste in females."

"I am afraid we need to focus less on speculation and more on fact," I said. "I say this having spent far too much time this afternoon indulging in the former." Rodney and Miss Fitzgerald approached us.

"Emily, could I have a word in private?" He looked exhausted.

"Matilda, you can entertain Miss Fitzgerald, can't you?" I asked.

"With pleasure." Matilda looped her arm through Cora's. "Let's get a drink and see what kind of trouble I can get you into."

134

Rodney and I stepped out of the room and into the great hall, which, depending on one's point of view, was either a masterpiece or a nightmare of Elizabethan carving and plasterwork. An enormous chimneypiece flanked by large family portraits dominated the long wall opposite the front windows, but it was the elaborate screen dividing the room from the entranceway that commanded attention. Two arched doorways surrounded by carved wood and pillars elevated to the ceiling its three tiers of plasterwork depicting mythological scenes. A single lantern illuminated the space, hanging over the center of a long Georgian table, and wood paneling covered the walls to the height of the tall mantel. It was not a space that seemed to yearn for intimate conversation, but that appeared to be just what Rodney required.

"What is the matter?" I asked. "You didn't even call Matilda 'Boudica'. Has Miss Fitzgerald overwhelmed you?"

"Something of the sort," he said, pulling at his chin. "I am glad I was able to distract her from her loss, but I cannot step in as a replacement suitor."

"Is your heart engaged elsewhere, Lord Montagu?"

"Perish the thought," he said. "I am trying to start a new life, Emily. I want to have a go at running the estate, and I want to do it well. I cannot afford any distractions right now."

He looked sincere, and for just a moment I felt almost sorry for him. "I understand. Did you explain this to Miss Fitzgerald?"

"I tried. She hears what she wants to. I have never before encountered someone simultaneously so naive and so sophisticated. She pulls a gent in with sweet girlish charm, and then before you know it she's making it all too clear that she's well aware of what might come next. She can change in an instant. It's almost hard to believe she is real."

I could not have said it better myself.

The next morning, I asked Cook to put together a basket of food while I gathered a large bunch of flowers cut from the walled garden. Every Tuesday when we were in residence I made the rounds of my own tenants, bringing whatever they might need, so Cook and I had the process down to a science. She would prepare heaps of hearty and nutritious fare, all portable, while I organized clothing, linens, and other useful items no longer required in our household. Today we operated on a smaller scale, as I would be visiting only one house, but this did not stop Cook from concocting a feast that would have made Tantalus cry. Two footmen loaded my bounty into the carriage, and I set off, stopping to collect Matilda, who had agreed to accompany me to the tenant farmhouse where Miss Fitzgerald claimed to have spent time the night Archibald died. The farmer's widow opened the door to us, but did not appear overly delighted to have guests. She curtsied to Matilda.

"It's very kind of you to come, Lady Matilda," she said, "but we is doing quite fine, I assure you. No need to worry about us."

"This is Lady Emily Hargreaves from Anglemore Park," Matilda said. "The vicar's daughter told her there was sickness in your house. We wanted to make sure you were in need of no food or supplies or anything else with which we can help. If you require the doctor, we shall send for him at once."

"My boy is well now."

"May we come in?" I asked.

"I suppose that would be all right."

The house was small and grubby. A pack of young children huddled in a corner, their faces dirty. They jumped to their feet in unison when they saw us, like bedraggled and unkempt soldiers who knew how to look sharp when required, regardless of the state of their uniforms. Whatever material comforts they lacked, their mother had not skimped on discipline.

"This is Lady Matilda of Montagu and Lady Emily," their mother announced.

"Good morning, Lady Matilda," they chanted in unison. "Good morning, Lady Emily."

We smiled at them and set to work. Matilda pulled the curtains back, letting light flood the room through dingy windowpanes. I filled a bucket with water and started to wipe them while Matilda swept the floor. All the while, we peppered the widow with questions.

"How long were the children sick?" I asked.

"It was only one of them, my youngest boy," she said. "It was nothing, really. Just a sniffle."

"It must have been a help to have Miss Fitzgerald on hand."

"I'm not sure as to what you mean," she said. "Miss Fitzgerald does visit at regular intervals. Since her mother died the vicar has no wife to check in on his flock. But she hasn't been here in weeks."

"Are you quite sure?" I asked. I had finished with the windows, pulled a cheerful checked cloth from my basket, and spread it over the table. This was good and satisfying work with tangible and immediate results.

"Well, thinking about it, I do recall her coming by when the boy was sick. She didn't come inside, though. Only stood at the doorway and asked if we needed anything."

"Why didn't she come in?" I began removing the food from the basket: several cheeses, a dozen Scotch eggs, a cold ham, two loaves of bread, meat pies, a selection of cakes, a bottle of milk, and a container filled with fresh lemonade. The children took quite an interest in all this, especially the cakes, and had soon surrounded me.

"We didn't need anything, and it was quite late. The children was already in bed."

"Do you know what time it was?" I asked.

"No, madam," she said. "I've got a clock, but it wasn't working till yesterday when me son fixed it. I can tell you it had already got dark. As I said, the children was asleep."

"How old is your eldest son?" I asked, noticing a tall, quiet boy who had remained to the side during all the commotion since our arrival except when, without having to be asked, he emptied the dirty water from the bucket I'd used on the windows.

"Thirteen, madam. He's a good boy. He's working with the men now, on the estate."

"Farming?" I asked.

"Yes," she said. "There's no other work to be had."

"He fixed your clock?" I asked.

"Yes, madam. He's handy with such things. His father taught him."

"I have been hoping to find a boy who could help with the clocks in my house. We've so many of them, and they need to be wound regularly. Do you think he would be interested? The pay would be a bit more than farming, I think."

Matilda smiled at me. "I don't know that the new marquess will much appreciate your taking in his tenants."

"He will survive the blow," I said.

"Would it really be all right, Lady Matilda? I wouldn't want to anger his lordship," the widow said.

"It will be perfectly fine," Matilda said.

"Have the boy come to Anglemore tomorrow morning. The butler will set him up with livery and work."

"Thank you, Lady Emily," she said. "Thank you so very, very much."

It was a small thing, really, yet I knew the additional income would be a boost for the family. We had so much and they so little, all due to the accident of birth. My place was to do all I could for them, and it was a duty I would not shirk. I took a last look around the little house and felt a wave of relief followed by a wave of guilt. How lucky I was not to be living here.

Downstairs

viii

The rooms above stairs were something of a shambles after the previous night. The dinner party had gone on and on, and Lily had thought they would never go to bed. The family and their guests had moved from the white drawing room to the dining room and then to the library, and that was where Lily was now, tidying up the mess they had made. Lady Emily trusted her to return the books to the right spaces on the shelves, and at least a dozen were scattered on tables throughout the room. Alice told her that once Lady Bromley had retired to bed, Lady Emily had stood on a chair and recited something Greek about a man trying to find his way home after some long-ago war. The gentlemen were nearly in tears laughing, and Lady Matilda had threatened them with a sword if they didn't pay better attention to the poem. Lily was sorry she had missed it, but instead she had seen Miss Fitzgerald's attempt at kissing Lord Montagu and how he himself had thwarted it. Miss Fitzgerald must have been mortified.

Mr Davis had already removed the decanters of port and whisky, and had been kind enough to take downstairs for her the glasses that had been strewn about as well. Someone had spilled something sticky near the fireplace. It was fortunate that it had not left a stain, but she was having a bear of a time removing all traces of it. She was on hands and knees scrubbing when Lord Flyte entered the room, startling her. She dropped her brush and stood up as quickly as she could.

"I am terribly sorry to have caught you off guard, Lily," he said. "I really must be more sensitive. I have interrupted you at a bad moment. We made a terrible mess last night, didn't we?" He looked around the room. "I didn't realize. I suppose none of us did."

"That's all right, sir," she said. She hadn't noticed before that his eyes were so very warm and almost a golden brown color that she'd never seen on anyone before. "Things always look different when you're in the midst of cleaning them."

"I have something for you," he said. "I hope you don't consider it inappropriate." He passed her a slim parcel wrapped in fancy paper.

"I shouldn't —"

"No, take it," he said. "I insist."

Her hands were shaking as she opened it. Inside was a book of paintings and sketches that showed page after page of famous places from all over the world: the Great Pyramids of Giza, the Paris Opera House, the Parthenon in Athens, the Coliseum in Rome. And more. More than she could count.

"I — I —" She stood for some time, unable to complete the sentence. When at last she found her voice, she looked straight into Lord Flyte's golden brown eyes. "It is the most beautiful thing I have ever seen in my life. Thank you, sir."

"I wanted you to have a bit of the world to look at until you can go to all these places yourself. I suspect that when you do travel, your own sketches will put these to shame."

"You are so kind," Lily said, clutching the book to her chest. "I will treasure this, just as I do your painting."

"I hoped you would," Simon said. "I am very pleased you like it." There was an unusual feeling swelling in his chest. He couldn't quite identify it, or even tell if it were pleasant or not. It was pressing and prickly and hot all at once.

"It is the most wonderful thing I have ever owned."

"I shan't distract you any longer," he said, "but I do look forward to seeing you again." He made a little bow to her — to her! — before he left the room. Lily was dizzy; her heart raced, and she thought she might faint with pleasure. She put the book down, eager to finish her work so that she might take her treasure upstairs and stow it away somewhere safe. Tonight, and every night after, she would look at each and every page when she was finished with work. Lord Flyte was like no other gentleman.

This observation rather frightened her. The room seemed to crash around her, the colors too bright, the sounds coming through the open window too jarring. Lily had heard more stories than she could count about how dangerous it could be for a maid to become entangled with a gentleman, no matter how kind he seemed. Nothing good could ever come of it. Lord Flyte had never tried to take liberties, though. Perhaps he was different. Or perhaps he was more patient. She felt her stomach clench, and she wondered if she ought to return the book to him, but she couldn't bear the thought. If he did turn out like so many others, she would be very, very sad, and then what would she be forced to do? She took a deep breath and started to consider her options, then realized she didn't really have any. Perhaps that was of no consequence. No matter what happened, she would still have the most magnificent book she had ever seen.

CHAPTER
NINE

Matilda and I were in high spirits when we left the widow's farm. It always felt good to be able to offer assistance to a family in need, and I hoped that bringing the boy into my household would enable him to have a better life and to provide the additional income so desperately needed by his mother and siblings. Service was a respectable occupation, and if he did well, he could eventually become a footman. If he worked hard enough after that, someday even a butler. I would speak to Davis about him. He might take the boy on as a special project.

That settled, I began to contemplate the lack of candor in what Miss Fitzgerald presented as her alibi for the night of Archibald's death. She was not telling the truth, or at least not the full truth, and I did not trust her. I wanted to speak to her again, but she was not home when Matilda and I called, so we returned to Montagu to inspect Charlotte's journals.

"I have not entirely given up hope that Mr Scolfield is a bastard," Matilda said, leading me to her grandfather's study, "but can Charlotte be the person who proves it?" The room was small, with stained-glass windows depicting scenes from the life of King Arthur.

The windows were lovely but did not let in much light, so we lit a dozen candles to illuminate the space. Matilda took a stack of old notebooks with worn leather covers and uneven pages from the desk and handed it to me.

"It is possible, of course, but perhaps it is best to consider what you will do should you have to accept Rodney as marquess," I said.

"I don't want to admit the possibility. It's too much to bear." She looked away from me. She stood up. She sat down. She stood again and walked to the window and back. "He is a decent-looking gent, isn't he?"

This stunned me. Surely she wasn't beginning to warm to her much-loathed relative, even just a bit? I had not mentioned to her my suspicion that our Rodney was not, in fact, the real Rodney. She did not need any false hope. Colin had taken him to London that morning, and we would have confirmation one way or another by the end of the night.

I decided to ignore Matilda's question. "Don't you want to read, too?" I asked, nodding in the direction of the notebooks.

"No," she said. "I am too nervous to put together the meaning of even two words in a row. I shall pace instead."

Charlotte's diary began when she was a girl, fourteen years old. The first entries were striking only in how similar they were to what a fourteen-year-old girl might write today, more than two hundred years later. She complained about her sisters, missed her parents when they were away, delighted in selecting fabric for new gowns, and despised her tutors. As she grew older, what she wrote became more serious. Her eldest brother, who would have been marquess, succumbed to cholera in the army, dying when Charlotte was sixteen. Now she stood to inherit, but this was knowledge she found keenly painful.

On a lighter note, she went on at length about not liking to ride, despite her mother's insistence on going out at least once daily. How unlike the older Charlotte depicted in her portrait, dressed in her habit, groom on hand with her horse, was this younger girl. She would have deliberately chosen how she would be portrayed in the painting, and would have elected to present herself in a manner she thought was either expected of her or would improve her image. Her diaries, however, offered considerably more insight into her true character.

By the time Charlotte turned twenty-one, her opinion of riding had reversed itself. Now she was spending as much time as she could on her horse, and I wondered what had catalyzed the change. That became evident in an entry dated 7 August 1779.

His name was Pearce. He initially appeared in the diary after having shown Charlotte how to better adjust her stirrups so that she would be more comfortable in her saddle, and then wasn't mentioned again until 25 October, when Charlotte described, in rapturous tones, how he came to her rescue when she lost control of "the evil beast Mother had forced upon me" and was thrown from the animal's back. Pearce was a groom in the family's stables. When the errant horse returned riderless, he set off at once in search of his master's daughter, and found her, bruised and scared, in a far-flung spot on the grounds.

From that day, Charlotte could not spend enough time on her horse. Her parents, she reported, were greatly pleased and encouraged her. They even went so far as to insist that Pearce accompany her after the accident until she felt right in her saddle again. As the savvy reader will have already surmised, Charlotte was not about to admit to feeling comfortable any sooner than absolutely necessary. By mid-November, she no longer mentioned Pearce by name, referring to him only as "My P". Her happiness was contagious. I felt buoyed reading her joyful accounts of long mornings spent with her love.

"You're grinning," Matilda said. "What have you learned?"

"Come." I took her by the hand and all but dragged her across the house to the portrait of Charlotte. "She was madly in love with her groom when she was twenty-one. I think this is he."

We both leaned close, wanting to get a better look at the figure in the background.

"He was tall," Matilda said. "And strong. Look at the hold he has on the reins."

"Handsome, too." I was on my tiptoes and starting to lose my balance. I pulled a chair in front of the canvas and stood on it. "I cannot make out the color of his eyes."

Matilda took something out of a table drawer and climbed onto the chair, holding me around the waist to keep us both from falling. "Magnifying glass," she said and held it up in front of the groom. "Pearce. I wonder what became of him."

"This was painted when she was twenty-five," I said, noting the date on the brass plaque on the picture's frame. "He must have stayed in her employ."

"What other option did he have? They could not bear to be apart," Matilda said. We were both giggling like schoolgirls. "Unless she scandalized society and married him?"

"No," I said. "First because it would never have been allowed at the time, and second because he is depicted as a servant. Had they married, he would have been her equal." I jumped down from the chair. "Who did she marry?"

"I cannot say I recall," Matilda said, "but it would be easy enough to find out. I've got all the genealogy at the ready."

We returned to the study. Charlotte, Marchioness of Montagu, had married Sir George Reynolds in 1780. "A pity it could not have worked out better for her," I said.

"Keep reading," Matilda said. "If she had Pearce in her portrait in 1783, the affair could have gone on for ages. Sir George may have rarely troubled her. He undoubtedly had a mistress of his own."

"I would like to keep reading," I said, "but I fear I must get back to work. May I borrow the diaries?" Charlotte had been prolific; there were seven volumes.

"Of course, so long as you promise to tell me everything about the divine Pearce."

"You may depend upon it," I said. "Can you imagine if she had lived in a different world, one in which ladies could marry whomever they wanted, even if that meant a groom?"

"That, Emily, is too radical a concept even for me to consider." She walked me to the front door, where my carriage was waiting. Just as we stepped outside, Rodney rode up on my husband's favorite horse.

"Good day, ladies," he called, lifting his hat. "What a pleasant surprise to find you both here."

"I cannot say the same about seeing you," Matilda said. Her voice was sharp, harsh even, but I detected the slightest hint of color in her cheeks.

"Boudica, don't be cruel."

Matilda bristled but made no comment about the name. "To what do we owe the disgrace of your presence?"

"Must I justify a visit to my own home?" he asked, his eyes lingering on his cousin's face longer than strictly proper. For a moment, I felt as if I were the intruder, stumbling into a private scene, but I dismissed the notion as nothing but foolish. Still, I could not deny that Matilda's eyes had rested as long on Rodney's as his had on hers. All at once she snapped out of what I could only imagine was a trance and spoke.

"You are infuriating." She turned on her heel before marching back into the house without another word.

"You have your work cut out for you, Rodney," I said. "I do not know how you will ever convince her to accept your role here."

He slid down from his horse and passed the reins to a waiting groom. "I like nothing more than a good challenge, Emily."

"I'm surprised you're already back from London."

"Only just," he said. "It is approaching seven o'clock."

"So late? I hadn't noticed."

"A good book will do that." He nodded at the leather volumes in my hand.

"Quite," I said. "I'm off home. Shall I see you there soon?"

"I think I shall dine with my energetic cousin. She keeps trying to goad me into fencing with her, but I thought I would try something more civilized first. If, that is, you take no offense to me abandoning you and Mr Hargreaves?"

"Matilda is the one who may take offense. I can only wish you luck."

The sky had gone dark and the air chilly by the time I reached Anglemore, and the soft light emanating from the windows warmed me even before I stepped inside. No home could be more welcoming, and I reveled in this knowledge for a moment before continuing on my way. I was eager to interrogate Colin on his day's work. Was Rodney Scolfield who he claimed? First, though, I went up to the nursery, kissed my dear boys, and had just started down the stairs when I ran into my mother coming up them.

"I am not entirely certain Lord Montagu is the sort of person one ought to welcome as a houseguest," she said, her voice low and serious, worry etching itself on the lines of her face which seemed to grow deeper by the minute.

"Have you only just come to that conclusion, Mother?" I asked.

"He is a man of extremely strange habits. And his valet?" She looked around as if it mattered whether anyone else heard her next words. "He is a Red Indian."

"I am well aware of that."

"He has pitched a tent next to your stables."

"Yes," I said. "Does that cause a problem for you?"

"It is unthinkably bizarre. What will people say?"

"He presents himself well enough. I saw him the other morning. He is a handsome, proud man. Davis tells me the servants like him and that he is a hard worker. At any rate, I don't see how it is any of our business. If Lord Montagu is content with him, we must be as well."

"But, Emily —"

"You must excuse me, Mother. I have not yet seen my husband since he returned from London." I gave her a little kiss and continued on my way, listening to her sputter as I left. I was, perhaps, somewhat more amused by this than I ought to have been. Some things cannot be helped. Colin, as I expected, was in his study when I found him, bent over a chessboard and looking rather confused.

"I don't remember leaving it this way," he said.

"You didn't." I wrapped my arms around his waist. "It was mate in five. I solved it after you left this morning."

"Dreadful girl." He covered my face with kisses. "Show me what you did."

"Not until after you tell me what you learned in London."

"I am afraid you will find it a crushing disappointment."

"He really is Rodney Scolfield?" I asked.

"Yes," Colin said. "We lunched at the Travellers. Not only did seven members recognize him and come speak to us, there was a photograph of him from the *New York Herald* displayed in one of the rooms. It had been taken when he set off on an expedition to the North Pole."

"The North Pole?"

"He made it no farther than the Yukon," Colin said. "The paper identified him in its caption, and there can be no mistake. The man in the photograph is the man we know as the new Marquess of Montagu."

I sighed and flopped down onto a chair. "I suppose it was too much to hope otherwise."

"Yes," he said. "Whisky?"

I shook my head. "No, thank you."

"What did you learn today?" he asked.

"Miss Fitzgerald lied about spending the evening of the murder at a farmhouse, and in the eighteenth century the Marchioness of Montagu had a passionate affair with her groom."

"Did she?"

"I'm reading the torrid details in her diary. It is rather titillating."

"What are you going to do about Miss Fitzgerald?" he asked.

152

"I shall go into Melton Carbury tomorrow and see what I can learn about her."

"I am still troubled by the coincidence of Miss Fitzgerald and Rodney Scolfield having met before his arrival here," Colin said.

"What other explanation could there be? Without, of course, slipping into dangerous speculation."

He propped his long legs up on his desk. "It could be there isn't one, but that doesn't sit right with me. I should like to speak with the vicar tomorrow. Will that interfere with any of your plans?"

"Not in the slightest," I said. "We can ride to Melton Carbury together."

He dropped his feet to the ground and sat up straight. "Heavens. You and your passion for riding. I don't need to be worried about any of the grooms, do I?"

"Don't be ridiculous."

"No?"

"Of course not."

He went to the door and locked it, a delicious glint in his dark eyes. "Prove it."

I slipped out of the study more than an hour later, my hair undone and my face flushed as if it were the hottest day of summer. Marriage truly is the greatest delight in life. "Dinner will need to be pushed back another half an hour, Davis," I said, not meeting his eyes as I passed him in the great hall.

"Yes, madam." If he noticed the state of my appearance, he made no visible show of it. "These wires have arrived for you."

"Thank you." I removed them from the silver tray he presented, with as much dignity as I could muster, and turned to go up the newel staircase, a showcase of Elizabethan wood carving, half tempted to laugh, half tempted to run in embarrassment. If marriage is the greatest delight, a discreet butler is perhaps the greatest necessity after the right husband. "Could you please send Meg up as well?" I cringed at the thought of her inevitable reaction to the state of my hair.

"Lord Almighty, Lady Emily," she said when she entered my room. "What on earth have you done to yourself? It's as if some sort of animal had at your hair."

"Something like that," I said.

"I see that sly smile. It was Mr Hargreaves, wasn't it?"

"Meg!"

"I thought you'd be pleased that I'm used to him now."

Meg, who had been with me from the time I made my debut in society, had taken a rather long time to adjust to my being married to Colin. Philip and I had only lived together for a short time before he died, so Meg had never before really had to deal with a husband. For more than a year after Colin and I wed, she had tiptoed around him, all but refusing to come into my room when he was there. Now that she had accepted him, she was wont to go overboard on occasion. Not that I minded. Her candor was refreshing. "You are impossible, Meg, but I simply could not do without you."

"What is milady going to wear tonight?" she asked.

"I don't mind. You pick something." I had opened the first wire, from a gentleman in France, an old friend of the Scolfield family, with whom Archibald and Mr Porter had stayed during their time abroad. His words were brief. The boys had stayed five nights. Nothing unusual happened. The second was from an innkeeper in Munich. He asked if I had access to a telephone and, if so, would it be possible to arrange that I ring him? This piqued my interest. We had no telephone at Anglemore, but Colin had one installed in Park Lane the previous year. Although I had numerous misgivings about the device in general, I rather liked the idea of making a call to Germany and decided to speak to my husband about it before dinner.

The third wire was from Mr Porter's aunt. She asked if I could possibly make my way to Dover, as there was much she would like to discuss. I was halfway through mentally planning a trip to London and then Dover when I noticed Meg standing in front of me waving two dinner gowns.

"No opinion, then?" she asked. "If you don't pay better attention, I may put you in a morning gown. Or perhaps a riding habit."

"Yes, that's fine, Meg," I said, hardly hearing her. She laughed, and I knew I was in the most capable hands.

Downstairs

ix

Pru was dragging a basket heaped full of potatoes to the kitchen when Lily came downstairs. "You ought to lift that," she said. "You'll leave a mark on the floor."

"What do I care about the floor?" Pru scowled.

"You'll care when you're the one up late cleaning it." Lily flounced past her into the servants' hall, ready for a cup of tea, pausing only for a second when she saw Lord Montagu's valet, the tall Red Indian, sitting quietly in the corner of the room. She couldn't decide if he scared or fascinated her. In the end, she determined to choose fascination over fear and asked him if she might sketch him. He obliged, and she sat on a chair across from him, pulling out the pad and pencil she kept in her apron pocket.

There was time for her to do this because Lord Flyte's gift had given her the energy of ten ordinary maids plus two, and she had finished her work quicker than usual, leaving her with a quarter of an hour before she needed to go upstairs and prepare the dressing rooms again. They would all be getting ready for dinner now, she thought, and she pictured Lord Flyte in his evening kit. She was glad she worked in a house where the footmen wore livery. Otherwise, she might think the gentlemen looked rather too much like the servants. This made her smile.

"You're awfully pleased with yourself," Alice said, bringing a pot of tea into the room and putting it on the long table. Her face was strained and pale.

"What's wrong?" Lily asked, stopping work on her drawing.

"Rotten day," Alice said and lowered her voice. "Johnny and Pru."

Lily looked at the Red Indian. He nodded, understanding, and rose from his chair. He crossed the room and sat again, this time near the fireplace, far enough away that the girls might speak freely without being overheard.

"No, that can't be right. Why would he like her when he could have you?" Lily put her drawing materials away and filled three cups from the pot, proffering one to the valet before sitting down with her friend. "What you need, Alice my dear, is a nice cuppa tea."

"He has no interest in me because he can do whatever he wants with Pru." She was whispering now, not wanting the valet to hear her. They had offered him tea, but he declined.

"Even Pru wouldn't be that foolish."

"She is." Alice spooned sugar into her cup. "One of the other grooms saw them in the stable. He'd just put the carriage away after collecting Lord Flyte from the train station."

"Just because they were in the stable together doesn't mean —"

"They were caught in the act." Alice flushed crimson.

"Well, they'd better hope Mr Davis doesn't get word of it," Lily said. "He'd send them both packing in a heartbeat."

"It won't happen," Alice said. "No one will say anything because everyone likes Johnny. All the grooms, that is. I can't say I'm particularly fond of him anymore."

"More likely the grooms want what Pru's offering." Lily took her friend's hand. "If they rat him out, she would go, too. I'm so sorry, Alice. You deserve better."

"Quite right I do," she said. "But what about you? You look as if you could fly today."

"I've had a present," Lily said, leaning close to Alice and keeping her voice a whisper. "When you're in our room next, take a look. It's in the top drawer of my dresser."

"Is it from whom I think?" Alice asked. She took Lily's blush as a yes.

Pru was watching them from the corridor, full of hate for Lily. Eavesdropping might be a sin, but sometimes a body had no other options. She knew what she needed to do next, and the evil look that heathen Red Indian was throwing her way wasn't going to stop her.

CHAPTER
TEN

Meg had laced me so tightly I could hardly breathe, let alone even consider bending over. The effect justified it, however, as since the twins had been born there was no other way to squeeze me into this, my favorite shell-pink silk Worth creation. It pained me to recall the death of the greatest clothier of the century, Charles Frederick Worth, the previous year. His sons had proven well capable of continuing their father's standards of design and innovation again and again, but I would miss the man himself, with his exacting opinions and flawless taste. I had started wearing more and more Liberty Gowns — my mother was continually criticizing my steps towards Rational Dress — but I would never want to entirely abandon the delicate beauty of haute couture. I adored tonight's gown, with its pointed corselet bodice and a skirt narrower than had been seen in years. Best of all, the grotesque voluminous sleeves of seasons past had at last deflated, their replacements long and almost skintight.

Colin had come upstairs, changed into evening kit, and gone back down in less time than it had taken Meg to finish retaming my unruly hair, and I wanted to speak to him privately before Simon and my mother joined us in the drawing room. I did not find him in the house, but a helpful footman directed me outside, where he was discussing something with one of the grooms. I pulled a wrap around my shoulders and went off in search of him. The stables, behind the house and to the east, formed a large compound situated around a courtyard. The stone buildings provided ample space for our horses as well as room above to house the grooms. I stood back some distance, before he had seen me, and watched him. His every move was an exercise in elegance. Adonis would have wept in shame to be compared with such a man.

When he turned away from the groom, I stepped forward, called to him, and gave a little wave, blushing at the memory of our time together in his study.

"My dear, your cheeks are a perfect match for your gown," he said, planting a soft kiss on my lips. "You grow more beautiful daily. Aphrodite would tremble in your presence."

"You are too kind." I could feel myself blush. "I need to arrange a quick stop in London followed by a trip to Dover, after tomorrow, of course, when I have exhausted any leads I find in Melton Carbury. And while in London, I shall need to telephone Germany."

"My, you are industrious," he said. "All this since you left me in my study? I cannot say I've accomplished anything beyond getting dressed for dinner."

"You were rather vigorously engaged when I last saw you," I said, "so don't be too hard on yourself. You needed some rest."

"London and Dover, eh?" he asked. "Do tell the details, and then I shall share with you what our industrious groom had for me."

"You first," I said. "Mine will take longer."

"Both Lily and Prudence have come forward and admitted they saw a figure outside the servants' entrance the night of the murder."

"Yes, I am aware of that."

"Lily is certain it was a man. Prudence isn't sure. But Johnny has just informed me that he heard a voice that night. A woman crying."

"Why did he say nothing until now?" I asked.

"He thought it was a cat."

"A cat? We don't have cats at Anglemore. Your foxhounds would eat them."

"I would allow nothing of the sort," Colin said.

"I am quite confident Bellerophon would eat *me* if you left me unguarded and alone in the house. I can have no faith in creatures bred to tear a defenseless fox to shreds."

"You know I share your opinion of fox hunting. That is why we don't allow it at Anglemore."

"Precisely why the hounds are likely to eat any available cat or unaccompanied lady. We have thwarted their purpose in life."

"You are most amusing, my dear," Colin said. "I should have married you ages ago. At any rate, cats were apparently rampant at Johnny's previous place of employment, and more than once he mistook their mewing for a child crying. A few hours ago, he mentioned to one of his fellow grooms that he thought it odd he hadn't heard the cat again since the night of the murder. At which time someone pointed out to him that there are no cats here. He realized his error and asked to see me."

"He is certain it was a woman?" I asked.

"Reasonably." Colin ran a hand through his thick, dark hair. "It is as unlikely that a man would be crying outside our servants' entrance as it is that someone would mistake him for a cat."

"Would you like me to speak to Lily?" I asked. "I could ascertain just how confident she is in her identification."

"That is an excellent idea. I don't believe I was intimidating when I spoke with her, but she might respond better to you."

"I shall have a chat with her after dinner."

"Now tell me about this proposed trip of yours. Why do you need to telephone Germany?"

"I have had a very interesting series of wires," I said. "Walk with me and I shall tell you all about them."

By the time we had finished discussing our options (and meandered no small distance through our grounds, taking in not only the formal garden but the walled garden, the lake, the abbey, and two follies as well before reaching the house, all the while Acastus and Pollux at their master's heel), my mother and Simon were already in the white drawing room waiting to go in to dinner. The meal itself was uneventful, despite my mother's constant insistence on discussing the numerous ways in which she found Rodney and his valet inappropriate until I told her that if she did not stop, I would retire to the Red Indian's tent. After port

162

and cigars (my mother being the only person who exited to the drawing room in favor of sherry), I left Colin and Simon and asked for Lily to be sent to me in the Spanish room, deciding the library felt too large for speaking to the young and sometimes timid housemaid. I wanted Lily to feel as comfortable and safe as possible.

"You called for me, madam?"

"Thank you for coming so quickly, Lily," I said.

"What can I do for you?"

"Take a seat, please," I said. "I want to speak to you about the night of the murder."

Her face went a shade paler as she sat on the chair across from mine, perching on its very edge, her back straight and her eyes unblinking. "I told Mr Hargreaves everything I could remember."

"I am interested in the figure you saw outside the house."

"He seemed bulky and was dressed in dark clothes," she said. "That's all I know, milady. I wish I had noticed more details."

"It would have been difficult to in the dark. Are you absolutely certain it was a man?"

"I was," she said. "He seemed too large and hulking to be a woman, but now that I've been asked so many times I'm starting to doubt myself. How can I be sure?" She was clenching her hands so hard her knuckles were white. "I didn't know at the time I was seeing something that mattered. If I had I'd have been more careful to better remember. I promise you that, milady."

"Don't worry yourself," I said. "I know you are doing the best you can, and it would be wrong of anyone to expect more. It is important that I make sure we know everything we can about that night. Did you hear any sound when you saw this person?"

She squeezed her eyes shut and then, after a moment, shook her head with an almost violent force. "No — no, I don't think so. The window was shut."

"You were upstairs. It is not surprising you heard nothing."

"Did someone else hear a sound?"

"Yes," I said. "One of the grooms, Johnny, thinks he heard a woman crying."

"Crying?" she asked. "No, I know I didn't hear that, and I doubt the person I saw would have been crying. I can't quite explain it, but he seemed more menacing than sad. Of course I couldn't see his face, so I could be completely wrong. Who do you think it was?"

"I haven't the slightest idea," I said. "If you and Prudence hadn't both seen someone, I would be inclined to dismiss it altogether. But you both did, and now we have Johnny's account as well. Can you remember if everyone was present and accounted for in the servants' hall when you went back downstairs?"

"I can't say that I particularly noticed," she said, "but I know I didn't think anything was out of the ordinary."

"Did anything else strike you as unusual that night?"

"Not until Lord Montagu collapsed."

"Thank you, Lily. Please do come to me if you remember anything else, even if it seems too small a detail to matter."

"I will, madam, I promise."

*　*　*

Colin and I were in Melton Carbury before nine o'clock the next morning. We started by interviewing the villagers, trying to learn whatever we could about the Fitzgeralds. We found they were much liked by their neighbors, who considered them to be helpful and pious. Cora taught Sunday school and was always available to assist children who were struggling with their lessons. The vicar was an integral part of every family, there for baptisms, marriages, and deaths. No one had much to say about the missionary work he had undertaken at the beginning of his career, but there was no reason to expect anyone to know much about it.

Confident that there was nothing else to be learned from the villagers, we went to the vicarage. While Colin spoke to her father inside the house, I went to look for Cora in the garden. She was sitting in an alcove formed by ancient yew trees, with a piece of embroidery on her lap, her head bent over her work. I called a greeting and sat next to her on the bench.

"I was wondering, Miss Fitzgerald, if you could tell me more about the night of Archibald's murder?" I asked. "I had occasion to visit the family you had previously mentioned to me. Lady Matilda heard of their plight and was concerned about the health of the children. She asked me to accompany her to the house."

"How kind of you," she said. "I wish you would have told me. I should have liked to go along as well."

"The widow said that only one of the children had been ill, and that he was already much better."

"What a relief. She must be very pleased. The poor woman has enough burdens without having to contend with disease ravaging her family."

"Hadn't you told me all the children were under the weather?" I asked.

"I always assume everyone is at risk when a family living in such close quarters is facing illness. Particularly children. They are so vulnerable." She tugged at her thread, which appeared to have got tangled.

"A very sensible strategy," I said. "Tell me about what happened when you arrived there that evening. It was evening, wasn't it?"

"Yes. The sun had long since set."

"Do you know what time it was?"

"Not precisely, no."

"So you got to the house. What happened next?"

"I went inside and examined the children," she said and thrust her needlework onto the bench beside her. "I must say, Lady Emily, I am getting the distinct feeling that I am being interrogated, and I do not appreciate it. I was doing my duty that night, helping a family in need. Why all these questions?"

"Were the children awake when you arrived?"

"Yes, of course. How else would I have examined them?"

"All of them?"

"Yes."

"Even the little ones?"

"I already told you, yes." Her tone was becoming more and more strained. "What are you really asking me? Do you think I killed the man I loved?"

166

"If I wondered that, I would ask you directly," I said, meeting her flashing eyes with my own calm gaze. "I do, however, know that you called on the farmer's widow quite late in the evening, and she told me that all the children were already in bed, fast asleep. She insists that you did not set foot in the house."

"So you are calling me a liar?"

"I am asking you to explain the discrepancy in the two versions of the story."

"How on earth should I know?" she said. "Did it occur to you that I might be the one telling the truth? Or do you take the word of an uneducated, overworked woman over mine?"

"Your stations in life have nothing to do with it," I said. "I do not see that the widow would gain anything by lying. You, on the other hand, do have a connection with the murder victim. I would be remiss in my duties if I did not come back to question you again after hearing the widow's story."

"You are welcome to do whatever you wish," she said, "but I cannot make up answers to suit your pleasure."

"So you stand by your original statement?"

"I do. Why wouldn't I?"

"And you have no explanation for why the widow has such a different memory of the evening?"

"None in the least. Perhaps I should have checked her own health more carefully. She might have been affected by the fever as well."

"Sarcasm does not become you," I said.

"You might consider, Lady Emily, that she could in fact have had reason to be less than candid, even if she did remember what actually happened. You arrive, unexpectedly, with Lady Matilda. Her house is in disarray — it is filthy — and her children are running wild. She is living there on nothing more than the goodwill of the Scolfield family. Lady Matilda's grandfather let her stay in the house after her husband died even though none of the children were yet of an age to be able to do enough work on the lands to justify the expense. Do you really think she is going to admit to even more weakness? Her only hope of remaining in her home is to make Lady Matilda — or now, Lord Montagu, but she wasn't to know that at the time — believe that her children are strong and healthy and mere months away from being of real use to the other farmers on her land."

"It is an interesting theory, Miss Fitzgerald," I said. "I shall give it due consideration." Miss Fitzgerald stared at me, her face unmoving, her eyes boring into my own.

"Thank you." There was no kindness in her words.

"I did not mean to offend you," I said. "You must understand the seriousness of the problem before us. We have to find justice for Archibald Scolfield. You of all people should see the value in that."

"I know." She dropped her head into her hands. "It is not so easy for me. I thought he loved me. I believed all the sweet words he said to me, and gave my love to him freely and wholeheartedly, only to find I have been a naive fool. How could I have ever thought he would want me when he stood to inherit a title and an estate? He needed a gracious lady with status and reputation, someone who could entertain political guests and help forward his career. Not the silly daughter of a vicar."

"You are too hard on yourself," I said. "There is nothing silly about you, and your experience assisting your father both here and during his missionary work would have been ample preparation to be the wife of a marquess."

"Be that as it may, he needed a wife with rank from a family at least as prestigious as his own. I knew that, or at least I should have done. I certainly did in the beginning, when I could hardly believe he loved me in any serious way. Yet he was so adamant about not wanting what was expected of him, not when it came to society. He insisted again and again that he wanted to rally the nation against social inequality and that he needed someone like me by his side in order to do it. By then, I believed him because I wanted to."

"He sounds like a young man in search of a mission," I said, "and that does not mean his feelings for you were anything short of sincere."

"I appreciate that you are trying to make me feel better, but it is not going to work. I should have found a more suitable husband."

"I didn't realize Lord Montagu was interested in a political career," I said. "What were his specific plans?"

"He never really talked about a precise strategy, but aren't all young men in positions like his interested in politics, especially once they've inherited? I should have thought his involvement a foregone conclusion."

"I think, Miss Fitzgerald, you give the upper class too much credit. Countless men like Archibald are content to do nothing but sit around their estates talking to their dogs and shooting birds."

"Archibald wanted to travel."

"You had mentioned that."

"I thought he perhaps wanted to be involved in the diplomatic service," she said, pulling a face. "I guess I did not know him so well as I thought."

"I wouldn't go so far as to say that he deserved to be murdered," I said, "but I think you may be better off not married to him."

"I should like very much to believe that," she said.

"Please forgive me for having upset you," I said. "I hope you can understand I am bent on finding whoever committed this heinous crime. If, in the course of the investigation, I ruffle a few innocent feathers, I consider it a small price to pay in exchange for justice."

"I do understand, Lady Emily, and I assure you I will do whatever I can to help you in the matter. In the meantime, I was wondering if I could speak to you about the new Lord Montagu? Are you aware of him harboring any romantic attachments? A lady in my unfortunate position is in dire need of any distraction she can get."

I was glad when Colin came to collect me in the vicarage garden. Miss Fitzgerald was quite unstoppable when it came to asking questions about Rodney. "I cannot decide," I told Colin as we climbed back onto our horses, "whether she is genuinely interested in him now, or if this is all a throwback to her girlish crush.

170

Nor can I tell what to make of it all in the context of her so-called fiancé's death."

"She can't be too broken up over the loss of him if she's so taken with someone else."

"Unless it is nothing more than a way of turning her grief into something more manageable."

"Do you believe she lied about her visit to the farm?"

"I do," I said.

"Why would she have lied?"

"If she did kill Archibald, her story would have provided an alibi, though not a good one if it is so easily exposed."

"She could have panicked when you initially spoke to her and told you the first thing that came into her head."

"Yet she did go to the farm," I said. "That could have been a deliberate attempt to give herself an alibi. She might not have thought the widow would have anything different to say to us."

"Most likely she assumed the widow would back up whatever story she had told. If you had merely asked for confirmation of what Miss Fitzgerald said, I have no doubt the widow would have given it without a second thought. Instead, you asked her what happened, which made her tell it as she remembered without any outside influence. Well done making her actively provide an answer."

"Thank you," I said. "What did the vicar have to say?"

"He told me about his years in India with Cora, two to be exact. He spent the better part of a decade as a young man doing missionary work and traveled all over the world. When he returned to England, he married, and his wife died soon after their daughter's birth. When he thought Cora was old enough, he wanted to return to his previous task, but after they had been in India a little over a year, he started to realize the girl would be better off in England."

"So they returned?"

"Yes, once a replacement for him could be found and he got the living here from Matilda's grandfather," he said. "As for Rodney Scolfield, he did not remember much about him at all. Denied the story of the tigers altogether."

"Do you think Miss Fitzgerald invented the whole thing?"

"It is possible she did, but I don't necessarily think so. It seems to me the incident was far more significant to her than to her father. He had myriad other things to worry about."

"So how do we feel about Miss Fitzgerald?" I asked.

"She remains a suspect," Colin said. "Her behavior has been not quite cricket."

"Something about her connection with Rodney is still nagging at me," I said, "but perhaps it's only that I don't want to think them having met in India and then again here is nothing more than coincidence."

"Humans always long for significance," Colin said. "Sometimes explanations don't provide the tidy endings we prefer. In this case, however, I am inclined to agree with you."

★　★　★

172

Colin spent the remainder of the day speaking to the outdoor servants at both Anglemore and Montagu. I went back to the site of the murder, hoping I might find some clue overlooked by him and the police. The abbey had not originally been part of the estate, and the family had not bothered to do anything with the building when the land had been granted during the Reformation. It had crumbled gracefully, its walls still standing, but the upper level and the roof had long ago collapsed. Remains of sculptures lay scattered across the cracked stone floor through which wildflowers now grew, their blooms returning color to a space that hundreds of years ago would have been full of it. The altar, marred and broken, stood at one end. Not far from it was a small pile of cigar ashes that had already been identified as Archibald's, but I found nothing else related to the night of the murder. I went back to the house and climbed the stairs to the nursery. All of the babies were awake, and all of them on the floor, playing, insomuch as babies can. Tom was back to his favorite trick of banging his rattle against a block. Richard was lying on his stomach and pushing himself up with his little arms, over and over. Henry, flat on his back, was looking at the ceiling, doing not much of anything.

"Is this Lily's work?" I asked, noticing a sketch of the boys that was sitting on a table.

"It is indeed," said Nanny. "She came up on her afternoon a few weeks ago. Said she wanted to capture them when they still had nothing to think about but smiling. It's a lovely likeness, isn't it?"

"That it is," I said.

"If you don't mind me saying so, Lady Emily, Lily is too bright to remain a maid. With a little education and some training in the social graces she would make a fine governess."

"That is an astute observation, Nanny. I shall give the matter serious consideration," I said, looking at the sketch again. "They are handsome boys, aren't they?"

"You are a devoted mother, Lady Emily. I am so glad of it. Some of these ladies today, well, I need not tell you. I have, after all, met Lady Bromley."

"Yes, I am so sorry, Nanny," I said. "I know she can be a bother."

"I have taken it upon myself to reform her. She wants me reciting the list of the kings of England to the boys three times a day, even now, when they're little babies. Says she wants to be sure they've learned it by the time they're able to speak. Thing is, madam, these are smart boys. They'd learn it in two days flat, if it took that long, and it will be much longer than two days before they can speak. Does she want me to bore them to death?"

"She can be difficult."

"I told her the Queen's nanny confided in me years ago that Prince Albert insisted on his children hearing German, French, and English in the nursery every single day so that they would be able to speak all three languages fluently."

"Did he really?"

Nanny looked up at the ceiling and gave a little shrug. "Well, madam, the truth is I've not the slightest idea. I've never met the Queen's nanny. I do know, however, that Lady Bromley prides herself on her French, and I followed up my little tidbit about the prince with the helpful suggestion that when she visits the boys, she should speak to them in French. She's so focused on that now that she leaves me more or less alone. She hasn't asked me once since then about the list of kings."

"My," I said, with a gasp of admiration. "Nanny, I am most impressed."

"Thank you, madam."

We both turned at the sound of gurgly laughter. Henry was no longer on his back, but flipped over onto his front, his smile indicating he was well pleased with himself. He rolled again, onto his back, and once more onto his front. He then pushed himself up and laughed heartily. I scooped him up in my arms and kissed his chubby cheeks.

"They are delightful, aren't they?" I said. "I don't know what I would do without them."

"That's the first time he's managed from back to front, madam," Nanny said. "They're all good strong boys."

"Indeed they are," I said. "Nanny, I came up to talk to you as well as to see the boys. Did any of the nursery staff notice anything out of sorts the night Lord Montagu was murdered?"

"You know we've answered all these questions already, madam. Our Colin was pleased as punch to show off his investigative skills to us. He was as eager as a little boy."

"I know, but it's possible you or someone else has remembered a detail that had previously escaped notice."

"I don't think so, madam. I'm sorry not to be of more help."

"Have you heard anything from the maid I dismissed?"

"No, Lady Emily, and I'm not likely to. She's probably in a factory now. Couldn't get another position in service without a character, and you know as well as I that she didn't deserve one."

I winced, knowing how bad factory conditions could be. She deserved no comfort, though, after deliberately neglecting and then hurting a child. This was a case of merit, or the lack thereof, determining a person's fate. "I know you are right," I said.

"Much though I would love for her to be guilty of the murder, the fact is she was up here with me all that evening."

"One other thing, Nanny," I said. "We've had it reported that someone heard a woman crying behind the house near the servants' entrance."

"None of us would have heard that all the way over here."

"Would you ask the nursery maids, just in case? One of them might have gone downstairs for something."

"I can, madam, but I must assure you that we all have revealed everything we know. Our Colin wouldn't have settled for a single word less."

"Thank you, Nanny," I said and gave Henry another cuddle before returning him to the floor. "And thank you for taking such good care of the boys."

Downstairs

X

Lily hadn't noticed anything out of place in her room when she had collapsed into bed last night. Exhaustion had overtaken her, and she hadn't even pulled Lord Flyte's gift from her dresser drawer. She had been too tired. She had been busier than usual yesterday, the house chaotic following the murder. Nothing seemed to be running smoothly. Three of the dogs had come in from outside through the front door — no one admitted to having left it open — and tracked mud all through the great hall and halfway up the stairs, so she'd had to wash up after them. The stairs were always the worst. They weren't quite deep enough to safely balance her bucket and always left her with a knot in her back.

Today, however, Lady Bromley was the only one home in the afternoon, and she had asked for her luncheon in her room, so there hadn't been quite so much to tidy after that. The dining room hadn't even needed a touch-up after she'd dusted in the morning, and this meant Lily had a few moments to herself after eating her own lunch. She slipped upstairs while the others were still sitting around the table over cups of steaming tea, listening to Lord Montagu's valet tell stories about his adventures in the wilds of the American West. She couldn't look at her painting, as one of the men on the estate had offered to make a frame for it, and he wouldn't return it for at least a fortnight, but she had enough time to study her wonderful new book.

Usually, Lily counted the steps from the servants' hall to the top floor of the house, partly out of habit, and partly to make the four long flights go by more quickly. Today she took them two at a time and was moving too fast to count. Truth was, she was moving almost too fast to breathe. She closed the door to the snug room she and Alice shared, a pleasant space with china blue walls and matching bedspreads. Lady Emily liked her staff to feel at home in their quarters and decorated their rooms accordingly. Some ladies gave their servants castoffs, but that was not allowed at Anglemore Park. She had allowed Lily to hang some of her drawings, and Lily liked to think of the room as her own little museum. She pulled the wooden rocking chair to her favorite spot in front of her small window and then went to her dresser to get her book.

She pulled open the drawer and was immediately consumed with a feeling of dread. Her stockings and spare cap, along with the handkerchiefs her mother had lovingly trimmed with lace, were a riot of mess — and her book, her beautiful book, was not where she had left it. She flung the contents of the drawer onto her bed but did not uncover it. Nor was it in any of her other drawers.

178

She hesitated, not wanting to disturb Alice's privacy, but she did find herself sorely tempted to riffle through her roommate's dresser.

"That will not do," she whispered to herself. "Alice would never have taken it and not put it back." She searched the rest of the room, under the two single beds, and in the wardrobe that stood next to the door, but the book eluded her. Tears smarted in her eyes. She hadn't even had a chance to thoroughly look through it. Her stomach churned and her face felt hot. She wanted to fling herself onto her bed and have a good cry, but she knew there was work to be done, and she'd already used up any free time she would have that afternoon.

Lily poured water from the pitcher into the basin and splashed her face, blotting it dry. She smoothed her skirts and her apron and, keeping Mrs Elliott close in mind, made sure her cap was straight before she returned downstairs. Her face was composed, but inside she felt nothing of the sort.

Today, someone had taken the world away from her, and she had a fair idea of the culprit's identity.

CHAPTER
ELEVEN

Colin had ordered a special train to take us to London the next morning, wanting neither to lose time making stops nor to have to wait for the first regularly scheduled departure. We arrived viciously early at our house, an elegant Georgian building in Park Lane, but had both agreed it was the best course forward. My telephone call to Germany was scheduled for nine thirty, and I did not want to miss my opportunity to make it.

The telephone both terrified and fascinated me. None of my friends had them installed in their houses — what would be the purpose? — so I had only used it on rare occasions, generally when my husband was working abroad and could ring me from an official building with a telephone of its own. The tinny voice coming over the black wires seemed half magic and half demon. If I tried to contemplate how the device worked, my head would start to hurt, but I nonetheless longed to understand it.

"What troubles me," I said to Colin as he centered the tall black object on his desk, "is how do we even know we are really speaking to the person we think we're ringing? Anyone could be on the other end of that wire and we would never even suspect." I looked at it suspiciously. It reminded me of a deranged candlestick.

"In this case, when you have never before heard a person's voice, that is entirely true," he said. "If you doubt the veracity of what you hear, we shall have to consider further options. Most likely, however, your Herr Gifford will give you a tidy bit of not quite useful information and this will prove to have been much ado about nothing."

"If we are lucky, much ado about very little."

"My dear girl, you look nervous. You're biting your lip."

"You know it unnerves me to speak into that thing," I said.

"I can speak to him if you would prefer."

"No, I shall do it." I forced myself to sit up straighter in my husband's desk chair and nodded to him that I was ready. He lifted the receiver, pressed three times the cradle in which it had hung, and then spoke to the operator. He put the receiver next to my ear and pushed the base of the phone towards me so that I could speak into it with ease.

I heard a crackle and then a voice, speaking, unexpectedly, with an English accent.

"Is this Lady Emily Hargreaves?" it said.

"It is." I realized I was shouting into the mouthpiece.

"This is Mr Ralph Gifford. I am so pleased you received my cable and were able to telephone."

"Yes, it is wonderful, isn't it?" I glanced at Colin, who nodded encouragingly. "What can you tell me about Archibald Scolfield and his friend Cedric Porter?"

"Mr Scolfield and Mr Porter stayed in my inn for a fortnight. I moved to Germany some years ago and frequently host Englishmen at my establishment. I like to provide a real home away from home. A bit of England in Germany."

"Was there a problem during their stay?" I asked.

"Not of which I was aware at the time. After they left, however, things changed. It came to my attention that Mr Scolfield had taken great liberties with my sister, Fanny, a girl of only fifteen. He ruined her, Lady Emily."

"Oh dear, how dreadful. I am most sorry to hear that, Mr Gifford. Did Mr Scolfield remain in touch with her?"

"No, he never contacted her again, which isn't much of a surprise," he said. "She never forgot him, though. I sent her to a school for young ladies in London shortly thereafter as she was in great need of a change of scene."

"I can well imagine," I said. "Did you not worry that he would seek her out in London?"

"It was eminently clear he had no interest in continuing the connection," he said. "What concerns me, Lady Emily, is that she disappeared from school just about a fortnight ago, and no one has been able to locate her."

"Give me all of the details, Mr Gifford, and I will see what I can do."

We only had the line for a few more minutes, so I gathered everything I could from him as efficiently as possible, not realizing I was shaking until I returned the receiver to its cradle.

"It is a relief to be finished with that," I said.

"It does amaze me, Emily, that you shudder before technology. I should have expected the opposite," Colin said. "Although I suppose one could surmise from your love of classical history and antiquities that you have limited interest in mechanical advancements."

"That, my dear, would be a most unwise assumption. I do not shudder before all technology. I have been meaning to speak to you for some time about buying a motorcar. I am desperate to learn how to drive."

"Thank heavens we are too busy to deal with that at the present time."

"Now who is shuddering?" I asked, feeling rather pleased with myself. I had scribbled down all the details Mr Gifford had given me of his sister, and Colin had read over my shoulder as I was writing. "Do we follow up on this now or continue on to Dover as planned?"

"I think Dover first, as we do not want to delay our appointment with Mr Porter's aunt," he said. "We will go by the Yard and make sure the girl's disappearance has already been noted. If the school filed a report, they may already have information that could prove useful to us. It is possible, though, that the school wanted the matter kept private."

"In which case we can call in there when we return from Dover," I said. "Should we warn them of our plans either way?"

"No," Colin said. "There is no need and no time. We shall have to hurry as it is. Come now, let's get a shift on."

We had time only for a quick stop at Scotland Yard. I always liked going there, particularly now that the force respected (somewhat begrudgingly) my abilities as an investigator. Today, however, I said very little, leaving it to Colin. The school had indeed filed a report, which was a welcome surprise, but so far no clues as to Miss Gifford's whereabouts had been found.

We hurried on to Victoria Station and narrowly avoided missing our train to Dover. I sighed with relief and collapsed into my seat when Colin closed the door to our compartment. I hated rushing and hated being late, and it always took me a moment to recover from having to hurry. The journey was not a long one, only a little over two hours, but I was looking forward to the time to read. I had brought with me Charlotte's diaries. I pulled a volume out of my satchel, cozied up next to my husband, and opened to my bookmark.

Charlotte's affair with Pearce was now in full swing, and as she fell deeper in love with him, she grew more daring. To start, they had seen each other only when she was riding, and their meetings were more or less innocent. Eventually, though, these trysts were not enough, and she took to going for long walks in the evening when her parents were out and wouldn't notice her absence. Pearce would meet her at a predetermined location. It was on one of these occasions that they shared their first kiss and he gave her the roses whose petals she had saved. Soon she had to come up with a different scheme to see him, as her parents started putting more and more pressure on her to marry and insisted on her participation in evening entertainments that were now geared to finding her a husband. She was too old, so far as they were concerned, ancient at twenty-one. I knew well what Charlotte must have been feeling. My own mother had once held similar opinions about me.

Charlotte resisted their machinations, however, and remained steadfast in her love for Pearce. She told her parents she felt the decision to marry was the most important of her life. She knew, she explained, that nothing was more essential than producing an heir for Montagu, and she did not want to rush into a marriage that might prove a disappointment. Surprisingly, her parents went along with her wishes, at least until the middle of 1780, when everything changed.

Charlotte did not mention the significant shift in her life that occurred sometime during that year. Not even the most careful reader could have been certain she and Pearce had consummated their relationship. Candid though she was in her diary, she could not have risked putting into writing such a shocking revelation. Frankly, I was stunned she had taken such a step before she was married.

Although my own marriage provided every sort of companionship and bliss for which a wife could hope, I knew that was not often the case, and common practice was for husbands and wives to seek affection — and love — elsewhere. For ladies, it was essential to delay any sort of affair until after having adequately filled the nursery, preferably with male babies. To embark on folly before then was to court disaster, and disaster is exactly what struck Charlotte. At first, she had no idea that the queasiness she started feeling early in the day was a sign of things to come. She mentioned it only casually. Even I, who had experienced the same myself, did not think anything of it when I first read her symptoms. It had never occurred to me she would have gone so far.

Eventually, though, she started to worry, and confided in her maid, who confirmed her worst fears. Charlotte was with child. She could not hide her condition forever, so there was nothing to be done but confess everything, or almost everything, to her parents.

Papa did not react quite so violently as I had feared, though I was afraid he was on the verge of striking me when I refused to tell him the name of my child's father. I would have withstood any blow to protect My Dear, Dear P. How could I bear to have him sent away from Montagu? I must have him near me. Papa yelled and bawled and quite lost his composure, and Mama's eyes looked like a summer storm. She will not forgive me for a very long time.

I shall have to be married, now, and as quickly as possible. Papa insists on it and I suppose he is right. I know better than to form opinions about any suitor now presented to me and it doesn't matter who it is regardless. I shall never love anyone but My P. Papa is even now arranging

things and says the business shall be settled
before the end of the week. I am not far enough
along, Mama assures me, to have to admit to my
condition. My husband will be a cuckold from
the start, and never know this child is not his.

Charlotte was naive to believe her parents would let
her hide her lover's identity for long. So far as I could
tell, they handled the situation as deftly as possible.
They remained calm, let her think she could keep her
secret, and arranged a quick marriage with Sir George,
who was pleased to know that his son, should he be
fortunate enough to have one, would someday be
Marquess of Montagu, quite an elevation from his own
knighthood.

The need for a quick marriage was explained away by
Charlotte's father's health. He had taken a nasty fall while
hunting the previous month and injured his leg. The
wound had become infected and wasn't healing well.
He told Sir George he feared he would die before seeing
his daughter married and ensuring that the Montagu
line would continue. No doubt Lord Montagu made it
abundantly clear to Sir George the necessity of ensuring
Charlotte would produce an heir as quickly as possible.

Sir George seems a pleasant enough man, but I
cannot bear to let him touch me. I shall have to,
I know, but the very idea sickens me. How have I
come to be in such an untenable situation? All I
want is to love My P. Is that so wrong? The next
Marquess of Montagu will be the son of a

groom, no matter what anyone believes. Why cannot my family accept the truth for what it is? Why must my life be one long, hurtful lie?

A fortnight before the wedding, Charlotte told Pearce what had happened and that she would have to marry at once. He begged her to leave with him and to run away, but she could not bring herself to abandon her dying father, not even for Her P. Pearce, devastated at her willingness to have another man as her husband, fled. He could not understand how she could let society do this to her. He could not understand the pressure she was under from her family. He could not understand that anything mattered more than their love. He disappeared before Charlotte became Sir George's wife.

"How sad," I said. "What a foolish, foolish girl."

"Do tell." Colin rubbed my hand while I recounted for him the story. "Foolish, yes, but doesn't it strike you as an absurd way to live, dividing people into classes and judging them more on their birth than their merit?"

"You need not try to convince me," I said. "I am well aware of your anti-aristocracy views, and you know I respect them. My mother is the one who was furious when you refused the dukedom." Colin had twice refused knighthood and once, more recently, a dukedom that had been negotiated by my mother. I knew full well Her Majesty was the less upset of the two ladies, but the Queen could not be described as pleased. My mother had still not given up hope that someday my husband would accept a peerage. From the day I was born, she had longed for nothing more than to see me a duchess. It was her life's ambition, and unfortunately for her, one I had never shared.

"Not half as furious as the Queen," he said. "She'll never forgive me."

"I shall let you believe what you want. Regardless, you are fortunate that she can't do without you," I said. "No one else in the empire has half your skill and discretion in handling difficult matters."

"I am more fortunate that you do not mind being banned from court."

"There is no court to speak of," I said. "Who would want to sit through those tedious dinners at Windsor being questioned, one at a time, for the whole table to hear?"

"Bertie won't be better," Colin said. "Different, certainly, but not better."

"More, shall we say, lively?" Bertie, the Prince of Wales, and his Marlborough House Set were not a crowd with which Colin and I chose to run. The Queen refused to allow her son and heir to engage in any sort of politics, and as a result he was a man wholly without purpose but in possession of all but unlimited resources. His excesses were notorious and his affairs a constant scandal, but he was congenial enough, if not particularly bright. I felt almost sorry for him, and wished his mother would let him come into his own. As it was, she was making it extremely difficult for him to learn to be an effective sovereign.

I had, not long ago, struck up a friendship of sorts with him, knowing that our mothers shared more than a few questionable qualities and thinking we could commiserate. Bertie, however, had other ideas and soon proved himself worthy of his playboy reputation. To his credit, he did not press the issue when I rebuffed his advances, and always treated me with the utmost courtesy. Nonetheless, I never felt wholly comfortable in his presence afterward.

"You are very polite, Lady Emily," Colin said, grinning and giving me a kiss.

I pulled away from him, my jaw dropping open. "You do realize what all this means?"

"Bertie? The Queen?"

"Charlotte," I said. "Matilda is the one descended from an illegitimate line, not Rodney."

"She will not be pleased."

"Maybe it will make her current situation easier to bear."

"You are assuming the groom's child survived infancy," Colin said.

"I've read past that," I said, "and then I skipped ahead to make sure. He inherited."

"And no one ever knew?" Colin asked.

"Apparently not. Charlotte's father died two months before the boy was born. That is why she was marchioness in her own right."

"Stories like these make me angry," Colin said. "She was forced to marry someone she didn't love just to ensure some ridiculous line continued without a visible blemish. And for what?"

"You cannot say the English system is completely without merit, Colin. Great families do much for their tenants and their households."

"Some of them do, but I don't think the lower classes should be forced to rely on the generosity of their landlords to ensure a decent living. It isn't right. Particularly when not all so-called great men do anything for their tenants."

"Dear me," I said. "I am afraid you are ready for armed revolution."

"I don't think it will take that," he said. "Our way of life has been changing since the beginning of the Industrial Revolution, and nothing is going to stop it. For that, I am immensely grateful."

"If you keep talking like this, my mother is likely to believe you are secretly a republican. Or even worse, an American. Do be careful. I don't want any more trouble from her."

The train slowed as it pulled into Dover Priory, and we gathered our belongings. I felt sad for Charlotte, but angry at the same time. She had put herself in a dreadful situation, and she had no one to blame but herself. Or did she? Gentlemen sometimes married their maids. It was unusual, but it did happen from time to time. A lady, however, would never be able to do such a thing. I might not agree with all of my husband's politics, but he was absolutely right about the inherent injustice in our way of life. It was a system too rife with immorality to be allowed to go on for eternity, but when it ended, where would we all be left? Change did not always lead to improvements, sometimes only to change.

Downstairs

xi

Alice had finished with Mr Hargreaves's room and was now in Lady Emily's pale blue dressing room. The walls were close to the same color as that in the room Alice shared with Lily, and she liked to think this was because Lady Emily was so very pleased with their work that she wanted them to feel more like family than servants. It was a foolish notion, but there was no harm in it. She had everything just about ready for her mistress to dress for dinner. Really for dinner tomorrow, or maybe luncheon, as she and the master were to stay overnight in Dover. Alice had been to Dover once and had picnicked below the great white cliffs, where she felt so proud to be English she had belted out every verse of "Rule, Britannia!" She wondered if Mr Hargreaves would show the cliffs to Lady Emily. She hoped he would. They were, she was certain, the best part of England.

Lily came into the room, breathless and flushed. "Good heavens, girl," Alice said. "What have you been getting up to?"

"My book," Lily said. "It's gone. Have you seen it?"

"No." Alice shook her head. "I know you told me I could look at it, but I felt funny taking it out without you there, so I thought I'd wait till you could show it to me yourself."

Lily was glad she hadn't gone through Alice's drawers. She knew she could always trust her friend. Alice was closer to her than her own sisters had ever been. They had even traveled to York together last winter, for a little holiday, and had walked along the old city walls, arm in arm, watching the people on the pavements below. It was one of Lily's happiest memories. "I think Pru took it."

"Pru? Why would she do that?"

"I don't really know, but who else? She can't stand me."

"What about Lord Montagu's Red Indian?" Alice asked. "He was brought up a heathen savage."

Lily crinkled her brow. "That is true, Alice, but he's behaved in no way that suggests he's still one. He's extremely polite and helpful. I like him much more than I thought I would."

"I am in absolute agreement," Alice said. "Still, it's something to think about. We don't really know him. I do have another idea, though. Lord Flyte gave it you, didn't he? The book, that is."

"Yes."

"Does Mrs Elliott know?"

"I don't think so. I haven't told anyone but you."

"I haven't told her, but she has a way of knowing things. If she did get wind of it, she might have taken it, deciding it wasn't appropriate for you to accept a gift from one of the master's guests."

"Do you think it's inappropriate?" Lily asked, pouring fresh water into a ewer.

Alice finished wiping the large glass over Lady Emily's dressing table before she answered. "I don't know, Lily. You're always so careful about things and are always warning me to watch myself with the gentlemen. Lord Flyte seems a nice enough bloke, but what can he really be after? You're not going to be a countess, though I do suspect you'd make an excellent one."

Lily's breath caught in her throat. "No, I would never expect such a thing. That would be silly." A wretched feeling coursed through her chest, going all the way through her stomach to her knees and back up again. Silly did not begin to describe it. It was naive and stupid to think anything good could come from such a friendship. She knew better than to get caught up in it.

"You've told me more times than I can count that gentlemen don't want to be friends with girls like us. They might be polite and they might even be kind on occasion, but if they go further than that, it can only mean one thing."

"I know," Lily said, turning her attention to cleaning out the fireplace. "I feel so foolish." She chastised herself, more disappointed than angry that she had allowed herself to be swept up in such a fantasy. For that's all it ever could be. It was shameful, really. She vowed to say four rosaries before bed that night as self-imposed penance.

"Don't be hard on yourself," Alice said. "Nothing's happened yet, right?"

"Of course not."

"And you're not going to let something happen?"

"No! I'm not Pru, you know."

"Lily, no gentleman is ever going to try to trifle with Pru."

This made Lily laugh. "I suppose not."

"Be polite and civil to Lord Flyte, but don't let yourself be compromised. You must make it clear to him that you're not going to provide him with anything beyond that."

"What about my book?" Lily asked.

"If Mrs Elliott's got it you'll know soon enough," Alice said, giving the brass fittings on the door a final polish. "And that will give you something new to worry about."

CHAPTER
TWELVE

Although I knew it had become something of a seaside resort once the railways had arrived, I had never given Dover much thought beyond its being the place where one leapt off the train and onto the boat when going to the Continent. Mrs Tindall, aunt of Mr Porter, now operated a charming inn there, perched above the white cliffs, with stunning views of the Channel. She welcomed us warmly and plied us with perfect tea and lemon cakes in a bright room lined with windows at the front of the building.

"I do so very much appreciate you both taking the time to come see me," she said. "I realize dear Cedric may be in more than a spot of trouble."

"He and Archibald Scolfield stayed with you before going abroad, is that correct?" I asked.

"Yes, they did," she said. "Mr Scolfield was a most pleasant gentleman. He flirted with me and flattered me and kept the house filled with fresh flowers the whole time the boys were here."

"You mentioned it was only later, after they had gone, that you discovered a problem?" I asked.

"Yes, five months passed before I noticed one of the girls in my employ — a housemaid — had got herself in a spot of trouble. She was with child."

"Archibald Scolfield was the father?" Colin asked.

"Yes. Not quite the gentleman he presented himself to be," she said. "I sent her to a home for girls in that condition, and she stayed there through her confinement."

"What became of the child?" I asked.

"I haven't the slightest idea," she said. "I heard no more news from her after she had given birth. I can only assume she returned to her family, wherever they were."

"Was Mr Scolfield informed about the baby?" Colin asked.

"No," Mrs Tindall said. "What would be the point? He wasn't going to acknowledge it. Trying to force him to would have done nothing but spark a scandal, and the poor girl didn't need more of that."

"Indeed," Colin said. "Forgive me, Mrs Tindall, but could you not have told us all this in a letter?"

"There is more, Mr Hargreaves," she said. "There were eventually rumors about what had happened to my maid, you see, as was inevitable. It turned out not many in town were surprised by the story. Mr Scolfield had trifled with girls in other establishments, more than I can count. Dressmakers' daughters, serving girls in taverns, and maids in several respectable households."

"I thought the boys were only in Dover a fortnight," I said. "Archibald must have been a very industrious man."

"He was," Mrs Tindall said. "Now, I am not gullible enough to believe all the stories, but I have no doubt some of them are true, and if he did even half of what he was accused of, you could find a right lot of suspects for his murder here in Dover alone. I'm sure his behavior didn't change when he reached the Continent. If anything, I would expect it to have been worse. Not all foreign girls have the strong morals of an Englishwoman." Her voice was so sincere. I did my best not to smile.

"Did your nephew know what his friend was getting up to?" Colin asked.

"I can't be sure of that," she said, the corners of her mouth turning down. "He tells me he did not, but I am not so innocent as to believe him without hesitation. Cedric was always a good boy. He worked extremely hard to earn that spot at Oxford, and he didn't come from a background where men were used to taking whatever they want."

"You do not believe he was behaving in a similar way?" Colin asked.

"Mr Hargreaves! My nephew would never act in such a base manner. He may not be from a family like the Scolfields, but current evidence would suggest that is not a bad thing, wouldn't it now? The Porters would never dream of lowering their morals so far."

"Forgive me, Mrs Tindall," Colin said. "I had to ask."

"I suppose so," she said, "but I do not have to like it."

"Mr Porter did not mention anything about this to us when we spoke to him," I said. "Why do you think that is?"

"Cedric would never do anything to impugn his friend's reputation, even after the incident at Oxford. He loved that boy like a brother."

"Enough to cover up his wrongdoings?" Colin asked. "Even after what happened at Oxford?"

"That, Mr Hargreaves, is precisely why I was concerned enough to want to speak to you in person," she said. "I don't know if I should continue."

"Do you think your nephew killed Archibald Scolfield?" I asked.

"I cannot imagine Cedric doing anything so violent," she said, "but at the same time, I cannot imagine anyone standing by and taking what he had to from someone he thought was his friend."

"I appreciate how sensitive this subject is, Mrs Tindall," I said, "but Mr Porter was sent down from Oxford more than four years ago. Why would he have waited so long to lash out?"

"Because, Lady Emily, his youngest sister had just entered service as a maid at Mr Scolfield's parents' house, and she had written to tell us she would be moving with Mr Archibald now he's taken up a residence of his own in London. It did not make sense to any of us that he would take such a junior servant with him, especially one so recently employed by the family, unless he had a particular interest in her."

"What does she say?"

"She insists nothing improper ever happened," Mrs Tindall said.

"Do you believe her?" Colin asked.

"I am not certain," she said. "I imagine she is terrified of losing her position if she says anything."

"The Scolfields wouldn't have had to know," Colin said. "She could have confided in her family, given notice, and found another position. Are they so hard to come by?"

"The Scolfields are a well-respected family who have a reputation for giving their staff decent conditions in which to live and work. Positions in those circumstances are never easy to come by. But she would never have dared say anything, regardless, Mr Hargreaves. She knows Cedric would never stand by, silent, if he knew someone had taken advantage of his sister. She knew that well. That is why I want you to talk to her. You might be able to figure out whether she's telling the truth."

"Where is she now?"

"Upstairs, waiting to speak with you. Shall I bring her down?"

"Please," I said, astonished that she had gone to such lengths, bringing the girl all the way to Dover.

When she left the room to fetch her niece, I pressed my palms against my temples. "Have you known anyone to have a more complicated life than Archibald Scolfield?" I asked my husband.

"He is not so different from many a profligate gentleman," Colin said. "I doubt he made as many conquests in Dover as is rumored. He may have tried, and been rebuffed, but it's likely he got nowhere with anyone but Mrs Tindall's maid. Such behavior is inherently risky. Archibald would have stuck with his

200

success once he found it and not bothered to look elsewhere."

"I wish I'd had a reply from the Scolfields' housekeeper," I said. "This is just the sort of thing I was inquiring about."

Mrs Tindall returned with her niece. Miss Porter was a slight girl, with dull, thin hair pulled into a chignon low on her neck. She fidgeted as she sat down, and could not seem to keep still.

"Thank you for seeing us, Miss Porter," I said, trying and failing to remember her from when we had interviewed the whole staff at Archibald's house in London. "I understand you have recently taken a position in service."

"Yes, madam."

"Are the Scolfields generous employers?" I asked.

"I can't rightly say, madam. I've no other experience to compare with."

"You know why we are here," Colin said, "so we may as well ask the hard question. Did Archibald Scolfield make inappropriate advances towards you?"

"Never, sir, never." Her voice was firm.

"Did he ever touch you?" Colin asked.

"Mr Hargreaves!" Mrs Tindall blanched.

"I am sorry, but we must know," Colin said.

"It is so important, Miss Porter," I said, leaning forward and taking her hands in mine. "Did he trifle with you?"

"He never, ever did, madam. I swear it." She blinked fast as if she were keeping tears at bay. "No one in the

201

household ever mentioned him doing anything like that. Why would I lie?"

"To protect a much-loved brother?" Colin suggested.

Miss Porter frowned. "This is an impossible situation. Lord Montagu never did anything wrong, but you won't believe me. I can't tell you anything else."

"My dear girl, if Cedric intervened on your behalf it's better that we know the whole truth," Mrs Tindall said. "It's the only hope he has."

"You think he's guilty, but he's not," Miss Porter said. "He had no reason at all to be angry with Lord Montagu."

Mrs Tindall looked at me, her face full of hopelessness. "I do not know what else to say, but I felt it important every possibility be considered. If Cedric is implicated, I do not want there to be any hint of impropriety on our part."

This surprised me. I could not decide whether she thought her nephew guilty or was truly concerned about his well-being.

"Quite right, Mrs Tindall," Colin said. "I thank you for your candor. Miss Porter, is there anything further you would like to tell us?"

"No, sir." She stared with great intent at the ground.

"Very well," Colin said. "Should that change, your aunt knows how to reach us."

We had planned to overnight in Dover, but that seemed unnecessary now that Mrs Tindall hadn't kept us as long as we had anticipated. Instead, we boarded the next train to London after Colin had wired ahead to alert the skeleton staff we always left in Park Lane that we would be staying over. They would open the house for us, pulling slipcovers off the furniture in the library and our bedroom, the breakfast room, and at least one sitting room. No doubt it was too much for a short visit, but the head footman, left in charge when Davis was in the country with us, insisted on seeing things done properly. If he had his way, he would have readied for us every one of the myriad rooms over all the floors. I often wondered what it was like, staying behind in an enormous London mansion when the family was gone and most of the rooms shut up. I would have been tempted to live like the master of the house, but I doubted very much any servant would dare.

"Was that not one of the oddest experiences of your life?" I asked as we sped towards the capital city. "Do you think she suspects Mr Porter of the murder?"

"My dear, I am at a complete loss," Colin said. "I do believe it may be simply as she said. If Porter is accused, and it comes out his family had hidden information that could have implicated him, it would make him appear even more guilty."

"That I can understand," I said. "What makes absolutely no sense in the least, however, is that the Porter family would allow their daughter to be employed by the Scolfields after what happened at Oxford."

"Unless Archibald was telling the truth all along and Porter did steal the essay," Colin said.

"In which case you would not expect the Scolfields to hire a Porter."

"Noblesse oblige, my dear," Colin said. "Although the truth is, they may not have even been aware of the incident. Archibald was not the one sent down, after all. He was the hero of the matter, turning in a cheater. His parents would never have had to get wind of any of it."

I dropped my head against the back of the bench behind me. "The Porters would not have allowed their daughter to work for the family that destroyed their son."

"The Porters do not consider their son destroyed, Emily. He has a respectable trade and earns a decent living. He has taken a step up from his father, and given the role his father's landlord played in his son's education, the father no doubt believes great families can do no wrong. If anything, his daughter working for the Scolfields may have seemed like redemption. By accepting her into their employ, the family was, in effect, forgiving her brother for what he had done."

"There is an unaccountable throbbing in my head," I said. "I cannot make sense of any of it." I closed my eyes. Colin was right, of course. I was making matters more complicated than they really were. The relationships between landowners and their tenants had not significantly changed in a thousand years, and what I considered outrageous and unfair was not necessarily universally accepted as such.

"I do not think Archibald trifled with Porter's sister," Colin said. "He would find that too distasteful for a variety of reasons."

"So this is nothing more than another dead end?"

"No," Colin said. "It has given us further insight into Archibald's increasingly bad-seeming character, and that is not insignificant. When we have a full picture of the man, we will have a better idea of who may have wanted him dead."

"Good heavens," I said. "You don't think we will turn up even more people with motive to kill him?"

Colin patted my hand. "We've only three so far: Miss Fitzgerald, Mr Porter, and Miss Gifford. That's not so many."

"Don't forget Mr Gifford," I said. "Given what happened to his sister, he has ample motive as well. It is not as if travel between England and Germany is difficult."

"A fair point, Emily. Four suspects."

"We shall know more tomorrow," I said. "Once we have visited Miss Gifford's school."

"I do hope you are willing to take the lead there, my dear," Colin said. "If there is one thing I have extremely limited tolerance for, it is the antics of overexuberant schoolgirls."

Downstairs

xii

Having vowed to remove herself from any danger of becoming overly fond of Mr Hargreaves's houseguest, Lily carefully examined the small changes she had made in her routine on his behalf. Since her first conversation with Lord Flyte, she had made a habit of getting up the fire in the cinnamon drawing room at the same time each morning, not too early, not too late. More specifically, within a quarter of an hour of the precise time she had first met Lord Flyte. Today she deliberately deviated from this uncovenable routine and swore she would never again return to the wicked habit. She went there when the kitchen was still quiet. She opened the shutters, before any pink light darted across the dark sky, and set to work. She had come close to finishing with the fire when she heard footsteps. It must be Lord Flyte, but she could hardly believe even he would rise so close to dawn. It took an effort, but she didn't look up to see him. Instead, she bit back her curiosity with a quick prayer.

"Lily?" His voice was soft and kind.

"Sir?" She still didn't look at him.

"Is something wrong?"

"Not at all, sir," she said, and stood up, all business. "Can I do something for you?"

"I just hoped we could talk," he said. "I so enjoyed our last conversation. How are you finding your book?"

Lily wanted to tell him that she, too, had enjoyed the conversation. She wanted to smile at him and to look into his golden brown eyes. She wanted to confide in him that someone had stolen the book and beg him to help her retrieve it. "I've lots to do this morning, sir. No time for idle chatter. Mrs Elliott would have my hide." She gave the coals a last poke and arranged the tools beside the fireplace before exiting the room. She felt tears pooling in her eyes as she closed the door behind her, but she knew it was the right thing. She steeled herself and went to tend to the fire in the next room.

Downstairs, Alice filled a bucket with water and soap to clean the marble floor in the great hall. Pru smirked at her as she walked by.

"Your friend Lily is going to be in a right heap of trouble," the kitchen maid said.

"How so?" Alice asked. "No one in this house works harder than Lily."

"That's not what I hear," Pru said. Alice had never seen anyone else whose smile was like an ugly slash across her face.

"What do you hear?"

"Wouldn't you like to know?" Pru asked.

"Not especially," Alice said. "I have no use for idle gossip." She started up the stairs only to be stopped by Mrs Elliott's sharp voice.

"Alice," she said. "A word in my room, please."

CHAPTER
THIRTEEN

Mrs Chelmsford's School for Young Ladies reminded me more than a little of a medieval dungeon. I exaggerate a bit, I suppose, and will admit there were no visible instruments of torture, but the dimly lit classrooms with their low ceilings and dirty windows pressed in like the walls of a cell. Mrs Chelmsford herself would have made an excellent jailer. A large ring of keys hung from her chatelaine, and I envisioned her locking up any girl who dared show the slightest bit of spirit. The schoolmistress's eyes were narrow and cold, with a streak of meanness in them.

Her students, wearing gray dresses by way of a uniform, could not have looked more miserable. With not a single eager face among them, they stood behind their desks, reciting in unison some sort of underwhelming poem. In the corner, a solitary girl stood on a chair, her back to the room.

"She is a very naughty one, that," Mrs Chelmsford said, closing the classroom door so that we could no longer peek in. "I take discipline very seriously, Lady Emily, and tolerate no nonsense."

"What was her offense?" I asked.

"She criticized the poem I chose for the girls' recitation. Impertinence is not a quality gentlemen look for in wives."

I knew better than to try to engage her in any sort of reasonable dialogue on the subject. Not now, at least. "I do hope you can tell me all about Fanny Gifford. Did she have a tendency towards impertinence as well?" If she did, I wouldn't be surprised in the least if she had run off to escape this desolate place.

"No, she was one of the most well-behaved girls I have ever had," Mrs Chelmsford said. "Kept her room tidy, never complained — not that my girls have any valid complaints to make — and always did well in her studies."

"What happened to her?"

"As I told the detectives from Scotland Yard, she simply disappeared. We realized she was gone when she didn't turn up for breakfast."

"It was right of you to contact them at once," I said.

"I was not about to have her family claiming I had been negligent," she said. "They searched the whole premises and found nothing. She must have just slipped out in the night."

"Why would she do that?" I asked. "Do you believe she was happy here?"

"Why wouldn't she be?" Mrs Chelmsford asked. "I take good care of my girls. You can see that."

It took a not inconsiderable effort to resist giving an honest answer to her question. I dodged it altogether, preferring to take the matter entirely into my own hands after I had finished learning all I could about Miss Gifford. "So why, then, would she leave?"

"Perhaps there was a young man," Mrs Chelmsford said, pressing her lips together in a thin line. "That is generally why young ladies leave school."

"Surely if there were a young man she would have told her brother, the only family she has."

"Who am I to judge?" she said. "Maybe she has no fondness for her brother."

I did not think I would get much else out of Mrs Chelmsford, but I did want to speak with the girl who had shared Miss Gifford's room. Mrs Chelmsford did not look happy at my request but agreed to send her to me. I waited for her in the girls' small bedchamber.

The room, no bigger than seven feet square, was in dire need of a fresh coat of paint. The sickly color that might once have resembled yellow was now peeling from the walls, and the sparse furniture in the space consisted of two narrow beds, a rickety dresser, but not even a single chair. The blankets on the beds were worn and must have made for exceedingly cold nights. There was no fireplace. I would have wagered my fortune Mrs Chelmsford kept herself in much greater comfort than she allowed her students to enjoy, and I vowed to do whatever I could to remedy the situation at the first opportunity.

Miss Gifford's roommate was a girl called Helen, a sweet thing, with beautiful dark hair and a pretty face. She was as pallid as her schoolmates, though, and far too thin. I introduced myself and gave her a packet of sweets I had purchased for the occasion. As I had hoped, this served to warm her to me. She smiled as if she hadn't seen candy in years.

"I know Mrs Chelmsford is dreadful," I said. "Please believe that I will share nothing you tell me with her. You can trust me absolutely."

"Is that true, Lady Emily?"

"You can rely on it."

"All right, I shall," she said.

"Do you know anything about your roommate's disappearance?" I asked. "It is crucial that we find her as quickly as possible."

"I know she wasn't happy here," she said, "but then none of us is."

"Do you know where she went?"

"I don't, truly I don't."

"Did she tell you she was leaving?" I asked.

"No," Helen said. "She —" Fear filled her eyes. "Are you quite certain it is safe for me to talk to you?"

"Helen, is it that bad here?" I asked, sitting next to her on the edge of her bed.

"Worse than you can imagine," she said. "You get punished for everything. If you are lucky you only have to stand on a chair for an hour, but usually you have a meal taken away. I'm certain it's to save Mrs Chelmsford from having to buy food. She's the stingiest person on earth. That I know beyond doubt. Have you read Mr Dickens's story about Ebenezer Scrooge? We all reckon she would be a fine match for him — before he met the ghosts, that is." She looked at me, her dark eyes almost too big for her face. "You won't tell her I said that?"

212

"Never," I said. "What do your parents think?"

"They don't know," she said. "Who would they believe? We're not supposed to complain, are we? Even if we did, Mrs Chelmsford would tell her side of the story."

"What is her side?" I asked.

"That her punishments always fit our crimes. She doesn't have to be truthful if it doesn't suit her. There's no one in authority to question her."

Institutions like Mrs Chelmsford's preyed on families who could not afford better educations for their daughters but wanted to be able to say the girls had been to some sort of finishing school. The fees were, most likely, lower than the cost of keeping them at home, a great temptation for many struggling parents. These were girls who had a station too high to work, but too low to be certain of being looked after properly.

"What would have happened to you if you had known of Miss Gifford's plan to flee?" I asked.

"I would have been locked in this room for two days with nothing but water."

"So I imagine your friend wanted to protect you?"

"That's just it, Lady Emily," Helen said. "That's what she said when —" She stopped again.

"It is all right, I promise."

"I woke up when she was leaving. Our door creaks just enough to disturb my sleep. She didn't take any of her belongings, only herself, and she begged me not to admit that I had seen her because she knew I would be in fierce trouble if Mrs Chelmsford ever found out. Fanny told me I was the best friend she had ever had, and that the only reason she hadn't confided in me was that she did not want to risk getting me punished."

"She didn't tell you where she was going?" I asked. "You are quite sure of this? It is so important that you be honest now, Helen."

"I swear she didn't. I begged her to, because I knew I would worry about her, but Fanny thought it was smarter not to. That way, no matter what Mrs Chelmsford tried, I wouldn't have anything to tell her. Fanny did promise, though, that she would write to me once she was settled."

"Have you had a letter?"

"I have not." Her voice was very small, and she gave a little sniffle.

"How were her spirits when she was leaving?" I asked.

"She was excited," Helen said. "She couldn't wait to be on her way. I hadn't seen her smile that much since I'd known her."

"Do you think she was meeting someone? A gentleman, perhaps?"

"I couldn't really say. I hope so, because I don't know what else she could do. It is not as if she can support herself, and I don't think her brother would have been pleased for her to leave school."

"Have you opportunities while you are here to meet young men?"

"Very rarely, yes," she said. "We are, in theory, being groomed for marriage, and Mrs Chelmsford hosts dances at the end of every term. We also go on outings once a month, usually to a museum, and we take walks in the park every Sunday afternoon."

I dared not imagine how deathly grim any dance hosted by Mrs Chelmsford would be. "Did Miss Gifford seem to have an attachment with anyone she had met?"

"Not that I was aware," Helen said, "but she was always popular at the dances."

"Would she have hidden such an attachment from you?"

"I really don't think she would have. Not at first, anyway, because she wouldn't have been planning to run away then, would she?"

"I would think not," I said.

"I wish I could be of more use, Lady Emily. I am truly worried about Fanny."

"I know you are," I said, "and I will do everything I can to try to find her. You must promise me that the instant you get word from her, you will get in touch with me."

"I will, I promise."

"Thank you, Helen. I hope to hear from you soon."

I spoke to Mrs Chelmsford again, briefly, on my way out. "I must say you keep your girls in appalling conditions. Do their parents have any idea how they are treated here?"

She bristled and scowled, then leaned closer to me, narrowing her eyes. I think she meant to intimidate. "Their parents are quite pleased with my results and would not deign to criticize my methods."

"Is that so?" I stepped closer to her, unafraid of a woman who was used to bullying young girls. "You shall be hearing from me in the very near future, Mrs Chelmsford, and I warn you to be prepared. I am not going to stand by and let you torment your students. This will stop."

"High and mighty ladies of your kind pretend to care about people like these girls, but you don't really," Mrs Chelmsford said. "Their families have enough money to take care of them, and they are not in need of your charity. Why don't you go to the East End, where people really need help?"

"What goes on in the East End does nothing to justify what you are doing here," I said. "As I said, you will hear from me again." I slammed the door to her office on my way out and, full of righteous indignation, was marching down the hall when one of the youngest students, who could not have been more than eleven, tugged on my arm.

"Madam, may I speak to you for a moment?" she asked.

"Of course."

"Can we go somewhere else?" Her eyes darted nervously. I took her hand and led her outside, to the barren garden behind the school.

"Will you be in trouble for having left your classroom?" I asked.

"I am already bound to be in trouble," she said. "I know you're here about Fanny Gifford. I saw her the night she left, in the street below my window. She was

216

with the most handsome gentleman I've ever seen. I think they were going to be married."

"Why do you say that?" I asked.

"Why else would he have come to collect her?"

"Did he have a carriage?"

"Not in front of the school, but there was one down at the end of the street," she said. "They walked to it."

"Could you see livery or a coat of arms on it?"

"No, it was too dark."

"That's all right," I said. "You've done very well to tell me this. Did anyone else see her?"

"I don't think so," she said. "No one else has mentioned a thing about it. Not that any of us would, I suppose. If she is found, you won't make her come back here, will you? Mrs Chelmsford would do I don't even know what to her."

"I don't think Miss Gifford would choose to return here under any circumstances," I said, pressing a packet of sweets into the girl's hand. "You are very brave to have told me all this. Let me bring you back inside and make sure that you aren't in any trouble as a result."

Colin, who had stayed behind in Park Lane, was suitably horrified when I returned home and described for him the conditions in Mrs Chelmsford's School for Young Ladies. "Do these parents visit?" he asked. "Do they not care?"

"I believe she convinces them the austere conditions allow the girls to focus on their studies and to learn a sort of discipline appreciated by the average husband. Many boys' schools are as bad, if not worse."

"It is reprehensible nonetheless."

"I am glad you feel that way," I said, "as I am going to see our solicitor before we return to Anglemore. I want to buy the school, fire Mrs Chelmsford, and move it to more suitable premises."

"Continuing your pursuit of social reform, my dear?"

"How can we not fix this situation?" I asked. "If we do nothing, we are as bad as that wicked woman withholding food from growing girls."

"Have you any idea what this will entail?"

"We will need a building, obviously, and a staff. What's the best way to find a good head teacher, do you think?"

"I haven't the slightest idea, my dear, although I have not a doubt in the world that you will not only find one but mold the school into a model of enlightenment."

"Of course I will," I said. "Would either of us stand for anything less?"

"Never," he said. "I assume ancient Greek will be a cornerstone of the curriculum?"

"You know me too well," I said. "*Whoso neglects learning in his youth, loses the past and is dead for the future.*"

"Homer?" he asked.

"Euripides."

"I should have known, but the fact is, my dear, you are the expert on all matters classical in this household."

"I have been toying with the idea of learning Egyptian," I said. "How do you feel about visiting the pyramids?"

"Let's get the matter of Archibald Scolfield settled first," he said.

"Of course. So long as you promise me a midnight excursion to Giza."

Downstairs

xiii

Alice got up a quarter of an hour before she had to each morning to ensure that she never completed any of her tasks late. She made a point of being conscientious, asking for additional work, and doing everything in her power to keep Mrs Elliott happy. This was not simply to pacify the housekeeper. Alice had aspirations of her own. She wanted to be a housekeeper someday, and Mrs Elliott's recommendation could go a long way to getting her there, especially if Alice stayed on at Anglemore until Mrs Elliott retired. That would be years and years from now, of course, but it would be worth the wait. Mrs Elliott's position was much envied, even by housekeepers at other great estates, in part due to the very fine accommodation she had at Anglemore. Her rooms were nothing short of beautiful. In particular, Alice was fond of the Pug's Parlor, as junior servants called the housekeeper's sitting room. It had high ceilings, walls painted a lovely pale green, and, being up six stairs from the level of the kitchen, windows with a sweeping view of the gardens behind the house. Alice rarely had any trouble from Mrs

Elliott, and as a result had no negative associations with the room. Today, however, she felt the tug of nerves as Mrs Elliott pulled the door closed and stood in front of her.

"I have heard some very disturbing things this morning, Alice," she said, "and as you are friends with Lily, I wanted to see if you can elaborate on them before I speak with her. I will need the truth, of course. Your continued employment in this house relies upon it."

"I would never lie to you, Mrs Elliott."

"That is as it should be," she said. "Someone has reported having seen Lily in an inappropriate embrace with one of Mr Hargreaves's guests. Do you know anything about this?"

"Lily would never do that, Mrs Elliott."

"Do you know the guest to whom I am referring?"

"Yes, Lord Flyte."

"Why is it that you can identify him if there is nothing inappropriate going on between him and Lily?"

"It's not like that, Mrs Elliott," Alice said. "Lord Flyte was kind to her, and he spoke to her while she was working, but nothing else ever happened between them."

"So I am to believe that another member of the staff has concocted a vicious lie?"

"I don't know anything about that, Mrs Elliott."

"It would be best for Lily if you tell me the truth."

"I am telling the truth, Mrs Elliott."

"Go find Lily and send her down to me," the housekeeper said. "I will not tolerate loose morals in this house."

★ ★ ★

Alice did her best to warn Lily about the reason for Mrs Elliott's summons, but she did not have the opportunity to say much. Lady Bromley was in the cinnamon drawing room, and as Alice was to take over Lily's duties there while she went downstairs, she could not hope for the privacy of the back stairs. The maids were able to exchange a few quiet sentences, enough to give Lily a serious bout of nerves as she descended the staircase, but they were not able to have a frank conversation. Lily took a deep breath and tried to compose herself. She knew Pru must have gone to Mrs Elliott, but whatever the girl had told the housekeeper had to be a lie. Lily had not let her morals be compromised, but the realization that deep down she desperately wished Lord Flyte would compromise her was terrifying, and she scolded herself for having such an inappropriate thought at such a moment.

Mr Davis nodded at her as she passed him in the corridor along the kitchen. He didn't look angry; Mrs Elliott must not yet have spoken to him. Lily's knees knocked together as she rapped on the door of the Pug's Parlor.

"Enter." Mrs Elliott liked to behave like the lady of the house. Lily stepped into the room. "Close the door behind you, girl."

"Alice said you wanted to see me," Lily said, trying to keep her teeth from chattering.

"I have had a very alarming report about you, Lily," Mrs Elliott said. "Is it true you permitted Lord Flyte to embrace you in the white drawing room yesterday evening?"

222

"No, Mrs Elliott, absolutely not," Lily said, finding her voice stronger than she had expected. "I would never do such a thing."

"You do not admit to having a special friendship with Lord Flyte?"

"He has been enormously kind to me, if that is what you mean, but he has never crossed a line that threatened my virtue."

"You have no business engaging any of the family or their guests in conversation. It is wholly inappropriate."

"Yes, Mrs Elliott." Lily bowed her head.

"So why did you converse with Lord Flyte?"

"I didn't know what else to do, Mrs Elliott," Lily said. "It would have been impolite not to answer his direct questions, wouldn't it?"

"You volunteered nothing to him on your own?"

Lily's face was hot and her palms were starting to sweat. Under the scrutiny of the housekeeper, she could hardly even remember the times she had talked to the gentleman. "I do not believe so, Mrs Elliott."

"I shall have to speak to Mr Davis about this, and I can assure you he will not be best pleased. As we have no corroborating evidence for either your version of the event in question or your colleague's, I shall leave the matter as it is at present. Do understand, though, Lily, that I shall be keeping a close eye on you. One step out of line and you'll be out with no character."

"I understand, Mrs Elliott," Lily said. "Thank you, ma'am."

If she had been shaking when she entered the Pug's Parlor, she was trembling twice as much when she left, but this time it was from anger, not fear. Lord Flyte had never embraced her. Neither the footmen nor the other housemaids could have seen anything alarming in the exchanges she had with him. Only one person in the house bore her a grudge, and that was Pru, who had no business being above stairs under any circumstances, let alone in the white drawing room.

Lily paused at the entrance to the kitchen, but stopped herself from going in to confront her enemy. Instead, she poked her head inside and called to Cook.

"I have never seen Lady Bromley look so pleased with a meal as she did the tray you sent up for her breakfast," Lily said, forcing a wide smile onto her face. "I thought you would like to know."

Cook flushed and grinned. Pru, bent over a pile of unwashed dishes, her arms in steaming water to her elbows, glowered. Lily simpered at her.

She was happy to have passed on the compliment and to have brightened Cook's day. More, though, she was sending a message. She would not let Pru think she was worried or scared, and certainly not give the girl a hint at the depth of her anger. So far as Pru could see, nothing she had done troubled Lily in the least.

CHAPTER
FOURTEEN

I called on Matilda the morning after we returned from London, having finished reading Charlotte's diaries on the train back to Anglemore. The butler led me up the many turns of the staircase to a long gallery on the top floor of the house. Rows of ancient weapons hung from the bare stone walls, and the vaulted ceiling was at least fifteen feet high. Beneath it, Matilda and Rodney had taken their bickering to a new level. They were fencing.

Literally. Matilda was charging at him, épée in hand, and I think she might have stabbed right through him had he not been wearing a thickly padded vest.

"Well done, Boudica," Rodney said, once she had lowered her blade and stepped away from him. "You do your namesake proud."

"The Empress Matilda did not fight with swords, so my namesake has nothing to do with it. I fence because my grandfather taught me," Matilda said. "You must stop this ridiculous habit of calling me Boudica."

"My dear girl, having witnessed firsthand your skill at swordplay, I have yet another reason I *must* call you Boudica."

She raised the mask covering her face, stepped right up to his chest, and glared at him.

"Do I need to be worried about another premature death in the line of Montagu?" I asked. Neither of them had noticed my entrance into the room until I spoke.

"No one is safe around this warrior queen," Rodney said, taking a dramatic step away from Matilda. "Boudica's temper is legendary. Any man not terrified of her is a fool."

"How refreshing to see that at last you have admitted you are a fool," Matilda said. "It was getting increasingly awkward to be the only one in the family in possession of that undeniable fact."

"Your cruelty might sting others," Rodney said, "but not so much as you'd like it to. As for me, I am immune to all your criticisms. Your every word is like music to me."

"You are immune to all sensible discourse," Matilda said, lowering her mask and lunging at him again with her blade. Rodney stepped neatly out of the way. Matilda, too far forward to catch herself, started to stumble, but managed to get her balance in check before she fell all the way.

"This is intolerable," she said, pulling the mask from her head and flinging it to the ground. "Emily, please tell me you have news for me."

"I do, although not anything about Archibald's death," I said. "May I speak to you in private?"

"Of course," she said, tossing her sword to her cousin. "I have been trying to get him to leave for hours. He is implacable. That is why I turned to violence."

226

"You have not once asked me to leave," Rodney said, hanging both swords on a wooden rack at the southern end of the room.

"A gentleman would have been able to tell from any number of my comments that I was desperate for you to go," Matilda said. "Which simply confirms my suspicions that you, Mr Scolfield, are not a gentleman."

Rodney made a little bow in her direction. "I shall leave you now with my deepest apologies, Boudica. Emily, I do hope I am not imposing too greatly on your goodwill to continue my stay at your house?"

"No one wants you anywhere near here, Mr Scolfield," Matilda said. "If you are trying to make me feel bad about not wanting to see you live at Montagu, don't bother. I feel no compunction in that regard. You have no one to blame but yourself for the inconvenience of your presence."

"I know when to surrender," Rodney said, removing his mask with a flourish and bowing low in front of his cousin. "I shall, however, return for a rematch." Matilda scowled as he left the room and then stood at the window so that she might continue to glower at him as he made his way on horseback down her drive. Once he had disappeared from sight, she removed her fencing kit, smoothed her skirts, and led me to a charming little room nearby, where we sat on a long window seat below a leaded-glass bay that overlooked the pond behind the house.

"My grandfather wanted to turn the pond into a moat," Matilda said, "but the engineering proved too difficult. Shall I ring for some tea?"

"You might want something stronger than that after you have heard what I have to say." I handed Charlotte's diaries to her. "I have discovered an irregularity in the Montagu line, but not where you had hoped."

"What do you mean?" she asked. She went very pale when I started to tell Charlotte's story, then turned deep shades of red as I got to the end. "So I am the one descended from a bastard?"

"It doesn't matter, Matilda," I said. "Everyone accepted Charlotte's son as her legitimate heir. No one denies your rights in the family."

"It does weaken my case against Mr Scolfield, doesn't it?"

"You never really had a case against him," I said. "Much though I regret to say it."

"You mean you don't like him either?"

"It is not a question of like or dislike," I said. "I understand perfectly not wanting to feel forced out of a house you love so well, particularly when you thought it belonged to you."

"It is a good thing they found him, though," she said, a single tear making its way down her cheek. "I do not deserve to be marchioness in my own right."

"I don't agree," I said. "Rodney's position aside, you are just as legitimate as every marquess who followed Charlotte. You know it is bad manners to point out an illegitimacy when everyone has already decided to accept it."

"I don't know what else I can do," Matilda said. "I have been a beast to Mr Scolfield."

"And he would be a cad not to have sympathy for your position. He has made it clear you can stay at Montagu."

"I might consider doing so if I did not find everything about him so very disagreeable. The man is vile." She frowned. "Promise me you won't tell him about Charlotte?"

"If you'd like, but I don't see how it matters."

"I do not want my position in regard to him undermined in the least. So far as I am concerned, he is marquess only because of the deep prejudice the nobility has against women. I am much more closely related than he to every marquess in the line, but relation matters less than gender."

"I will not recite for you all the reasons it was arranged that way, but only because I agree completely that it is outrageous."

"Tell me about something more cheerful," she said. "Where has the investigation of Archie's death led you?"

When I returned to Anglemore, I found Colin and Simon entrenched in a game of chess in my husband's study. They were using his favorite chess set, with delicate pieces carved out of ivory that his father had bought for him on a visit to India when Colin had been only nine years old. My husband stood, gave me a kiss long enough that Simon had to pretend difficulty in lighting his pipe so as not to appear having noticed, and then greeted me with news of Miss Gifford. A lady fitting her description had booked passage two days after the murder on a Channel ferry from Dover.

"How many ladies in England could fit Miss Gifford's description?" I asked.

"Countless, no doubt," Colin said, "but this one was a bit odd. She claimed to be traveling on her honeymoon, yet bought only one ticket. She said her husband already had one."

"That is odd."

"Quite. The clerk remembered her precisely because of it. He does not often see a young lady traveling unaccompanied."

"Her husband was not with her at the ticket counter?"

"Apparently not, and neither was anyone else."

"So she might have left school, murdered Scolfield, and fled the country," I said. "After carefully waiting two days, lest the police be checking the ferries. Why two days?"

"A schoolgirl's guess as to how long is long enough?" Colin suggested.

"Can we do anything to track her beyond —"

"Calais?" Colin finished for me. "I have a good man on the task already. Now do tell us about your day."

"You must admit it is rather alarming that Matilda considered a murder investigation more cheerful than primogeniture," I said, after recounting for them all that had happened at Montagu.

"Alarming, yes," Colin said, "but not wholly unexpected. Perhaps your initial instincts were correct.

Do not forget you strongly suspected she had Montagu killed so she would inherit."

"I know I did," I said.

"Do you repent now?" Simon asked. "Or is it that as you have grown to know her better, you find her less and less capable of such a crime?"

"Nothing of the sort," I said. "I am looking at evidence. Yes, Matilda had motive — at least she believed so at the time of Archibald's death — but we know she could not have murdered him herself. Countless witnesses placed her at Montagu for a good hour before and after the murder. Furthermore, we have uncovered nothing to suggest she had hired someone to do the job for her."

"Quite right, Emily," Colin said. "Focus on the evidence."

"I just wish less of it were circumstantial," I said. I left them to their chess and started to go through my mail. Most of it was unremarkable, but I did, at last, have a response from the Scolfield family's housekeeper.

Dear Lady Emily,

I was distressed by your letter as it made me fear you think Mr Archibald's death could have been, in a way, the result of some character flaw of his own. I assure you, nothing could be further from the truth. I have known Mr Archibald — do please forgive me for continuing to refer to him by the name by which he was known in this house rather than his new title — from birth, and have never seen him exhibit the slightest disrespect to any of his family's servants. No maid has ever come to me with a complaint about his behavior, and his father would never have tolerated the attitude of entitlement that often leads young gentlemen astray when it comes to such matters.

Do not think, however, that I gave your missive anything short of the greatest and most serious consideration. I have spoken to the steward and the underbutler, as well as all of the maids, the cook, and the girls who work in the laundry, and no one has experienced or heard anything that would impugn Mr Archibald's reputation as the finest sort of gentleman.

Had I learned otherwise, I would not hesitate to pass the information along to you, as I consider it one of my most important duties to protect and take care of the household staff. I would never stay in a house where inappropriate behavior on the part of the master's son was allowed. Furthermore, I would share with you anything I uncovered because, no matter how terrible that sort of behavior is, it does not merit death as its penalty. I, like everyone here, want to see Mr Archibald's killer brought to justice.

I am your humble servant &c.

I drew my eyebrows together and considered her words with the utmost care. She seemed credible, I decided, and then I thought more about Archibald. Before I could make any headway on a study of his character, Davis entered the room and asked to speak to me in private.

"Do forgive me, madam," he said after we had retired to the library, "but I thought this matter required your immediate attention. One of the kitchen maids, Prudence, has informed Mrs Elliott that Lily has been" — he cleared his throat — "seen in a compromising position with Lord Flyte."

"Dear me, Simon?" I was aghast. "Are you quite certain?"

"Not quite, madam, which is why Mrs Elliott has done nothing more than give Lily a sharp talking-to. Prudence has a deep dislike of the girl, and should not have been in a position to witness what she says she did. She ought to have been in the kitchen when it occurred. None of the other members of the staff saw anything out of the ordinary."

"What does Lily say about it?" I asked.

"Lily admits to having something of a friendship with Lord Flyte, madam," he said. "As I am sure you can understand, I find this sort of thing most alarming, as it can never lead to a good end for the girl."

"No, of course not," I said. "Lord Flyte has a habit of being overly familiar with his own servants, though I assure you never in the way that Pru is suggesting. I shall speak to him at once and ask him to leave Lily alone."

"Thank you, madam. I was hoping you would offer as much. Lily is a good worker, and, if you'll forgive me, while I do believe you are sincere in what you say about Lord Flyte, my own experience has shown again and again that one never can be sure what sort of gentleman might trifle with a maid. I would not want to see Lily ruined."

Simon moaned, sending Iphitos tearing from the room, and threw an arm over his face when I returned to the study and relayed the details of my conversation with Davis to him.

"Emily, Simon would never —"

"I am not saying I doubt Simon," I said, "but —"

"No, no," Simon said. "I appreciate that you both trust me, but I do admit to having taken liberties of conversation with Lily. I would never have tried to corrupt her, but I do like her exceedingly well and want to know her better. Did you know that in London she used to go to the National Gallery on her free afternoons? That she is a self-taught artist, who has learned by copying great masterpieces? She is trying to make something of her natural talent. Are you aware that she dreams of becoming a lady's maid so that she might travel?"

"I do not believe you are in need of a lady's maid, Flyte," Colin said.

"I am not attempting to be lighthearted," Simon said. "Lily is a woman of undeveloped talents. I want to enable her to make more of her life than she can as a housemaid."

"I agree, Simon, that she has much promise," I said. "Nanny thinks that if Lily were to receive an education she would make an excellent governess. There is no doubt she has the capability to be more than a maid. She has a sense for the aesthetic that not many in her position possess. Her eye for beauty, her talent for

234

drawing, and her voice — she sings like an angel — are extraordinary. Furthermore, she possesses a natural elegance of movement that complements her extremely attractive features. I cannot say I am shocked that you should find her appealing."

"I want to know her better," Simon said.

"Flyte, you know you cannot do that," Colin said.

"I don't see why not," Simon said. "It's not as if I am trying to seduce her."

"You cannot have a friendship with a maid," Colin said. "What would it do to the poor girl other than distract her from her work, which can lead to all kinds of trouble and spark jealousy, as it has already done?"

"More than that, though, Simon, it gives her false hope," I said. "It is not as if there is a chance you would marry her." I paused, studying his face. He was not entirely composed. His complexion flushed, and a deep crease showed between his eyebrows. There was a general air of nervousness about him. "Is there?"

"How can I know if I am not allowed to spend more time with her?"

"Flyte, you cannot possibly be suggesting —" Colin started, but Simon raised a hand to silence him.

"I know I have been remiss," Simon said, "but isn't it time that we admit our servants aren't so far below us? I want to know Lily better. I should like to spend her next afternoon off with her, walking the grounds at Anglemore together. What harm is there in that? Who is to say I can't have a meaningful friendship with her? I would hardly be the first gentleman to embark on such a journey."

"Sir Henry Meux married a woman who was generously described as an actress," I said, "and we have all heard stories of gentlemen who became . . . entangled, shall we say . . . with their children's governesses."

"A governess is a far cry from a housemaid," Colin said, "despite what Nanny may feel about Lily's potential."

"I am not married with children," Simon said. "Surely what I suggest is more respectable?"

"Do either of you remember the story of Sir Harry Fetherstonhaugh? It happened years ago. He fell in love with a dairymaid on his estate. I believe it was her singing voice that first attracted him." I raised an eyebrow and looked pointedly at Simon. "He proposed to her almost the moment he learned her identity from his housekeeper."

"Did she accept?" Colin asked.

"Of course she did!" I laughed. "Can you really think anyone would prefer dairy work to being mistress of an estate? She was sent to Paris for some time before the wedding and given an education, and after the marriage they were notoriously happy."

"Was she accepted by her husband's friends?" Colin asked.

"By some," I said. "The enlightened ones. Ones like you. As for the rest, and, I imagine, some of the servants, the arrangement was viewed as a catastrophic mistake."

"If the couple were happy, what matter the views of the rest?" Simon asked.

"I will not argue that it matters in any fundamental way," I said, "but it does make for a more difficult road."

"A fact of which I am well aware," Simon said.

"If you are determined to spend more time with Lily while you are at Anglemore, what will happen when you go back home?" Colin asked. "Where will that leave her?"

"In the same position it leaves you, Hargreaves. We can write to each other."

"It is different with a lady than with a man," Colin said.

"That's not necessarily true," I said. "I have gentlemen with whom I correspond in a completely nonromantic way."

Colin started to pace. "I do not want the girl trifled with."

"Nor do I want to trifle with her," Simon said. "She has a sharp mind and a desire to see the world. I can tell her what life is like beyond the shores of England. In fact, I have already started to do just that. I gave her a book."

"A book?" I asked.

"I should have told you before," he said. "It was nothing much, just a small series of sketches of places abroad. If you could have seen the way her face lit up when she opened it . . ."

"Flyte! What can you have been thinking?" Colin asked.

"I should have asked your permission, perhaps," Simon said. "Though I must confess I did not think she was your feudal serf."

"Point taken," Colin said. "Emily, do you object to this friendship, so long as it crosses no bounds of propriety?"

"No, I can't say that I do, and I shouldn't think you, with your radical views about the evils of aristocratic society, would either."

"Then, Flyte, you have my feudal — or futile — permission," Colin said. "But act with extreme care."

"Of course," Simon said. "You have my word as a gentleman."

"Perhaps . . ." I paused, hardly knowing how to continue. "If things go well between you and Lily, and you both — it is essential you both agree on the matter — desire to continue the acquaintance, we might be able to arrange things in a more suitable fashion."

"How so?" Simon asked.

"I am thinking of Sir Harry and his dairymaid," I said. "Perhaps we could find a situation that would enable Lily to acquire the social graces necessary to you furthering your acquaintance while also making it possible for you to court her in a more traditional manner."

"Have you something in mind?" Simon asked.

"Colin, your mother is preparing to set up house in London, is she not? She might appreciate having a companion with her, especially as she has been out of society for so long. Lily does have an aptitude for art and music, both of which your mother appreciates, and might very well get along famously with her. I could write to your mother and see if she would consider Lily for the position."

238

"You think Lily would make a suitable companion for a well-respected widow?" Colin asked.

"I do," I said, "considering your mother's borderline revolutionary views about most political matters. Lily is polite and attractive and would benefit enormously from the sort of education your mother could offer. Your mother would derive great pleasure from the scandal her choice would cause among the old dragons of London society."

"My mother would very much enjoy having someone to educate," Colin said, drawing his brows together, "and enjoy even more tormenting the ton."

"Companions are often ladies from families whose financial fortunes have turned. Lily is not so very different from them, is she?" Simon asked.

"She is in service, Flyte," Colin said. He had started to pace. "That is an altogether different thing. I agree, however, that she is, so far as I can tell, as worthy of the position as anyone else society would deem acceptable."

"Darling," I said, touching his arm, "your mother would be mortified if she thought you believed she wanted a companion deemed acceptable by society. She would much rather view herself as Lily's rescuer."

He nodded. "Quite right."

"I shall write to her when the time comes," I said, "assuming the time does come. Simon, you shall have to be very, very charming."

Downstairs

xiv

Lily was thankful it was so easy for her to avoid Pru, and for the first time since her arrival at Anglemore Park she took great and almost smug satisfaction in the knowledge that her own position in the household was so far above that of kitchen maid. It was uncharitable, she knew, but Pru got nothing less than what she deserved. She could have taught herself, as Lily had, to behave in a way that would have enabled her to work upstairs, or she could pay better attention to Cook and start making her way up in the kitchen. If she had any ambition, she might already be a pastry cook or be doing sauces. Instead she whinged and meddled in other people's lives. Then there was the matter of Johnny. It was only a matter of time before Pru's antics in the stables got her in real trouble.

Lily was halfway up the stairs to assist the footmen with their preparations for the evening meal in the dining room when Mr Davis stopped her.

"Lady Emily wants to see you immediately," he said. "She is in her dressing room."

This could be nothing good. Lily felt her insides curdle as she thanked the butler and made her way to the wide corridor along which the family bedrooms ran. She should have told Mrs Elliott about the book. That had to be what this was about. Her sin was one of omission rather than a direct lie, but no employer was going to take her side in that argument. A maid's character was as important as her efficiency. Lady Emily could find ten girls capable of doing Lily's work as well as she without having proven themselves lacking in virtue. Lily took a deep breath and weighed the options before her. She would not be given a character, and without that would be unable to get another job in service. There was factory work to be had. She could go back to London, or perhaps Sheffield or Manchester. It wouldn't matter, really. She hated the thought of cramped, dirty conditions, the sound of whirring machines — she was certain factories were full of whirring machines, though she was not sure why — and a workday without a single moment of pleasure. She had grown so fond of Anglemore and its beauty, but it was all about to end. She would never be a lady's maid now. She would never see the world.

Lady Emily's dressing room door loomed before her. Lily blinked back tears, furious with herself for having behaved so stupidly, and straightened her lace-edged cap. She pulled herself up as tall as she could, ready to face her penalty, and knocked on the door. Meg opened it, smiling as she ushered her inside. Lily couldn't believe Meg knew nothing about her imminent downfall. How could she be smiling? Meg had always been kind to her before.

Lily realized she needed to stop the rush of thoughts in her brain and focus on her mistress, who had already started to speak.

"Thank you for coming so quickly, Lily," Lady Emily said, fastening a pair of heavy ruby earrings. "Meg, would you leave us for a moment?" Once the lady's maid was gone, she continued. "I have just had a rather lengthy conversation with Mr Hargreaves and Lord Flyte."

"Yes, madam, I know that you must be frightfully angry with me about the book," Lily said, tears streaming down her face. "I ought to have told Mrs Elliott, but I was so afraid —"

"Good heavens, Lily," Lady Emily said. "I had no idea you were so upset. Come, I can finish with this jewelry later." She took Lily gently by the arm and led her out of the dressing room into her bedroom. Lily's best efforts to stop her tears were failing miserably.

"I am truly sorry, madam," Lily said. "I don't know what's got into me."

They sat on a pale blue silk chaise longue tucked into the alcove formed by a bay window, and Lady Emily took hold of Lily's hand. "There is no need to apologize. You have done nothing wrong. Mr Hargreaves and I were talking to Lord Flyte about his relationship with you."

"It's not a relationship, madam, really it's not."

"Dry your eyes and do try to calm down," Lady Emily said. "Lord Flyte admires you and would like to have a real friendship with you, but we are all sensitive to the fact that such a thing between two people of different ranks can be viewed as inappropriate."

"Is it inappropriate?" Lily asked.

"Not if you are behaving in a virtuous way, which I know you are. Lord Flyte has asked if we would allow him to see you on your days off. Would that be agreeable to you?"

Lily looked down and closed her eyes as she nodded. "Madam, it would."

"I shall let him know you are amenable. He will be most pleased," Lady Emily said. She looked Lily over with a great deal of scrutiny. "I am aware that you are interested in becoming a lady's maid."

"Yes, madam, but that is not to say I am dissatisfied in my current position," Lily said.

"I do appreciate that," Lady Emily said. "It is admirable that you have ambitions, and even more so that you want to pursue your interest and talent in art. It is these qualities, Lily, that make you stand apart from the rest of the staff and that have drawn Lord Flyte's attention. Frankly, it is those same qualities that impressed me when you first came into my employ."

"I never intended to make a spectacle of myself."

"I am well aware of that." Lady Emily raised Lily's chin so that she could see her face. "Lord Flyte explained that he gave you a book. Why did you think you ought to tell Mrs Elliott about it?"

"I thought she would be angry that I accepted it."

"You have every right to accept any gift you deem appropriate," Lady Emily said, "regardless of what Mrs

Elliott thinks. It sounds like a beautiful book, and I know Lord Flyte is very much looking forward to hearing your opinion of it. I shall talk to Davis and apprise him of our conversation and have him make sure you face no obstacles from Mrs Elliott. It is most unorthodox to encourage such a friendship, Lily, but I do believe it is the right thing."

Lily swallowed hard. She wasn't going to tell Lady Emily the book was gone; that would only cause more trouble with Pru. She worried, though, about what she would say to Lord Flyte. She would have to tell him the truth. Once he knew how careless she had been, it would be doubtful he would ever want to speak to her again. Perhaps that was for the best. Lady Emily had assured her there was nothing inappropriate in his attentions, but could that really be true? The desperate feeling of longing in her belly made Lily know that, inappropriate or not, there was nothing she wanted more.

CHAPTER
FIFTEEN

The expansive grounds at Anglemore provided more walks than one could take in a lifetime. Directly behind the house was an elegant formal parterre, where a fountain featuring a statue of Apollo driving his chariot stood in the midst of geometric beds of flowers edged by low hedges. To the west was a dense wood Colin assured me had never been cut. He claimed, with the fervor of a little boy who earnestly believes everything his nanny tells him, that it was the most ancient wood in all of England. In the eighteenth century, a series of serpentine paths had been cut through it and classical sculptures, cascades, fountains, and two summerhouses placed in its midst. It was virtually impossible not to get lost in the woods, even, as my husband had proved on more than one occasion, after having spent one's youth exploring them.

Directly to the east of the house was another formal garden, primarily hedges, and a long, narrow pool that provided an excellent view from the windows of the wing of the house overlooking it. South of that was the walled garden, lush with roses and everything Cook might need in the kitchen. The walls of this garden were heated, making it possible to grow exotic fruit on them, even in the winter. Between the walls and our hothouses, we had pineapples, nectarines, pomegranates, and even bananas on the estate.

North, beyond the parterre, stood a pretty wilderness that met the woods at the edge of the lake. Nearer the lake, on the top of a gently rolling hill, stood a lovely little temple, the prettiest folly on the grounds, dedicated to the muses. Inside it was a single room, more window than wall, with sweeping views of the countryside in every direction. One would be hard-pressed to find a better spot for a picnic on a day that suddenly turned rainy, or a more suitable place to curl up with a book when one craved silence and solitude.

The ruins of the abbey were on the opposite end of the lake, just beyond the woods. I had spent the hours since dawn that day, the rainiest in recent memory, trudging through the mud to as many of these places as I could in search of gardeners and grooms to whom I could speak about the night of the murder. Colin had talked to them in the immediate aftermath, but we often found it helpful to interview people a second time, when they'd had longer to process the events and to remember details that might have initially escaped their notice. Furthermore, I was searching for a specific member of Anglemore's Gang who had gone away from the estate the morning after the murder. The Gang, as they were called, was comprised of men who had worked on the estate but were now more or less retired. In exchange for continued housing and a small wage to supplement the pension Colin paid them, they walked the grounds and kept them tidy. They swept leaves, made sure the paths were clear, and helped the gardeners pull weeds. It was a common arrangement on large estates, and a way for much-loved employees to feel they were continuing to make a contribution after harder labor became too difficult.

Our Gang were a congenial lot, always ready with a quick joke and a smile. Today was no different. I came upon the man for whom I was looking and one of his compatriots as I crossed the wilderness back in the direction of the house, the hand not holding my umbrella thrust deep into the pocket of my gabardine raincoat in a vain attempt to ward off the damp, chilly air. They hailed me with shouts of welcome and hearty waves, and scolded me in a most affectionate manner for being out when the weather had turned so wet.

"I would never go outside at all if I waited for it to stop raining," I said, "and I assure you I am doing everything possible to keep myself dry. How are you two faring today?"

"Fine, fine, Lady Emily," one of them answered. "It is good of you to ask."

"Better now that we've seen you."

"Thank you. I know Mr Hargreaves has already talked to you about the night the Marquess of Montagu was murdered."

"No, madam, he hasn't," the first said.

"Yes, he did." The second gave the first a friendly shove. "Has your mind gone?"

"I was away the next morning, wasn't I?" The first shoved the second back. "Me grandbaby was being baptized. I only just got back from my daughter's in Shropshire last night."

"Yes, I realize that and was hoping you could perhaps help me now. Were you working that evening? I know some of you helped Lady Matilda prepare her grounds for the party she hosted for Lord Montagu."

"I did assist with that," he said, giving a vigorous nod. "Nothing of note to report on that count, but I can tell you something else that might be of interest. There was a lady walking in your grounds with a gentleman I believe was Lord Montagu. I saw them late that night, long after the party had started. I had stayed on at Montagu once I finished working, as I'm friendly with some of the gardeners there. Dined with them and shared some ale before walking back home. I cut through the grounds, Lady Emily, to make the way shorter. I do hope that's all right."

"Of course it is. What time was this?"

"Round about ten o'clock, I'd say, but don't take that as reliable as the Queen's word," he said. "I already admitted to the ale."

"I understand," I said. "Are you certain about what you saw?"

"Yes, madam, I wasn't tight. Not like that."

"Where were they?"

"They was heading towards the old abbey, where Lord Montagu met his end."

"You are quite sure?"

"I don't know that they ever made it there, but they were only a good hundred yards away when I saw them."

248

"Can you describe the lady?" I asked.

"She had light hair and wasn't wearing a fancy dress — not fancy like a costume, but whatever it is you ladies call those contraptions you wear to balls. He was all gussied up, but she wasn't. Looked rather ordinary."

"Could you see her face?"

"Only enough to say she looked right pretty to me," he said, "slim and nice, but I wasn't close enough to make out details. That big harvest moon was the only light, you know."

"The moon was exceedingly bright that evening," I said.

"It was indeed," he said, "or I wouldn't have seen anything at all."

"You have been a great help," I said.

"I was planning to tell Mr Hargreaves all this today. This useless one" — he motioned to his companion — "said the master was right fierce about making sure we all spoke to him as soon as we could. Would've done it earlier if I hadn't been away."

"Thank you," I said. "I shall pass all this on to Mr Hargreaves. He will be in touch if he needs anything further."

"Very good, madam," he said. "Anything else we can do for you?"

"No, thank you. I hope to see you both again soon. Take good care of yourselves."

Miss Fitzgerald did not seem particularly pleased to receive me that afternoon. I had rushed back to the house, changed into a riding habit, and gone at top speed to the vicarage in Melton Carbury, where I found her at home. She looked better than she had when I first met her, just after the murder. Her complexion was still pale, but her hair was less wild, and her appearance generally neater. However, she was no longer wearing mourning, and I asked her about this.

"I stopped," she said. "Archibald, well, I hardly know what to think of him now. Do I mourn as a fiancée or as an acquaintance? I decided on the latter."

"Has Rodney Scolfield's turning up provided comfort?" I asked.

"I thought it might," she said. She blushed, just a little, and frowned. "I tried to force the issue, but got nowhere with it. He doesn't much like me, you see."

"I am sorry. You are in a miserable situation."

"It is to be expected. Why should he like me? We hardly even know each other, and I suspect I was always more fond of him than he was of me. I had hoped he could provide a distraction from this dreadful business. Nothing cures a broken heart like new love."

"I hate to have to dredge up the night of the murder again, but I have some new information that pertains to you."

"Me?"

"One of the workers at Anglemore saw someone walking with Archibald that night, and his description of the lady is a perfect match for you."

Miss Fitzgerald's features were motionless. She stared straight ahead, seemingly focused on nothing. I did not press her to reply, wanting her to take the time she needed. Eventually she spoke.

"I was there," she said and took a deep breath. "Archibald had been at Montagu for days and hadn't come to see me. I thought I would be invited to the party, not as his fiancée, but as the vicar's daughter. The old marquess had always included me in such events."

"Was your father invited that night?" I asked.

"He wasn't," she said. "I am not sure why Lady Matilda left us off the list. It may have been nothing more than an oversight, but I was hurt, particularly as Archibald didn't notice and extend the invitation himself."

"So you went to confront him?"

"No, nothing so dramatic as that," she said. "I sent him a note that afternoon and told him how I felt. He replied with a gracious apology and said that there was not much he could do given the lateness of the hour, but if I came to him when dinner would be finished, we could go for a walk. So I did."

"Why did you leave Montagu and cross onto our grounds?" I asked.

"I hardly noticed we had done until we were nearly upon the old abbey."

"There is a wall, Miss Fitzgerald. You would have had to go through a gate to pass through it."

"Yes, I suppose we did, but I cannot say I was paying particular attention to my surroundings until we reached the abbey."

"Did you go inside?"

"No, we did not."

"You did not go inside, not at all?"

"I told you we didn't."

"What did you discuss while you walked?"

"If you must know, Lady Emily, there rather wasn't a lot of talking. We were under that gorgeous moon. Did you see it? It reflected so beautifully in the lake by the ruins. Can you blame me for wanting kisses more than conversation?"

"Only kisses?"

"How can you ask such a thing?"

"A murder occurred shortly thereafter. Of course I am going to ask."

"Yes, only kisses," she said. "I am not foolish enough to go beyond that."

"Even though you were engaged?"

She sighed. "I suppose I may as well admit that I had started to believe I was more in love with Archibald than he was with me. He was so hesitant about discussing wedding dates, and you were right when you questioned his sincerity after learning of the plans we did make. I had never dreamed of eloping. What girl does? I had always wanted my father to perform my marriage ceremony in his church."

"Had you told Archibald that?"

"He said it wasn't grand enough."

"But eloping was?"

"No, eloping was on an altogether different scale, and therefore more acceptable, or at least more understandable. If we were to have any sort of public ceremony, it would have needed to be at St Paul's or Westminster Abbey or at least St Margaret's in London, with hundreds of people I had never met and

252

hundreds of people Archibald had told me he couldn't stand. He wanted something small, and knew that would only do if we eloped. He said it would disappoint his mother, but she wouldn't take it as a direct insult."

"What time did you leave him that night?"

"I couldn't say. I wasn't wearing a watch."

"Have you an idea of how long you were together?"

"Perhaps an hour, maybe a bit more," she said. "I'm not sure."

"Did he escort you home?" I asked.

"No, he had to return to the party."

"How did you get home?"

"I'd left my pony trap at Montagu."

"Did he accompany you back there?"

"Most of the way, but before we were in sight of the house someone called to him," she said. "We parted then so he could talk to his friend."

"Who was this friend?"

"I didn't recognize his voice."

"It was a man?"

"Yes."

"Did you then go straight home?"

"Of course," she said. "What else would I have done?"

"I thought you had gone to the farmer's widow?"

"Yes, yes, how stupid of me to forget."

"Miss Fitzgerald," I said, "I am not sure what to make of any of this. You didn't admit previously to having seen Archibald the night of the murder. Now that someone else saw you, you admit it, but then you forget your alibi. What do you want me to think?"

"What are you suggesting?"

"You may very well have been the last person to see Archibald Montagu alive, and you have not been honest."

"You think I murdered him?"

"I think it is possible, yes," I said, "and I should prepare to have a frank conversation with the police if I were you."

"They're not going to arrest me, surely?"

"Why shouldn't they?" I asked.

"Because I didn't kill him!"

"Your story hangs together with the barest of threads, Miss Fitzgerald. You need to tell me the truth. All of it."

"I have, Lady Emily. Yes, I omitted some detail before because I was frightened. Is that so surprising? What if I had told you straightaway about having met with Archibald? Now that you know about it, you're all but threatening me with arrest. It seems I was right to withhold the whole truth. I didn't kill Archibald, but I don't know how to prove it to you."

"It is not your place to prove your innocence," I said. "I am only worried that as more comes out about that night, you may find yourself in a position where others are trying very hard to prove your guilt. If you do not tell me everything that happened, I cannot help you, Cora."

"There's nothing else to be said."

"Why did you go to the widow's house so late?" I asked. "I can't imagine you make a habit of visiting parishioners at such an hour."

254

"I didn't want to go home."

"Why not?"

"I was floating, Lady Emily, filled with love and wonder and more kisses than I could count. I felt so fortunate to be loved by Archibald, and it was that feeling that spurred me to go to the widow's. She has not been so lucky as I, and I thought I should see if there was anything I could do for her."

"Did you know before you got there that her son had been ill?"

"Yes."

"Were the children awake when you arrived?"

"No."

"Why did you lie about this?"

"I thought I might need an alibi. I may have been one of the last people to see Archibald alive, but not *the* last, as you suggested. I had to take action to protect myself."

"So you went to the farm because you thought you might need an alibi?" I asked.

"No, Lady Emily," she said, "you will not find me quite so easy to catch out. I went to the farm because I didn't want to go home, and I did know that the widow should be checked on. Once I knew Archibald was dead, and once you came around asking questions, I came to understand the concept of 'alibi', and didn't see any harm in blurring the details. I didn't kill Archibald, and I was, in fact, at the widow's."

It was possible, of course, that Miss Fitzgerald was now being wholly candid with me. Yet the innocent, if they have not been accused directly of a crime, rarely worry so much about looking guilty. They assume the truth will protect them. Which made it all but impossible for me to take what Miss Fitzgerald said without a great deal of cynicism. I could not trust her.

Downstairs

XV

Rain always meant more work. More mud tracked through the house, more smudges on the windows, and more wet coats leaving a trail of drips through the great hall. Lily often felt on rainy days that she ought to keep a mop and bucket fastened to her side. Today was like that, gray and wet, but the house, so far, was quiet. Lady Emily had gone out early, dressed in a waterproof coat and the odd-looking boots she had ordered specially made for her, insisting they be both sturdy and comfortable. She must have been doing something more to investigate Lord Montagu's murder. Lily had watched her from the library window as she crossed the parterre and started down the steps to the grounds below and out of sight. Lily turned back to her work, preparing the fire, and she wondered, just for a flash, what it must be like to be the mistress of Anglemore, to walk across these grounds, knowing they were yours. It must be grand. She shook off the fantasy and returned to her work.

She had just lit the fire when she heard the door open. She thought her heart might stop and she was almost afraid to look up and see if it was Lord Flyte.

"Lily."

It was he. His voice, so elegant, made her flush.

"Good morning, Lord Flyte," she said, a shy smile on her face.

"That will never do, Lily," he said. "You must call me Simon."

"Oh, sir, I couldn't —"

"And we shall have no more of that, either. Simon."

"I shall try," she said.

"I know you are busy, and I do not mean to distract you, but I wanted to ask if you would like to join me for a picnic on your afternoon this week. I am hoping the weather will improve."

"That would be lovely, sir, I mean Simon." Simon. The word felt foreign and forbidden, exotic and delicious.

"I look forward to it," he said. Then he did something Lily would never have expected in all of time. He picked up her hand, raised it to his lips, and kissed it.

"I almost fell over dead, I did," Lily said, telling Alice every delicious detail as they carefully returned the Sèvres dinner service to its shelf, each piece back in its place. "He kissed my hand. Me — a maid. It's unthinkable."

"I'm starting to think I might not be fine enough to talk to you," Alice said. "Isn't it grand?"

"You know, when Jones, the old head housemaid, retired, she had been in this house more than thirty years. She worked for Mr Hargreaves's father. She was the one in charge of this dinner service that we're putting away now, and she never would let anyone else touch it, because she was sure someone would cause a chip. In all those years, not a piece was broken. I think of that every time I handle it, and I always used to believe that it would be so nice if I could call Anglemore my home for all my life, like Jones did, and make sure the service lasted another thirty years without a chip."

"And now you're wondering what Lord Flyte's estate might be like?"

They collapsed into giggles.

"What's all the commotion in here?" Pru asked, stepping through the door, a scowl on her face.

Lily and Alice fell quiet. "Nothing that concerns you," Alice said.

"You should watch yourself, Miss Lily," Pru said. "You know I'm watching you. You think you're so high and mighty, but I'm onto the truth about you. I know what you're up to." She turned to go, and as she did, she paused, looked directly at Lily, and flicked a teacup off the counter, smiling as it shattered on the floor. "Guess you won't be getting those thirty more years out of that now, will you?"

CHAPTER
SIXTEEN

In recent years, breakfast had become a favorite meal of mine. When I was younger, I had considerably less appreciation for it, viewing it primarily as the evil instrument that prevented me from a nice lie-in. Now, though, I had more control over both the time it was served and the hour at which I retired in the evening, particularly when we were not in London for the Season, and I had grown fond of the soft morning light with its golden waves. Today the sun was fighting a meandering mist for control of the gardens, and had already reached its inevitable victory before Colin had appeared. While a gentleman's toilette took considerably less time than a lady's, he was much slower moving than I in the morning. When his schedule permitted it, he preferred to linger in bed, reading the paper and taking a cup of tea before coming downstairs. This morning, I had grown impatient waiting, wanting very much to discuss Miss Fitzgerald's dishonesty. I felt it boded very ill for her continuing freedom, and, ready at last to face the world, my husband agreed.

"Not," he said, spooning a creamy heap of kedgeree from a silver dish on the sideboard, "that it would have made much difference in the end. She hasn't done herself a service, though. If she is charged and stands trial, her lies will not earn her any mercy."

"What do we do now?" I asked.

"Try to confirm the bits of her story we can. Go back to Montagu and see if any of the servants remember seeing her. One of the grooms will have handed the pony trap back to her. He may be able to give us a time, if nothing else."

"Anything new on Miss Gifford?"

"The woman we suspect to be her traveled to Lyons by train after arriving in Calais."

"Alone?"

"Alone." He took a seat at the round table next to me. "There is something else as well. The Yard has informed me that Matilda recently deposited a sum of money into a bank account belonging to none other than Cora Fitzgerald."

"Money?" I asked. "How much?"

"Not an enormous amount, but enough to feel significant to someone in Miss Fitzgerald's position."

"I shall speak to Matilda about it today."

My mother came into the room. "Do you know, Emily, that I think little Tom is trying to speak French. He distinctly said Maman today."

"To you?" I asked.

"Yes, to me." Though I am sure she would never have admitted it, she looked rather pleased with herself, all plumped up with pride.

"He must have taken quite a liking to you," I said. "What a compliment."

"You know I do not approve of him," she said, "but I am doing my best to accept your stubbornness on the matter."

"It is much appreciated," I said.

"Do not think for a moment I will alter my broader views on the subject. Children of murderers do not belong in polite society." She could be severe when she wanted to. "No matter how charming they may be."

"So you find him charming?" Colin asked.

"I suppose anyone would," she said. "He's rather cherubic."

"Perhaps a good English education could redeem him from the misfortune of his birth," Colin said. "Eton works wonders."

"Hrmphf."

They continued to banter, and as they did, an idea struck me. It would require my mother's assistance, but I could think of no one better qualified for the job. First, however, there was work to be done at Montagu, work Colin was leaving to me. His plan for the day was to dart down to London to go to Scotland Yard in order to follow up on the lone traveler we believed to be Fanny Gifford.

Yesterday's rain had been swept away by blue skies and puffy clouds, leaving us with one of those rare days when a person knows, in her heart, there is nowhere in the world more beautiful than the English countryside. Given the fine weather, I decided to ride to Montagu, and set off soon after finishing breakfast.

Matilda had already been up for ages, cataloging family treasures. The butler brought me to her in the great hall, where she was writing down critical information for each tapestry and every sword, shield, and spear hanging on its walls.

"I need to make sure that wretched Mr Scolfield doesn't get rid of anything," she said. "Which would, of course, be difficult if one doesn't have accurate records of everything. How would I ever know what was missing?"

"How can you stop him regardless?" I asked, glancing through the heap of papers she had left on a table. She had already done all of the paintings on the ground and first floors. "He does legally have the right to do whatever he wishes."

"I can attempt to shame him into keeping everything just as it is," she said.

"Do you have reason to think he wants to sell anything? Does he have financial problems? It certainly didn't appear that way to me. He's able to fund his numerous expeditions."

"Do not, Emily, force me to be rational. I need something to keep myself occupied or I shall go out of my mind."

"It is never a bad idea to keep orderly records," I said. "These country houses are full of art and precious objects often lost because no one realizes what they are."

"Thank you," Matilda said. "I do appreciate the support, even if it is nothing more than a veneer."

"Quite the contrary," I said. "I spent more than a year doing just what you are now, only I was cataloging art at a number of estates. It's a tragedy, really, the number of valuable and significant pieces all but lost in country houses. I thought it important to track down as many as I could so that scholars would know where to find them. It drove my mother to distraction. She found the whole project mortifying. She could not imagine inviting herself into someone's home and asking to go through their things. What could be worse?"

"She would think just that." Matilda gave a little laugh.

"The National Gallery and the British Museum did not agree with her," I said. "They were delighted when I sent them my archives. I managed to locate two Michelangelo drawings, a cache of Greek pottery, and at least seventeen Old Master paintings that would have gone moldy if they had been left in attics much longer."

"I imagine their opinions did nothing to sway your mother," Matilda said. "What are you embroiled in today? Can I offer any assistance?"

"I have some new information about the murder and was hoping I could speak to your grooms and some of the other servants."

"Of course," she said. "The grooms will be in the stables, and the butler can help you find anyone else. What have you learned?"

"Archibald met with Cora Fitzgerald during your party," I said.

"The vicar's daughter? She wasn't invited."

"No, and she was quite put out about that. They rendezvoused in the grounds and went for a walk after dinner."

"And you want to know if anyone saw them?"

264

"Precisely." I stacked her papers neatly on the table. "I don't suppose you did?"

"Alas, no. There was a chill in the air," she said. "I never set foot outside. Hardly anyone did."

"I thought as much," I said, remembering I had thought it exceptionally warm that evening. Was Matilda misremembering or deliberately attempting to hide an excursion she had taken from the house that night? "Now I must ask you something else, something quite awkward. It has come to my attention that you gave Miss Fitzgerald a sum of money."

"Yes, yes, of course," Matilda said. "It was for her charity work. I thought she could use it however she saw fit to assist the parishioners."

"You had it deposited into a bank account in her name, rather than one in her father's? Or the church's?"

"What difference does it make?" she asked. "Miss Fitzgerald is evidently the person who will put it to use. Why shouldn't she have direct access to it?"

"I see," I said, and I did. Still, it was odd. Definitely not the ordinary way to handle such a thing.

"I suppose you think it makes me look guilty, don't you?" She was smiling now. "Perhaps I paid Miss Fitzgerald a miserly sum in exchange for murdering my wicked cousin so I might inherit Montagu myself, but then my evil ways were undermined when Mr Scolfield turned up. This narrative could be rather useful, you know. If you would let Mr Scolfield know all the sordid details of the plot, he might decide to flee in order to preserve his life."

"It is not funny, Matilda."

"It most certainly is," she said. "If I were going to pay someone to commit murder on my behalf, I would choose someone much more competent — and much stronger — than Miss Fitzgerald, and I would pay him much better. You can't be too careful when it comes to these things."

"I suppose not." I decided not to press the issue at the moment, partly because her explanation, while unusual, was not impossible, and partly because I thought it unlikely I would be able to get anything else out of her. "I shall leave you to it, Matilda, and will let you know if I discover anything."

I left the great hall. Originally, I had been determined to head directly to the stables, but now I had a desire to search Matilda's room. An uneasy feeling about her had crept into my mind, fueled, I suppose, partially by the knowledge that in our last case, the murderer had turned out to be someone close to me. I did not want to make the mistake of ignoring suspicions because of friendship. Matilda had given me free run of the house, but it felt wrong to march into her room and comb through her possessions, even if, technically, it was the correct thing to do. The friend in me wrestled with the investigator, the friend wanting a better excuse for what I knew I had to do.

There was a commotion on the steps, and I heard a footman talking to the butler, imploring him to do something about a laundry issue that had become heated below stairs.

"The housekeeper will have to take that up with Lady Matilda's maid," the butler said, reaching the bottom step near where I stood. "She's upstairs now, dealing with some of her ladyship's clothing. When she is finished, I will ask her to address the trouble."

This was the perfect opportunity. Speaking with the maid, which was something I had wanted to do that day, was the salve the friend in me needed to feel better about going to Matilda's room.

"Did I hear right?" I asked. "Lady Matilda's maid is in her room?"

"Yes, madam," he said. The footman scurried off.

"Splendid. I've a few questions to ask her, so I shall need to go up straightaway. Lady Matilda told you, I believe, that I would be working here today?"

"Yes, madam, she did. I shall take you there at once," he said. I followed him to the bedroom, where Matilda's maid was returning a stack of recently mended gowns to a tall wardrobe. Before leaving us, the butler explained to her that Lady Matilda wanted all the staff to assist me in any way possible.

"I know you have been asked about the night of the murder already," I said, "but I was hoping to hear about some of the more personal parts of the evening in the hope that they may reveal something of significance. How were Lady Matilda's spirits that day?"

"She was quite happy, madam," the maid said. "She was excited about the party."

"Was she happy to have Archibald here?"

"Of course," she said. "They've been close since they were children."

"Do you remember what she wore that evening?"

"Her cerise gown, madam."

"May I see it?"

"I suppose so." She looked puzzled, but pulled the gown from its hanger. Though I knew it would already have been cleaned, I made a show of inspecting it nonetheless.

"Was there much mud on it?" I asked. "It's amazing you were able to get it out."

"It wasn't so bad, madam. Just around the hem."

"I shall have to have Meg speak to you." I flashed her a winning smile. "She has such trouble with mud. You wouldn't mind sharing your tricks, would you?"

Now she looked even more confused. "Mud isn't all that difficult, madam."

"Perhaps not for you." I smiled again. "I would be most grateful if you'd share your secrets with Meg. Will you do that for me?" I must remember to warn Meg before this conversation or she would think I had lost my mind.

"Of course, madam, if that's what you wish. Is there anything else I can do for you?"

"No, no," I said. "Don't let me keep you from your work."

She scuttled out of the room. I'm sure she thought I was the worst sort of out-of-touch eccentric aristocrat who was too stupid to realize that even the newest lady's maid would know precisely how to deal with mud on a gown, but that did not bother me. The police would have searched Matilda's room the night of the murder, but I thought it unlikely they had done much beyond giving it a quick once-over, and now I was in it, prepared to do just that. They would have been loath to disturb a lady's privacy, and I did not remember Colin telling me he had taken any interest in that particular part of the house.

I felt a bit underhanded doing it now, and a bit guilty at going through my friend's possessions, but I could not discount her as a suspect, especially now that I knew she had almost certainly lied about going outside on the night of the murder. I worked quickly, making my way methodically through the chamber. The first thing that sparked my interest was a folded paper I found hidden in the pages of a book, but it amounted to nothing more than a list of gowns she planned to order for next year's London Season. In the drawer of her bedside table I found a diary, but I could not bring myself to open it. That would be too much of a violation.

I did not feel the same, however, when I came across a bundle of letters tied with a pink ribbon and tucked into the back of a drawer filled with silk undergarments. A prick of disappointment came when I recognized the handwriting on the envelopes as that of Archibald, and I worried that Matilda, like his American fiancée and Cora Fitzgerald, harbored romantic feelings for him. I started at the sound of footsteps in the corridor, afraid Matilda would find me, but they continued along, fading in the distance. I was relieved, even though I knew I was doing what the investigation required.

With trembling hands I untied the ribbon and flipped through the envelopes, looking for the latest one. Fortunately, they appeared to be in chronological order, with the most recent on top. I opened it, spread it out on my lap, and read.

My darling dear cousin,

I am gladder than I can say to learn you don't object too strenuously to the change in our plans. I know how you adore Montagu, and I would love nothing more than for you to live there for the rest of your days. I have, however, promised myself to a young lady bent on playing mistress of the manor, at least for a while, and you know she is too headstrong to be put off. I thank you, thank you, and thank you, again and again for being understanding. You know Grandfather would be delighted at your generous spirit, and I promise not to make any changes to the house that are not easily reversed.

I am so touched by your continued kindness despite what could have been an awkward, if not painful, situation about the house. Here you are, disappointed, and yet offer to host a party for me. How could I refuse? You're right that I should address the staff as marquess and do everything the proper way, so I shall, and we shall celebrate as you have suggested.

No, I shan't be bringing her. She's still in New York, with no plan to return to England until the Season next year, and we will be married the following Christmas. Which means, dear Matilda, that you can stay, content, in Montagu until then. I shall keep you informed of renovations and will do my best to inconvenience you as little as possible.

Do choose one or two things of Grandfather's to take with you to the house in London. They will serve to remind you of Montagu.

I remain your ever-devoted servant,
Archie

I folded it quickly and shoved it back into the envelope. Matilda was as prone to lying as Cora Fitzgerald. Making a quick decision, I slipped the incriminating letter into my reticule and returned the rest to the drawer. Matilda knew of Archibald's plans to marry, and she knew she was going to be pushed out of the house she loved. She had lied about all of it to me. Was that enough to drive her to murder a cousin for whom she had such affection? Enough to make her pay Miss Fitzgerald to do the deed for her?

I hesitated, then pulled the bundle back out of the drawer. I wanted — needed — to read the rest of them, so I took them all and headed for the stables. I would talk to the grooms and then find somewhere quiet to read. If I was lucky, I would find a way to return the letters before their owner noticed they were missing. I did not want to confront her until I was ready.

The stables were extensive, covering a huge swath of land. The head coachman was extremely helpful, although he protested that they all had already told the police everything about the night of the murder.

"I have a very specific question for you," I said. "One that the police would have had no reason to ask. There was a young lady who came to see Lord Montagu that night. She had not been invited to the party, and as such wouldn't have been dressed in evening clothes. She wore a simple gown and was driving a pony trap. Could you see if anyone remembers her?"

"I'll do my best," he said. He returned a quarter of an hour later with one of the grooms.

"Do you mean Miss Fitzgerald, madam?" the groom asked. "The vicar's daughter?"

"Yes, did you see her?" I asked.

"I tied up her horse when she arrived. She's a most pleasant young lady."

"How long was she here?"

He blew a long gust of air from his lungs. "It would be hard to say, madam. She arrived just before the guests had finished dinner, which was somewhere in the neighborhood of half nine, and left before midnight. The police were here shortly after midnight. She was gone before they arrived."

"Do you have any idea how long before midnight?"

He thought for a while. "I remember one of the guest's coachmen telling me it was already half eleven and commenting on the fact that no one had left the party. We always notice when someone goes off early in a huff, madam. It makes the time pass more quickly."

"But no one went off in a huff that night?" I asked.

"Sadly, no," he said. "The coachman was looking at the big clock over the stable gate, so he knew the time, and I am certain I had handed the pony trap back to Miss Fitzgerald before then."

"How can you be so sure?"

"Because Lady Matilda came out with her, and for a moment I thought it might have been someone leaving in a huff, so upset that the mistress had to escort her out, but it was no such thing."

"Did you speak to her?"

"Only to wish her a good evening," he said.

"Was Lord Montagu with them?"

"No, madam."

"Did you see him that night?"

"No, but then I wouldn't have had cause to."

"Of course," I said. "Thank you very much for your assistance. It is much appreciated."

I stalked back towards the house, anger bubbling up in me. Cora Fitzgerald and Matilda had been together so close to the time when Archibald was murdered? Suddenly reading my friend's letters didn't seem like such a crime.

Downstairs

xvi

Pru was finished with that uppity Lily. The girl thought she was better than everyone, and now that she was supposedly *friends* with Lord Flyte, she was more unbearable than ever. Throwing it in everyone's face, she was, and it was causing unrest among the staff. Mr Davis and Mrs Elliott should never have allowed it, especially as Lily was most probably the sort of girl who always had friends she shouldn't. Even Johnny could see that. He admitted as much. Of course, he had admitted it when he was trying to get Pru to let him undo the bodice of her dress, so his opinion might not be entirely honest, but Pru was willing to overlook that.

Lord Flyte wasn't the sort of gentleman a girl could trust. He had looked at her in that way — that unmistakable way — when she spoke to him near the stables. Oh, he was right careful not to give anything away, but Pru knew what he wanted. She'd seen it before. She knew what to do. All that was left was to figure out how. She couldn't go upstairs like the others. Her work was all in the kitchen and its environs, so she had no easy way to put herself in front of Lord Flyte again.

274

Lily acted like she had high morals, and Pru knew that was smart of her. If you didn't put on a show of virtue, you'd be in a heap of trouble. There was so much to be gained by going with a gentleman, though, no matter the risks. Lily would be getting lots out of Lord Flyte, and as far as Pru was concerned, she ought to be the one reaping rewards, not some cheeky housemaid. She suffered enough in the kitchen and deserved a bit of fun.

Alice walked past her and scowled.

"Sorry you lost old Johnny, are you?" Pru taunted. "Guess you don't have what he wants."

"If what he wants is something you have, I'm glad to lose him," Alice said. "You should take better care, Pru, or you'll wind up in the kind of trouble you can't get out of."

"I'm not the one who's headed for trouble," Pru said. "It's Lily you should worry about." Pru smiled. Alice didn't know anything, especially what Pru had planned for her nemesis. They would all treat her with more respect when she was finished. They'd be afraid not to.

CHAPTER
SEVENTEEN

Rage was not an emotion with which I had much familiarity, but that was exactly what consumed me when I stepped back into Montagu Manor. Fortunately, I saw reason and decided to calm myself before I confronted Matilda about neglecting to mention having escorted Miss Fitzgerald to the stables shortly after the murder. Not wanting to be disturbed, I went to the servants' hall, took a seat at the long table in the center of the room, and read the rest of Matilda's letters from Archibald. Twice, panicked maids approached me, wondering why I was downstairs, and I felt a little bad for having invaded their space. It had been the right thing to do, however. No one asked me what I was reading, and no one could have recognized the bundle of letters.

Finished with them and feeling bolder than I had when I had removed them from Matilda's room, I went back upstairs and returned all of them but the last to their drawer. Unfortunately, none of the rest proved interesting to the case. After this, I spoke to three of the footmen before I realized I was stalling. It was time to confront Matilda. She had finished in the great hall and had moved on to the picture gallery, where it appeared

276

she had abandoned her project in favor of taking tea with Rodney. This would have surprised me more but for the fact that they were sitting at opposite ends of one of the longest tables I had ever seen.

"Goodness," I said. "Can you even hear each other speak?"

"Why would I want to hear him speak?" Matilda asked. "It is tiresome enough to have to look at him."

"Boudica's beauty is enhanced when you can't hear her voice," Rodney said. Their eyes met, and I started to feel as if I were interrupting something.

"Matilda, I apologize for disrupting your respite, but I need you to be candid with me," I said. "I believe you have left out some details of the night of the murder. Could you tell me again everything you know and be careful to omit nothing?"

Matilda's face fell. "I did not hold anything back from you, I'm sure of it. How could you accuse me of such a thing?"

"You did not tell me about Cora Fitzgerald." I folded my arms across my chest and leaned against the table near to where she sat.

"We just spoke about her not an hour ago."

"You neglected to mention that you walked her to the stables that night."

"Did I? No, I don't remember that at all. I didn't mention it because I didn't do it."

"Your groom is confident you did."

"Perhaps I did, then. How am I to remember everything? I had a not inconsiderable amount of champagne that night, you know, and then had to contend with the unexpected and violent death of a dear cousin. Details may have eluded me."

Rodney rose from his seat and walked around the table to stand behind Matilda, resting his hand on the back of her chair, his posture verging on protective.

"What did you and Miss Fitzgerald discuss on the way to the stable?" I asked.

"I don't recall any conversation."

"She wasn't a guest at the party," I said. "How did you wind up with her? You said you didn't go outside at all during the course of the evening."

"I said so because I didn't go outside — the groom is wrong." She screwed her eyebrows together. "I am sure of it."

"Why was there mud on the hem of your dress?"

"There wouldn't have been. Gracious, Emily, you aren't accusing me of something more than a bad memory, are you? You can't think I killed Archie? Or that I paid that dreadful Fitzgerald woman to do it?"

"There is no need to accuse anyone, Emily," Rodney said. "We all know Boudica wouldn't have killed her cousin."

"I don't think she killed him," I said, deliberately not addressing Matilda's second question. I needed more evidence before I confronted her about that. Her shoulders relaxed.

"Thank goodness for that," she said. "You gave me such a start."

"I do, however, need you to explain the discrepancies in your story."

278

"Truly, Emily, I have no memory of speaking to Miss Fitzgerald. She must have been with someone else who looked enough like me to confuse the groom from a distance. If I had seen her, I would have been forced to invite her in — which would have been awkward under any circumstances after I hadn't included her on our guest list."

"The groom spoke to you."

"It wasn't me, Emily."

"Why did you lie to me about Archibald's engagement? And about his plans to renovate Montagu? Then there's the little matter of him having told you his fiancée wanted to play lady of the manor and that you would have to live in London."

"Oh, Emily! You read that old letter, didn't you?" She shook her head. "That is old news. Ancient. Archibald had changed his mind about all of it ages ago."

"The letter was dated a fortnight before he died."

"Whole worlds can change in a fortnight."

"She is absolutely correct, Emily," Rodney said. "We have no idea what transpired between Archibald and his fiancée before he died."

"Nothing changes the fact that Matilda lied. Do you realize how bad that makes you look?" I asked, facing her.

"I know." She rolled her eyes and sighed. "I panicked. Archie was dead and I was afraid that admitting to having known any of that would make me appear guilty. I can offer no further explanation. It was foolish and irresponsible."

"What about Miss Fitzgerald?" I asked. "I shall be speaking with her as soon as I leave here. Is she going to tell me that you escorted her to the stables?"

"Not if she has an honest bone in her body," Matilda said. "Although I am not sure that is something upon which one can count."

"Matilda, this is no time to joke. Most of the evidence in this case is circumstantial, and quite a lot of it suggests that you would have liked to see your cousin dead. You certainly benefited from his demise."

"Not now that Rodney has turned up," she said. I had never before heard her call him by his Christian name.

"How many times have I implored you to see how my presence benefits you, Boudica?" Rodney asked. His voice sounded almost teasing.

"Rodney may be here now, but he wasn't here before the murder, and there is nothing that proves — or even hints — you knew he would inherit instead of you. One might argue your plot had accomplished nothing."

"Good heavens, you are accusing me."

"I do not like this, Emily," Rodney said. For the briefest instant, he dropped his hand onto Matilda's shoulder, then removed it just as fast, presumably before she could bite it off.

"No, Matilda, I am not making an accusation. I do not believe you killed Archibald, but I do have my doubts about Miss Fitzgerald. I need to know when she was here and, more importantly, when she left. If you walked with her to the stables, you might be able to help."

"I wish more than anything that I could," she said. "I've made such a mess of all this, I know that, and I'm humbly sorry. I was wearing a cerise gown that night. I shall go through the guest list and give you the names of every lady of my coloring who was also dressed in red. Someone was with Miss Fitzgerald, someone other than me, and I will do everything in my power to identify her."

"I cannot exaggerate how important this may prove to be," I said. "If Archibald was in the house after Miss Fitzgerald left, then it is unlikely she killed him."

"And if no one did see him after that?" Matilda asked.

"Then Miss Fitzgerald has a great deal more explaining to do."

Before calling on Miss Fitzgerald, I returned to Anglemore, where I summoned Meg and changed out of my riding habit, selecting my finest and most demure afternoon dress. Meg worked her usual miracles on my hair. Deeming myself presentable, I went in search of my mother and was surprised to find her in the nursery with Tom on her lap, while Richard and Henry were playing on the floor. I kissed the twins and gave Tom a pat on the head.

"I must say, Mother, this is unexpected."

"Do not, Emily, draw any false conclusions," she said. "The boy shows signs of an aptitude for French. No doubt this is only because he is older than Richard and Henry, but I feel I should nurture his burgeoning skills."

"So you are conversing with him in French?"

She flushed. "I am telling him the names of nursery objects. It is nothing more than any grandmother would do."

I raised an eyebrow but did not push her on the point. Nanny shot me a knowing smile.

"You look rather respectable this afternoon, Emily. If anything, I would say *that* is unexpected."

"I am in need of help, Mother, and could not think of anyone better suited to the task than you."

"Oh, how lovely," she said, handing the baby to Nanny. "What can I do?"

"Terrify a young lady into better preserving her virtue."

"You are quite right," she said, nodding smugly. "There is no one better suited to the task."

I briefed her on the situation as we went downstairs to the waiting carriage. The sun had broken through the clouds, so I had asked that the top be removed for the drive to Melton Carbury. My mother loved little better than lording herself over her tenants. I hoped Montagu's and Anglemore's would suffice for her today. With a brisk movement she opened her parasol and nodded to the footman as he clasped the door behind us after having helped us up to our seats. When she thought I wasn't looking, she gave a little wave to Davis, who was standing on the front steps. The gesture was repeated less subtly whenever we passed someone on the road to the village.

Once we entered Melton Carbury, it was as if she were holding court, smiling and waving. "It is so very

282

important, Emily, to be friendly with those less fortunate than yourself. It gives them such a feeling of joy to be noticed by a great lady, and costs nothing to you."

"I tend to go for more tangible assistance, Mother. A basket of food or a doctor's visit is often of more use than a wave."

"I am perfectly well aware of that, you silly girl," she said. "I do at least as much charity work as you, but it is essential to be sure to wave as well." She pulled herself up into so regal a posture I think the Queen might have objected had she been present. I suppressed a giggle.

Miss Fitzgerald received us in her cozy sitting room and offered tea, which my mother refused. "I am not here in search of libation, Miss Fitzgerald. I am on a mission of mercy. I have very great concerns about your reputation and have decided to take it upon myself to save you. We shall start by hearing from you a free and full account of your relationship with the deceased Lord Montagu."

Miss Fitzgerald's eyes opened wide and her jaw hung slack. "I . . . I . . . was engaged to him."

"Silly girl," my mother said. "Of course you were not engaged. You are the daughter of a vicar. He had inherited Montagu. The engagement was never announced, and his mother knows nothing of it. You are lying."

"I realize it was not the usual sort of engagement," Miss Fitzgerald said, all the color having drained from her face, "and I have come to understand I made very bad judgments when it came to Lord Montagu."

"He was toying with you, no doubt in order to have his evil way with you while he allied himself with that hideous American girl whom we all know to be interested in nothing but his title. He would need something better than her to keep him sated." She turned to glower at me. "Do not look at me in such a manner, Emily; you know it is perfectly true. An English rose will always be preferable to colonial trash, no matter how much money the trash brings with her."

"Lady Bromley, I —"

"I did not ask you to speak, Miss Fitzgerald," my mother said. "Did you let Lord Montagu have his evil way with you?"

"Never, no, of course not."

"Then what was he doing at the abbey ruins the evening of his demise? Reading the *Sunday Times*?"

"He kissed me, Lady Bromley."

"You should never have allowed such a thing," my mother said. "It is reprehensible and a disgrace. What happened then?"

"I had to leave," Miss Fitzgerald said, lowering her eyes, her voice little more than a whisper. "There was no other course of action."

"I understand your meaning full well. And what did Lord Montagu think of your decision to leave?" my mother asked. "Was he pleased?"

"No, he wasn't," she said, her voice barely audible.

"So he did not behave like a gentleman?"

"No, he did not."

"He let you see his frustration?"

"Yes."

"He did not escort you back to Montagu Manor and your pony trap, did he?"

"No."

"Where did he go? Do not bother me with the lies you told my daughter about being summoned by some nonexistent gentleman."

"I didn't see him go anywhere," Miss Fitzgerald said. "I left him by the side of the lake."

"Was he angry?" I asked. My mother glared at me. She had specifically instructed me not to speak, but I had never been good at following instructions.

"Very," Miss Fitzgerald said.

"Did he sever his connection with you?" my mother asked.

"He did, but I know he would have come back to me."

"And you would have been a fool to let him," my mother said.

"Who escorted you back to the stables?" I asked.

"No one," Miss Fitzgerald said. "I was on my own. The guests were all inside."

"The groom saw you with a lady in a red dress."

"He is mistaken, Lady Emily," she said. "Of that I am certain beyond doubt."

"Why, after all this, did you go to the widow's farm?" I asked. "I should have thought after being so upset you would have wanted to go nowhere but home."

"I was more upset than I have ever before been in my life," Miss Fitzgerald said. "Home, however, was the last place to offer solace. My father, Lady Emily, is a vicar. Do you think he would welcome the knowledge of what had happened between Lord Montagu and me?"

"You would not have had to tell him," I said.

"Of course she would," my mother said. "Don't be ridiculous, Emily. What else could she do?"

"You are quite right, Lady Bromley," Miss Fitzgerald said. "I would not have been able to help telling him had I gone home, and I did not want to do that. So I refocused and fixated on something else that might provide distraction."

"The widow and her ailing child," I said.

"Yes."

It was a plausible explanation, but not all I would have hoped. "One more thing, Miss Fitzgerald," I said. "Lady Matilda gave you a great deal of money recently. Could you tell me about that?"

"It was nothing out of the ordinary, really," she said. "I organize the charitable relief work we do in the parish, helping families when they need it. My father is better suited to talking people through their problems than dealing with the financial side of the work."

"Your father was a missionary for years," I said. "Surely he is no stranger to organizing more than conversation."

"He's perfectly capable of doing it, but he prefers to leave it to me now that I am able to help."

"Why did Lady Matilda put the money into an account in your name?" I asked.

"Why wouldn't she?" Miss Fitzgerald asked. "You are perfectly welcome to look through my records. I am very thorough."

"I for one have heard quite enough," my mother said. "Money? We are to sit here and talk about money? It is not to be tolerated."

I bundled her out of the house, but not before taking Miss Fitzgerald up on her offer to see her records. There was nothing in them that aroused suspicion. Still, I was not wholly convinced.

"That was very nicely done, Mother," I said as we drove back to Anglemore.

"You tricked me, didn't you?" she asked. "You were not worried that Miss Fitzgerald is at risk for immoral behavior. You think she killed Lord Montagu, and that, Emily, is something in which I will not be involved. I do not do what ought to be left to the police. I do not dirty my hands when it is not necessary. And I never, ever would let anyone think a countess needs work to fill her time. Do not pull me into your sordid world again."

"But you are so good at it, Mother."

"I will discuss it no further." She looked away from me.

I felt like a naughty ten-year-old and was not much enjoying the sensation.

"She knows something more," my mother said, still not looking at me. "He was angry, and he did not just stand there watching her leave. Why won't she tell us what happened?"

I bit back a smile, worried that any show of enthusiasm would stop the conversation. "I do not believe she killed him," I said.

"Why on earth not? He probably grew violent with her. He may have even struck her."

"He was not in the habit of striking his paramours," I said, "and Miss Fitzgerald is not some maid he thought he could toy with."

"It is all very well and good that you consider her a lady and someone near your station, Emily. That is your bizarre and incomprehensible way of dealing with the world. However, there is a natural order to things, and like it or not, a vicar's daughter is nothing more than a glorified servant to a marquess."

"I don't agree. He told her he was going to marry her."

"A bit of fun that his friends probably laughed with him about. Mark my words," she said, "something more happened by that lake, and if you want to know who killed Archibald Scolfield, you are going to have to figure out what it was."

I shuddered. Could my mother prove an adept investigator? Every sense revolted.

Downstairs

xvii

Lily had never felt so nervous in her life as she did now. She had finished her morning work and had gone upstairs to change out of her uniform so she could meet Lord Flyte — *Simon*, she corrected herself — for the picnic he had promised her. She wished she had a nicer dress to wear, but at least her blue serge was flattering. It was well cut, and the color suited her. There was a sharp rap on her door, and for an instant she wondered if it was Mrs Elliott, telling her she would have to work this afternoon.

"Yes?"

"It's me, Meg," came a voice from the other side. "Lady Emily thought you might like a bit of assistance with your hair."

"Come in," Lily said.

Meg opened the door. "Heavens! You're a fright! Do you mean to scare off Lord Flyte?"

"It's my best dress," Lily said.

"I am not talking about your dress," Meg said. "I am referring to the stricken look on your face. This is supposed to be fun, you know. Sit down and let me get to work."

Meg pulled the pins from Lily's hair and started to brush it.

"I'm just so awfully scared," Lily said. "I don't know what I'll talk to him about. He's traveled everywhere, you know. He's a man of the world."

"The world isn't so different from England."

"Is that true, Meg? You've been all over with Lady Emily. Tell me something I can say to make him think I'm well informed." Meg was twisting and turning Lily's hair in ways she had never before seen, at least not on her own head. "I've got to come across as something other than wholly ignorant."

"I didn't like to travel at first, you know," Meg said. "I was fierce with Lady Emily about being as English as possible when we were away from home. I couldn't understand why anyone would want to leave our lovely island, but there her ladyship was, traipsing off to Paris and Vienna and all those other places. I despised it. Everything seemed so different. The food, the people, nothing was familiar. Then I got to know a lady's maid in Paris. She works for one of her ladyship's friends, and, oh, how I do adore her! She showed me Paris, and I fell in love with the place. It took me a while, but I suppose that's not so unusual for a person who hasn't traveled. In the end, Paris is just a city, like London, and you used to live in London."

"Yes," Lily said, "but now I stay at Anglemore even when the family's in Park Lane, so it's been ages since I've had what one might call a cosmopolitan experience. I did go to York once, as well, but I suppose that's nothing like Paris. I can't imagine Lord Flyte would be interested in hearing about York. How I wish I'd been to Paris."

"That's all right. Paris is beautiful, but I have come to see the world is more about people than objects or buildings," Meg said, sticking the pins back in Lily's hair. "Lord Flyte wouldn't have struck up a friendship with you if he was concerned with things more than people. You caught his interest, and you don't need to be anything but yourself with him. That's what he liked in the first place."

"I can see the sense in that," Lily said, "but are you really sure I shouldn't try to be cultured?"

"You can't pretend to be more cultured than you are. He knows you are a maid."

"I can talk about art with him some, but how am I to know if I'm saying the right thing? I don't want to put him off."

"How is one to know what is the right thing?" Meg asked. "Look at Lady Emily. She's got all those strange paintings in the white drawing room. Called Impressionist, they are. What sort of impression they make I'd like to know. Not a good one, I'd say."

"I wish I paid better attention when I dust the antiquities. It's possible I could have been able to think of something to say about them. Might be easier than art."

"You have nothing to worry about. If Lord Flyte weren't already charmed by you, he wouldn't be taking you on a picnic," Meg said. She tugged a little more at Lily's hair. "There. Take a look. What do you think?" She passed Lily a looking glass. Lily gasped. She looked like one of those elegant ladies in the fashion plates. Well, at least her hair did, all piled up and curled. She hardly recognized herself.

"Meg, I've heard Lady Emily say at least a thousand times that you work miracles. Now I know it's true."

"You would've known it sooner than now if you'd ever seen her hair when she wakes up in the morning. Sometimes it requires more than a miracle. Now go meet your young man and enjoy yourself. I expect a full report when you get back."

CHAPTER
EIGHTEEN

My mother's words in the carriage struck a chord with me. I believed she was right: Something else had happened beside the lake. What remained uncertain was whether Miss Fitzgerald had been on hand to witness it. Colin had not yet returned from London, and Simon had taken Lily on his much-touted picnic. Rodney was my only hope. He had spent the morning shooting and was now in the library, reading.

"Sorry to disturb," I said, "but I am in need of a gentleman's perspective on a delicate subject."

"Sounds enticing." He closed his book. "What is this delicate subject?

"Suppose a gentleman were, shall we say . . . entangled . . . yes, entangled, with a young lady to whom he had a close relationship. Suppose they reached a point beyond which no respectable young lady would go. Suppose, further, this angered the gentleman. What would he do?"

"There is nothing he could do," Rodney said. "He must respect the young lady's wishes. Moreover, if he was in any sort of relationship with her, he would not want to put her in a situation that might compromise her reputation."

"But he was angry. Would he have fought with her?"

"You're talking about Archibald Scolfield, aren't you?"

"Yes. Who else?"

"From everything I have heard, he was used to getting what he wanted, but not from anyone close to him, if you catch my meaning. He would not have pressed a lady to . . ." He looked at me and winced.

"He was angry and frustrated. Would he have gone back to Matilda's party after such a thing had happened?"

"What other option did he have?"

"He could have looked for someone not in a position to refuse him," I said, an ugly image forming in my mind.

"That's a whopping accusation, Emily," Rodney said.

"He has a history of involving himself with girls below his station. He trifles with them and then leaves them. Just never ones in his own household."

"Not all of those sorts of relationships stem from undue pressure," Rodney said. "I am not suggesting he wasn't a beast for taking advantage, but girls like that sometimes let themselves believe something more might come of it."

I thought of Lily, setting off almost this minute with Simon on her picnic, and wondered if I had made a grievous mistake. Was I being naive, trusting that a gentleman, even one as enlightened as Simon, could have a genuine interest in getting to know a housemaid? Had I put Lily in a position bound to cause her hurt and pain? I did not believe Simon would trifle with her, but his good intentions, however noble, might lead Lily to hope for more than was possible.

"Thank you, Rodney. I do appreciate your thoughts, more than you can know."

"Do me something in return?" he asked.

"Of course."

"Be a little easier on Boudica, would you? She's more sensitive than she lets anyone know. It is grinding her up inside to think you are suspicious of her."

"Why do you say that?"

"We had a long talk over breakfast this morning. Do not mistake her bluster for a lack of vulnerability."

"You had breakfast with her? This morning? I thought you were shooting here."

"I went to Montagu," he said. "They are my birds, after all."

Breakfasting together? This, though fascinating, was not something I could contend with at the moment. I needed to speak to Davis about Archibald's predilection for women below his station. "Would you excuse me? I need to speak to my butler in private, and this is the room —"

"Don't say another word. I'm already gone."

Davis responded to the bell and brought with him a wire from Colin, who explained that his colleague had caught up with the woman we had thought was Miss Gifford. She was someone else altogether. We would have to start our search all over again. I turned to my butler.

"I am afraid I have something very difficult to speak to you about." While he listened to me, Davis's face was as grave as I'd ever seen it. "I do not want to alarm you," I said, "but I think I should speak to each of the female staff privately. Can you arrange that in a manner that won't too badly disrupt you all below stairs?"

"Of course, madam."

"Have you heard any talk of such goings-on in the house?" I asked.

"I have not, madam, and I would like to believe such a thing could not go on without me taking notice. I have some concerns about Prudence in the kitchen and Johnny, one of the grooms. They seem to be gravitating to each other in a most unsavory fashion. Not the sort that would lead to marriage, madam, if you grasp my meaning."

"I do, Davis."

"I shall start sending the girls up to you at once. It is Lily's afternoon, so she'll be last, when she returns. I imagine port would be desired afterward?"

"Thank you, Davis."

"I might even be persuaded to allow you a cigar, madam. I cannot imagine this series of interviews will be anything short of trying."

Davis was spot on. Each of the maids squirmed uncomfortably as I questioned her. We were all embarrassed. Of everyone so far, only Alice kept her head high.

"Lily is frequently lecturing us about this below stairs, madam," she said. "She's always on about virtue and not doing anything to jeopardize our positions. May I be direct, madam?"

"Please," I said.

"We've not had cause to worry much about that sort of thing in this house. Mr Hargreaves is a fine gentleman, and it seems that most of his friends are, too."

"Most of them?"

"Well, I am not ready to pronounce a verdict on Lord Flyte, madam. He seems honest and upstanding, but I can't quite believe he wants to picnic with a housemaid."

"I can assure you, he does," I said. "He's one of the most honorable men I have ever known."

"They're always honorable to ladies like you, madam, but some of them treat the likes of us very differently."

"I do believe you, Alice," I said, "but I have a great deal of faith in Lord Flyte."

"Yes, madam." She bobbed a curtsy.

"You will tell me, though, if anything untoward happens? Anything that alarms you? I do not want Lily to be hurt."

"Of course, madam," she said. "I would make sure Lily came straight to you."

"Thank you, Alice. That is all." I rubbed my forehead as she left. The door opened almost as soon as she was gone. "Hello, Prudence," I said. "Do sit down. I need to speak with you about something rather difficult. It has come to my attention that someone among the staff may have suffered at the hands of Lord Montagu before he was murdered. Do you know of what I speak?"

"I sure do, madam," she said. "I should have come to you sooner, I suppose, but I didn't think there was any harm in it."

"Please tell me what you know."

"Well, it was Lily, wasn't it? She's always had an eye for the gentlemen, and I saw her near the lake that night. Johnny's my sweetheart, he's one of the grooms."

"Yes, I know who he is."

"We'd gone for a walk when I'd finished the washing up, and I saw Lily was out, too. Her work is generally done much before mine, madam."

"Was she alone?"

"She was." Prudence drew a sharp breath. "I don't think she would have done any harm to a man like Lord Montagu, madam. But I did see her alongside the lake, right near the old abbey."

"Did she go inside?"

"I don't know, madam. I wasn't there long enough to see."

"When was this?"

"Close to eleven. I looked at the clock before I went to the stables to find Johnny. We was only out twenty minutes or so, maybe not even that long. I have to get up before dawn, you know, and there was still all the copper and brass to polish."

"Prudence, I need you to be absolutely honest with me. Who did you see outside the servants' entrance later that night? The person you spoke to Mr Hargreaves about?"

The poor girl. She squirmed in the chair and tugged at her cap. I noticed her apron was a dingy shade of gray, and I made a mental note to have Mrs Elliott give her a new one.

"Did you recognize the figure, Prudence?" I asked.

298

"I did, madam, and I know I should have told you before. I was so scared, though, with a dead body in the house and murder all around us. It was Lily, madam, come back from the lake, a look of sheer terror on her face. I'm sorry I didn't say so before, but I was afraid of what she might do to me."

None of the other maids had anything to say about Lord Montagu, though I was gratified to see how much they respected Colin and enjoyed working for us. When I had finished with all nine housemaids, the stillroom maid (who begged for a second to help with her work), two dairymaids, the other kitchen maid, the vegetable maid, three scullery maids, and the entire nursery and laundry staffs, not to mention Mrs Elliott, Cook, and Meg, I went up the back stairs to Lily's room. It was exceptionally tidy, as I expected, knowing Mrs Elliott would tolerate nothing less. Lily's uniforms hung next to Alice's in the wardrobe, her work shoes below. Aprons and caps were neatly folded in a drawer. She did not have many personal possessions: a Bible, a packet of writing paper and envelopes, a souvenir card from the Queen's Golden Jubilee, and a well-worn handmade doll carefully wrapped in an even more worn blanket fashioned from the softest wool. Finally, in a small box, there was a rosary. I had forgot Lily was a Roman Catholic. I did not find the watercolor Simon had told me he had painted for her.

The contents of the top drawer of her dresser alarmed me. There, beneath her folded undergarments, was the book Simon had given her, but it was in no state to be read. Every page had been torn from the binding and ripped into small pieces. The cover itself had been rent into three ragged chunks. I was taken aback. Had I been entirely wrong about Lily's character? I had believed she cared for Simon and that she had been delighted to receive his gift. He certainly had believed so. But this — this suggested a violence I had not expected. I gathered up the sad remains of the book, took them to my desk in the library, and rang for Davis.

"I am holding you to your promise of a cigar," I said, "but not until you tell me everything you can about Lily."

"Lily is a hardworking girl, madam, and has never given any trouble," Davis said. "I have found her to be a conscientious member of the staff, dependable and trustworthy, always ready to go the extra mile."

"This was in her room." I showed him the shreds of paper. "It's the book Lord Flyte gave her. And now Prudence has admitted to having seen Lily near the abbey shortly before Lord Montagu died."

"Prudence is no friend of Lily's," Davis said. "Does anyone else corroborate her story? I have seen nothing in Lily's character to make me believe she would be violent."

"Johnny, the groom, was with Prudence, so I shall see what he has to say. Tell me, Davis, do you think Lily resents her station in life?"

"She has never exhibited any signs of doing so," he said. "She very much admired Jones, you know, who was a maid here for many years, and so far as I could tell, did her best to emulate her. She visits Jones sometimes, and I've heard her say she hopes she can stay in this household until she retires."

"Could she be harboring secret feelings of resentment?" I asked. "The state of this book makes me think she might."

"I am shocked at what she has done, if indeed she has done it," Davis said. "It makes me unsure what to think."

"Would you please fetch Johnny for me? I want to question him here." I paced as I waited for the groom, ill at ease and unsure what to think. Johnny looked more uncomfortable than I felt when he arrived. It was likely he'd only been above stairs the day he had been hired. "Thank you for coming, Johnny," I said. "Please take a seat."

He did as I asked, clutching his cap tightly in his lap. "Have I done something wrong, madam?"

"I wanted to speak to you about the night of the murder," I said. "I am aware you had some free time late in the evening. How did you spend it?"

"I went for a walk with one of the kitchen maids, Pru."

"Where did you go?"

"Through the big meadow and over to the lake. We was looking at the moon."

"Did you see anyone else? Perhaps Lord Montagu?"

"No, madam, I didn't see him, but I did see Lily. She's a maid, madam. She was down by the lake as well."

"What was she doing?"

"I couldn't rightly say, madam," he said. "She was by the old abbey. I figured she was waiting for somebody, a sweetheart maybe."

"Why do you think that?"

"It's a good spot for a bit of romance, isn't it?" His eyes twinkled. "Nothing out of order, madam, of course."

"Yes, Johnny, nothing out of order," I said. "Which does put me in mind of something. I should like to remind you that Mr Hargreaves and I will not tolerate anything out of order. I would like to suggest you carefully consider some of your recent behavior. We have never stood in the way of our staff getting married. Should you decide to do so, we would happily put you and your bride into a cottage on the estate. But there are to be no underhanded dealings with the female staff. Do you understand?"

"I do, madam," he said, swallowing hard. "I take your meaning quite well."

"Very good. Did you see Lily leave the lake?"

"No, madam, we only walked by quickly. Pru had to get back to work."

"Is it possible that the person you heard crying that night — the one you initially mistook for a cat — could have been Lily?"

"I couldn't swear on it, madam, but it might have been her voice."

"Why didn't you tell Mr Hargreaves that you had seen Lily by the lake when he initially spoke to you about the murder?"

He leaned forward and looked very serious. "I know I should have, madam. It was nothing but wrong of me not to. Only Pru was afraid, you see. She saw her — Lily, that is — coming back to the house, all upset. Then when she knew the gentleman was dead and it was murder, she worried Lily would remember seeing us by the lake. Right by where he was killed. We could be in a heap of danger, madam."

"I can assure you we will not let anything happen to either of you for having come forward with this information. Is there anything else?"

"No, madam. That really is all. I am awful sorry about not telling it sooner."

"I'm glad you have told it now, Johnny," I said. "You may get back to work. Thank you for your assistance."

Downstairs

xviii

At precisely noon, Lily had gone down the back stairs to the ground floor and then made her way to the great hall, where she was to meet Lord Flyte — *Simon, I must really try to remember to call him Simon,* she reminded herself. The house looked different to her today, as if she were seeing it from an entirely new perspective. For the moment, at least, she did not look at the rooms and quickly evaluate them to see what needed dusting. Instead, she considered them merely as pleasant spaces through which a lady — not that she was putting on airs, she knew she would never be a lady — might drift in a lovely gown on her way to meet a gentleman for a picnic. She made a quick stop in the white drawing room to look at the paintings, hoping she might be able to come up with something interesting to say about them to Simon, but found herself at a loss. When she arrived in the hall, he was waiting for her. They went out the front door — the front door! — and he, an earl, was carrying two large picnic hampers, which Lily tried to take from him.

"Don't be ridiculous," he said. "You are not here to work."

"Yes, sir."

"Lily." There was a pleasant sort of growl in his voice that gave her a thrill.

"Simon."

"That's better." He smiled. "You look lovely. Blue suits you. It brings out your eyes."

"Thank you, Simon."

"I thought we could go to the vista I told you about, near the Temple of the Muses. I'd so like to show it to you. Then, after we've eaten, we could stroll through the gardens. The roses may be long past their peak, but the rest won't disappoint."

"That sounds perfectly lovely," Lily said.

When they reached the vista, Lily gasped. "It's so beautiful, even more stunning than I had imagined." She caught herself and continued on quickly. "Although it looks no more beautiful than it did in your painting. You did a wonderful job with the light. You made it look as if the scene were alive."

"You are too kind," he said. He opened the hamper and pulled out a thick wool blanket that he spread neatly on the ground, smoothing it with great care. "Now you, Lily, are to sit, and I shall get everything ready for you."

She did as he instructed and watched as he produced marvelous thing after marvelous thing from the hampers. Cook must have outdone herself. There was mousse made from foie gras, salmon with some sort of green sauce on it, and cold beef. Simon placed two dishes of salads on the blanket next to a bowl of fruit and arranged biscuits and cakes on a platter. There was a flask of tea and a flask of coffee, but those were for later. First, Simon insisted on opening the champagne, Bollinger, Mr Hargreaves's favorite. Lily recognized it.

Simon poured her a glass and clinked his against it. "I am so pleased to be here with you, Lily."

"I couldn't be happier," she said.

"Start eating and tell me all about your week."

"My week?" Lily almost laughed. "You can't possibly want to know about my week."

"Why not?"

"It would bore you to death, sir . . . Simon. You already know how I spend my time. We should talk about something interesting. You are, after all, something of an artist. Tell me how you learned to paint."

"I am sadly an amateur artist, if I could even be called that," Simon said. "As for learning, before I went to school I had a governess who taught me a few basics, and I honed what little I knew when I was on my Grand Tour."

"I can't think of a better way to record magnificent places," Lily said. She stretched out on the blanket and watched geese flying overhead in a perfect vee. "Imagine, setting up an easel in front of the Acropolis. It must have been heaven."

"I suppose it was, though at the time I'm afraid I took the experience entirely for granted. That is one of the things I love about spending time with you, Lily. You make me rethink everything. I have had a life in which much has been handed to me. I better appreciate all of it when I see it through your eyes."

She blushed. "I am very flattered, sir. Simon."

"Tell me about yourself. Do you like your work?" He was spreading the foie gras mousse on a piece of triangle-shaped toast. Lily followed his lead and did the same.

"I do. It's satisfying. I like seeing the results and take great pride in a well-tended-to room."

"I can understand that," he said. "Tangible results are deeply satisfying."

"There's a way in which it's not unlike my drawing," she said. "Immediate results whose quality depends on the care taken with the task."

Simon's gaze rested on hers. How did this girl, without the benefit of much education, manage to make such meaningful observations? He wanted to kiss her, to tell her he adored her sharp mind and wanted to help her hone her abilities. It was too soon, though. Wasn't it?

"How do you spend your time?" she asked. "Other than paint, that is. You don't maraud about the country taking care of matters for the Queen like Mr Hargreaves does, do you?"

"Oh dear." He laughed. "I'm afraid I am not so useful as my friend. I manage my estate, take care of any problems my tenants are having, and I spend a certain amount of time in London at the House of Lords. I don't like it much in town, but one must do one's duty."

"It sounds very elegant and exciting."

"Believe me, it's not."

"Do you like Anglemore?"

"It's one of the best estates in the country," he said. "Can you picture a better scene? Look at the hills, the lake, the immaculate gardens all around us. Hargreaves takes dashed good care of it, and of his people. I admire that."

"What do you do when you're here?" she asked. Then, feeling cheeky, she added, "Live the life of leisure?"

Now he really laughed, a great guffaw. "Yes, I suppose I do. I have some work to attend to, things that can be done from a distance, but I've been spending most of my time taking long walks, shooting birds, painting, and reading. Emily has an incomparable library. Did you know she owns the books, not Hargreaves?"

"No, I didn't," she said.

"He gave them to her — went so far as to deed them — when he was trying to persuade her to marry him. I still goad him, saying she liked the books better than him."

"No!" Lily gasped. "I think she adores him. He's so handsome, how could she not?" She covered her mouth. "I shouldn't have said that."

Simon laughed. "Believe me, I'm immune to all references to the handsomeness of our resident Adonis, and you're right, Emily does adore him. I was only teasing."

"Oh," Lily said. "I'm silly."

"You're not. Not in the least."

"You're very kind. Do you get bored staying here?" Lily asked, moving her hand lightly over the grass just past the edge of the blanket. It was cool and starting to feel the slightest bit damp. "It seems like not a lot to do."

"Never," he said.

"I wonder if I might be bored if I had so little to do. I don't think I'd be good at shooting birds," she said. "Is it difficult?"

"I shall teach you and you can decide."

"Sir!"

He glowered at her with false menace. "You must call me Simon," he said, and leaned closer to her, "or I shall be extremely put out."

She sipped her champagne. "As you say, Simon." She loved the sound of his name on her lips, forbidden and exciting.

"How did you like your book?" he asked.

This question all but made her heart stop. They had been having such a lovely time, and now she would have to spoil it by telling him she hadn't read it. "I'm afraid I haven't been able to take a good look through it."

"Why not? Is Emily working you too hard? I thought you had time in the afternoon to yourself."

"Oh, I do," she said, eager to distract him. "Usually, Alice — she's one of the other maids — and I have a cup of tea in the servants' hall and put our feet up. That is to say, not actually up on the furniture, you know, but we do get to relax. We read the newspaper and catch each other up on any interesting letters we've received from our families."

"And in the evening, when you've finished working?"

"That's generally when I sketch or read," she said. "Lady Emily is lovely about letting us borrow books from the library. I've not been in many other ones, but I do agree hers is quite wonderful."

"What do you like to read?" Simon asked.

"I quite like Mr Dickens," she said. "*Oliver Twist* and *Great Expectations* are my favorites."

"When do you plan to read the book I gave you?"

"Oh, sir." She turned away from him. "Simon."

"What is it? Is something wrong?"

"It's just that, you see, I can't read the book you gave me."

"Why on earth not? Mrs Elliott didn't take it away from you, surely?"

"No, she didn't, but I'm afraid someone else did."

"Who?"

"I'm not certain, but I do have a suspect."

"A suspect? You sound like your mistress. Tell me what happened."

"I had been saving it, you see, wanting a good proper look at it when I wasn't too tired and had a nice bit of time to myself. So I put it away in my dresser. I was very careful with it, I promise you. But then when at last I went to fetch it, it was gone."

"Gone?"

"Vanished."

"So whom do you suspect?"

"One of the other maids. She's in the kitchen."

"Why her?"

"She despises me," Lily said.

"What's her name?"

"Pru."

"I have met her," Simon said. "Outside the stable." He remembered how she had made it clear she would be available to him for any bit of fun. He had never liked girls like that.

"I can't prove it, of course, and I don't want to cause trouble by accusing her when I've got nothing more than a feeling about it."

"You didn't tell Mrs Elliott? Or Mr Davis?"

"No, sir, only Alice."

He didn't correct her "sir."

"I am so sorry," she said, her heart sinking. "I hope you can forgive me."

He smiled, and relief washed over her. "You've done nothing wrong. I'm sorry that your book is gone. Don't worry, though, I shall get you another."

"You can't! It's too much."

"I shall be the judge of that," he said. "Now, you've hardly touched your salmon. Tuck in at once or you'll be in danger of losing it to me."

And that was it. He wasn't mad. He didn't think she had been careless. She hadn't let him down. More importantly, Meg had been right. He was happy to talk about whatever she wanted to and was interested in her world, not in trying to make her something she wasn't. Lily thought she might die of happiness.

The champagne was gone, and the biscuits and cakes demolished. Lily had just returned her empty teacup to its saucer when Simon leaned close, over their plates. "I can't remember when I've enjoyed an afternoon more," he said.

"I know I never have," Lily said, feeling herself start to lean towards him.

"You are a magnificent girl, Lily. I am so pleased we had this time together."

Then the most extraordinary thing happened. He leaned forward even farther and kissed her, right on the mouth. Lily had never felt anything so soft and warm as his lips, and she wished with everything she was that she could forever be suspended in this, the most wonderful moment of her life. No matter what happened in the future, no matter what she had lived through in her past, she would always have this moment, this kiss, this perfect, perfect kiss. No one had ever told her life could be so sweet.

CHAPTER
NINETEEN

Simon and Lily would be returning to the house soon from their picnic, and I was not looking forward to seeing either of them. I was in the library, reading Herodotus until I came to a passage that made me close the book: *The worst pain a man can suffer: to have insight into much and power over nothing.* I rang for Davis and reminded him of his promised cigar. When he brought it without argument, my heart sank deep into my abdomen. He, too, knew the gravity of the situation. I stopped him as he opened the door to go.

"Davis, I would like you to join me," I said. "Fetch yourself a cigar, and I'll pour port for us both."

"Madam, I —"

"You know better than to argue with me."

He nodded, disappeared, and returned a short while later with a second cigar. He cut it, warmed it over a match, and lit it, rotating it in a fluid manner that suggested experience.

"I am most distressed," I said, handing him his port. "I want to run a happy household, and I thought I did until this wretched business with Lily. Are the staff generally pleased with their situations?"

"I believe they are, madam. You must not chide yourself simply because of one girl with an ill temper." He took a sip from his glass. "This is a fine port."

"It is," I said.

"It feels very odd to be drinking it in the middle of the afternoon."

"I promise it will feel less odd once you have finished your glass," I said. "Are you content with your life in service?"

"I am, madam. I have been working since I was a boy of eight, when the Viscount Ashton — your late husband's grandfather — took me on as a page."

"And you've worked your way up to running the whole show," I said.

"I will say, madam, I never thought I'd leave the Ashtons."

"I am very glad you did."

"Service is a good life, madam. I am well looked after, I eat well, have comfortable rooms, and get a great deal of personal satisfaction from my work. If Lily is less content, she cannot blame you."

"I know you are right, but I cannot help feeling guilty all the same. It is down to nothing more than an accident of birth that I am the one inviting you to sit in this library instead of the reverse."

"Why should that trouble you, madam?"

"It seems so unfair."

"I don't agree in the least," he said. "The great families of this country possess their land and their rank because they have proven themselves time and time again. Your ancestors distinguished themselves in

314

grand manner. Mine did not acquit themselves in such glorious fashion. That is not something for which you should feel bad."

"But it was our ancestors, not us."

"If I may be so bold, you have been taking Mr Hargreaves's revolutionary ideas too far to heart, madam."

Then, for one of the very few times in all the years I had known him, Davis smiled. A real smile. Not the hint of one, not a small grin in an unguarded moment. A real smile.

"So you do not believe that Lily has a legitimate complaint?" I asked.

"No, madam. If she doesn't want to be in service, she doesn't have to be. There are other jobs to be had."

"But in what sort of circumstances? Would working in a factory be a step up?"

"To some it is, madam. I have argued more than once with men who consider me less than they because I serve a gentleman — and a gentlewoman, of course. They prefer a factory, where they believe they serve no one but themselves. They are as much in service as I, but they don't view it that way, perhaps because they are responsible for their own lodgings and live away from where they work. I am not suggesting one way of life is better than another, but we all have choices, madam. Including Lily." He took a last puff on his cigar before putting it out in a silver ashtray. "I should like to stay longer, madam, but there is work to be done. Many thanks for this respite."

"Thank you, Davis," I said. "You have given me much to think about."

After he had gone, movement outside the window caught my eye. Simon and Lily were returning from their picnic, their faces animated and smiling. He held two hampers on the same side, one tucked under his arm and the second's handle firmly in his hand, so that he could keep the other free to hold hers. I shuddered. Did she plan to do to him what she had to Archibald? It was impossible to believe as I watched her. Nothing in her countenance gave away even a hint of displeasure or resentment. Could I be wrong? There might be some other explanation for the book and her presence at the lake that night. I would pass no judgment on her until I had spoken to her myself.

Simon had gone directly to his room upon his return, and I hoped he wouldn't rush to come back downstairs. It was cowardly, I knew, but I could not bear to take away the happiness so evident on his face when he was with Lily. I glanced at the clock on the mantel. The train from London would have already arrived; Colin would be home soon. Alice brought tea to me, and I knew Simon could not be long behind her. I braced myself, wishing Colin would beat him to the library.

It was not to be.

Simon flung open the door in a most exuberant manner, grinning. "My dear lady, I have never — ever — ever in my life had such a delightful afternoon. Lily is all charm. She is the most unaffected creature, completely unspoilt. Her mind is sharp, and she possesses an admirable curiosity. She does not belong in service."

"Did she tell you that?" I asked.

"Lily? Heavens, no. I don't think she would even like to hear someone else say it."

"Why is that?"

"She waxed rhapsodic about her work," he said, dropping onto a leather sofa and accepting the cup of tea I offered him. "Bloody gorgeous day. This weather cannot possibly hold."

"No, I imagine not."

"You are grim," he said. "Apologies. I am so wrapped up in my own triumph I didn't ask how you are. Have you made any progress in the investigation?"

"I'm afraid I have, but it brings me no joy."

"Emily, what is it?" he asked.

"One of the kitchen maids admitted today that she saw someone near the lake close to the time of the murder."

"Dear me."

"It gets worse, Simon," I said. "She saw Lily."

"Ridiculous. If she was by the lake, I am sure there is a completely innocent explanation. I can assure you that Lily had nothing whatsoever to do —"

"There is more. I found this in her room." I had put the sorry pieces of the book into a small box, which I passed to him. All the color drained from his face.

"Bloody hell," he said. "She told me someone had taken it. I don't know what she'll do when she learns it has been destroyed."

"She told you someone had taken it?" I asked.

"Yes, this afternoon. She was mortified by the whole incident. It was very sweet, really. She thought I would be angry."

"Perhaps she felt that way because she knew what she had done to the book."

"You cannot think she had anything to do with this," he said. "She loved this book. If you could have seen her eyes when she opened it —"

"Simon, I want more than anything to believe you, and I would never doubt your sincerity, but this is rather strong evidence she is not quite so pleased with you as you think. Consider also that she has been placed at the scene of a murder, the murder of a man in a position comparable to your own."

"Lily is not going to kill me. Good Lord, do you not see how absurd this is?"

"I am not suggesting that we know it for a fact," I said. "I haven't yet spoken to Lily."

"She told me the book was missing, and she thinks a kitchen maid took it."

"Prudence?"

"Yes, how did you know?"

"Prudence is the one who saw Lily at the lake."

"Prudence hates Lily."

"Davis told me they are not friends," I said. "However, one of the grooms saw Lily as well."

Simon nodded, and I detected the slightest change in his countenance. He seemed less confidently certain. "This is an extremely serious situation."

"Indeed," I said, reaching for his hand, "and I am more sorry than I can say to see you embroiled in it in a way that may cause you hurt, or even heartbreak. Anyone could read on your face how happy you were

318

this afternoon. It is possible that Prudence has not been truthful."

"Prudence may be the one with something to hide," Simon said. "I don't like the girl."

"You know her? When on earth did you see her?"

"Outside the stables when I returned from London," he said. "She made what I considered some rather awkward advances to me."

"Did she?"

"I recognized what she was doing at once."

"I was under the impression she was involved with one of the grooms," I said.

"And was it he who was with her by the lake and confirmed having seen Lily?"

"Yes, and before you say anything, I realize that they both could be lying. That is why I want to speak to Lily at once." I rang for Davis and asked him to bring her to me. Simon remained. He wanted to hear for himself what she had to say, and, I suspect, he wanted to offer her what moral support he could.

The door opened, and we both stood straight up. I almost knocked over my chair. I must have been more on edge than I realized. Colin laughed.

"You two are a sorry sight," he said. "Have I interrupted something untoward?"

"Far from it," I said and was about to start to explain when Davis entered the room.

"Madam, I am most sorry. Lily is nowhere to be found. All of her possessions are gone from her room. I'm afraid she has fled."

Downstairs

xix

Alice had spent more than two hours during Lily's afternoon off in the China room, carefully dusting every piece of porcelain displayed in the built-in cabinets that lined the interior walls. When she emerged, stepping into the great hall, she wondered if Lily had returned yet from her picnic, but was almost immediately distracted from the thought by the clatter of footsteps that seemed to come simultaneously from every staircase in the house. She heard voices calling from upstairs but couldn't make out what they were saying. She went directly below stairs and popped her head into the Pug's Parlor. "What's all this commotion?" she asked the housekeeper. "It's chaos here."

"Lily has gone missing," Mrs Elliott said. "I have no doubt Lady Emily will want to speak to you about it presently. In the meantime, please continue to see to your duties. The fact that Lily has decided to shirk hers should not be felt upstairs."

"Of course, Mrs Elliott," Alice said. "I'll start with the fires and then go do the dressing rooms." Alice's heart was thumping in her chest. Something terrible must have happened with Lord Flyte. She knew it had been foolish to trust him. Gentlemen like that always wanted the same thing. Lily had told her just that, more times than Alice could count.

She closed Mrs Elliott's door but hesitated before going to the drawing room to stoke the fire. Instead, she went into the kitchen, where Cook was starting preparations for the family's dinner.

"What do you want?" Cook asked. "Can't you see we're busy here?"

"Have you heard anything about Lily?" she asked, throwing a look at Pru, who was kneading dough. "I know you have, Pru."

"We know she's gone, that's all," Cook said.

"It's not all," Pru said. "She's gone because she can't hide her guilt any longer."

"What do you mean by that?" Alice asked.

"I couldn't lie for her any longer," Pru said. "Not with Lady Emily questioning all of us again. I saw her down by the lake right before Lord Montagu was done in."

"You can't think Lily —"

"It's not my job to think," Pru said, "only to tell the truth about what I saw."

Alice did not stay to hear another word. She raced upstairs, not to the family rooms, but all the way to her own, where she found Mr Davis looking very serious indeed.

"Do you know anything about this, Alice?" Mr Davis asked.

"About Lily? About her being gone?"

"Yes."

"No." Alice felt tears in her eyes. "Is it really true?"

"She's taken everything," Mr Davis said. "Had she said anything to you?"

"No, sir, she hadn't," Alice said. "I haven't seen her since she came back from her picnic. It seems to me, Mr Davis, that something must have happened to her this afternoon."

"What are you suggesting?"

"Has anyone spoken to Lord Flyte? Or is he too grand to be capable of doing something wrong?" She was crying now. "Lily is the best girl I've ever known, and she wouldn't harm a hair on anyone's head. Can you say the same about Lord Flyte?"

"This has nothing to do with Lord Flyte, Alice. This has to do with the murder," Mr Davis said, handing her his handkerchief. "Dry your eyes. Do you have work to do?"

She nodded and sniffed.

"Best return to it. I shall take care of things here."

"She didn't do it, Mr Davis," Alice said. "You can't believe Pru."

"You've nothing to worry about on that count, Alice," he said. "We all know that we must take Prudence's word with a very serious pinch of salt. But this — Lily running off — is very grave indeed."

"It had to be due to something that happened with Lord Flyte. I'm sure of it, Mr Davis."

"I shall speak to Lady Emily about it. You, child, get back to work."

She held his handkerchief out to give back to him.

"Keep it," he said. "This is bound to be a most trying evening."

CHAPTER
TWENTY

Once we knew Lily had vanished, Anglemore descended into a state of near-chaos. Rodney shocked me by asking if I would promise to go to Matilda as soon as reasonably possible and keep her abreast of any updates so he could accompany Colin and Simon when they gathered up a search party of men from the estate and set off to find Lily. They delegated the estate men to comb the grounds while they themselves raced along the roads, stopping every coach and carriage they found. She could not have got far in this short time, so we were all hopeful that she could be located. I spoke to each of the servants again but learned very little. Simon had brought Lily in through the front door, so none of them had seen her return. Only Alice had made a plea on her friend's behalf. She was convinced, utterly and completely, that Lily would not have fled if something terrible hadn't happened between her and Simon that afternoon.

"I saw them coming back, Alice," I said. "Lily was the picture of radiant happiness."

"When she was passing your window, yes," Alice said, "but she may not have known everything then.

What if Lord Flyte threw her over just before they came back into the house?"

"I would think Lily possesses a strong enough constitution to stand up to being thrown over."

"Not if he'd compromised her, Lady Emily."

I could see Alice had been crying, and my heart went out to her. "Lord Flyte assures me nothing of the sort went on between them, and I believe him."

"You people always stick together."

Her words stunned me, and I could see they stunned her, too.

"Madam, I'm so sorry," she said, starting to cry again. "I should never have said that."

"It's all right, Alice. We are all under a considerable amount of stress. Now go see if Mrs Elliott needs you for anything. I promise I shall inform you the moment Mr Hargreaves finds Lily."

I felt at loose ends, discontent to be left useless, waiting for news, and was glad I had promised Rodney I would go to Matilda. I called for the carriage and arrived on her doorstep a short while later.

"You're calling at a rather inconvenient time, aren't you?" Matilda asked. Her voice was stern, but her face was not. "I'm only teasing. Has something happened?"

"Yes, and Rodney insisted I come to you at once so you would know. He was rather concerned about you."

She rolled her eyes. "He is concerned I won't leave him alone once he takes possession of Montagu." There wasn't much sincerity in her barb, and I was beginning to suspect her feelings for Rodney were more complicated than she let on. "Now tell me what brings you to me."

I explained to her all that had happened with Prudence and Johnny and Lily.

"Do you really think she killed Archie?" she asked.

"I didn't," I said, "until she ran off."

"It does seem to be a sign of a guilty conscience," Matilda said, "and now that I mention it, I must admit that I have one, too."

"How so?" I asked.

"I did speak to Miss Fitzgerald when she was leaving Montagu the night Archie died. I don't know what on earth possessed me to lie about it."

"What did you talk about?"

"Nothing of consequence. She seemed tense and didn't have much to say."

"Why did she lie about not having seen you that night?"

"That's why I paid her, Emily. I was afraid you would suspect we were up to something nefarious."

"So you bribed her?"

"I'm not proud of it, but I have been brought up to believe I can buy my way out of most trouble."

"Matilda, this is a disaster! Do you see how guilty this makes both of you look?"

"Of course I do. Once again, I panicked. You were asking so many questions and seemed to suspect me of something or other. I wasn't sure why Miss Fitzgerald was on my grounds that night. I hadn't invited her. She looked a shambles, all discombobulated and her eyes swollen — when I thought back on it, I wondered if she had something to do with what happened to Archie. If she did, I worried what might happen to me if it got out that I had spoken to her that night."

"Why did you tell no one you suspected her?"

"'Suspected' is an awfully strong word, Emily," she said. "I wondered what she had been doing, but had no information to justify reporting. Who would believe I had nothing to do with it if I was talking to her — a possible suspect — so soon after the evil deed?"

"This was all very badly done, Matilda."

"I am well aware of it, but I've very little experience when it comes to dealing with murder and trying to preserve one's reputation. Miss Fitzgerald was somewhat shocked by the money and agreed to take it only with the understanding that it would be used for charity work. It has proven to be money very badly spent, as it doesn't matter anymore, now that we know who killed Archie. Where do you think Lily went?"

"The men have fanned out, covering as much ground as they can," I said. "We have also contacted the railway station. As yet, she has not bought a train ticket, but there is still time for her to get on the last train to London."

"Was she on foot?"

"Yes, but I can't imagine she'll continue that way for long. I wonder — could we check to make sure nothing's missing from your stables?"

"An excellent idea."

We raced outside and questioned one of the grooms. Nothing was out of place. "Let's think this through carefully," I said. "If she is on foot, she can't have made it very far. It's miles to the railway station in Melton Carbury from Anglemore and farther still in the other direction to the next village. She could not have reached any of those places on foot in so short a time, and she would know it to be impossible. She could be hiding somewhere nearby, biding her time."

"Which makes it more likely the men will find her."

"Unless she has managed to persuade someone passing to give her a lift." I frowned. "Her family are in Wales. I have already wired them and asked that they contact us at once if they hear from her. What would you do if you were in her situation?"

"I would never be in her situation," Matilda said.

"That's hardly helpful."

"You can't expect me to know what it would be like to be a maid."

"Alice is her closest friend, and I do believe she has no idea where Lily's gone. Lily must feel so alone, and after such a heady day, when it seemed as if everything was right with the world."

"So you don't believe she tore up the book?"

"I don't know what to think," I said. "Do you have paper? I need to organize my thoughts." Matilda motioned towards a writing table. I sat down and took out two pieces of paper, labeling one "hates simon" and the other "loves simon".

"That's a bit coarse, don't you think?" Matilda asked.

"Undoubtedly," I said, "but I do not want to waste time coming up with something cleverer. Now, if Lily did destroy the book, she may bear a serious grudge against those whose positions in society are above hers. She may have flirted with Archibald, led him to the ruined abbey, and murdered him."

"And if she loves Simon?"

"Then she came home, found herself on the verge of being accused of murder, and, terrified, ran away. Where would she go?" I tapped the pen on the table. "Simon. If she trusts Simon and cares about him and believes that he cares for her, wouldn't she seek his help?"

"She didn't speak to him before she left, did she?"

"No, he had no idea she was going."

"If I were Lily, I'd be inclined to go to Simon's estate and find somewhere there to hide," I said.

"How would she get there? She couldn't possibly walk all the way to Yorkshire."

"No, and she couldn't get a train going in that direction until tomorrow. I don't think she's left Anglemore. At least, not the grounds."

"Then the men will find her," Matilda said.

"No, I don't think they will. Want to come with me?"

"Absolutely."

When the carriage turned into Anglemore, beneath the gate with ELEUTHERIA — ancient Greek for "freedom" — carved into the stone at its top, I asked the driver to take us not to the house, but to the path that led to the ruins of the abbey. I knew Colin would have had someone search there, but I wanted to do it again myself. Sure enough, two of the gardeners were leaving as we arrived.

"She's not here," they called to us. "We've looked everywhere."

"I don't doubt you, but there is one place in particular I want to check." They accompanied us, holding their torches to light our way. It wasn't yet dark, but the moon had waned after its spectacular showing the night of the murder, and the shadows of twilight were already long. The sun would disappear altogether soon. We picked our way through the rugged stones of the ruins, until we came to a stone spiral staircase that rose up to meet a floor no longer above us. I started to climb it, and the gardeners balked.

"Madam, I don't think that's safe, and it don't go anywhere. She can't be up there."

"Don't worry," I said. "The steps are quite sound. I've been up here before." I was careful, holding one of the torches myself, my other hand balancing on the wall to my left. Halfway up there was a narrow outlet, just large enough for a lady to fit into. I had discovered it during one of my early explorations of the ruins. Because the floor above was missing and the walls rose to varying heights, the space, which was little more than a platform, provided a charming view and a place to sit. I sometimes read there when the weather was fine. In the dark, no one looking up from the ground would notice someone there. I brandished my torch, fully expecting to see Lily.

She was not there.

Deflated, I went back down. "No luck," I said. "There must be something, though. Something to tell us where she would hide."

330

"Most likely she jumped on the first wagon that went by and is miles away already," Matilda said.

"I don't think so," I said. "She would be putting herself at the mercy of a strange man, and that is not like Lily. She's more cautious than that."

"Caution goes out the window when one is trying to avoid being hanged for murder," Matilda said.

"Let's go back to the house," I said. "I thought I was onto something, but I was wrong."

Cook sent up a cold dinner for us, and Matilda and I picked at it while I tried to come up with something productive to do. I did not trust Prudence, but doubted I could get her to tell me anything more than she already had. If she disliked Lily as much as Davis and Alice suspected, she could have taken Simon's book. She might have torn it up and only then returned it to Lily's drawer. Of course, I had no proof other than Lily's word that the book had been stolen. One would think she would have reported the theft to the housekeeper. Unless there hadn't been one.

Still, something was nagging me about Prudence. I recalled Simon having told me that she had made overtures to him. His ensuing friendship with Lily was ample ground for Prudence to be jealous.

"I have an idea," I said. "Come upstairs with me?"

Matilda and I climbed to the servants' quarters. Prudence shared a room with one of the other kitchen maids, and so far as I could tell, they weren't particularly friendly to each other. Cook was constantly telling them to stop bickering, and Mrs Elliott had informed me that none of the other girls in the house was close to Prudence.

Their room was on the opposite end of the corridor from Lily's and Alice's. I'd done it up in sage green, and the view out the window stretched over the gardens. It was a pleasant space. Prudence's clothes weren't quite so neatly folded as Lily's, but her Sunday shoes were polished like a soldier's boots. She had a stack of letters from her mother and a collection of newspaper clippings of pictures of the Prince of Wales. There was nothing else.

I went through everything one more time, including the pockets of her spare apron and her coat, and then back to the dresser drawers, scrutinizing everything. This time, I noticed the paper lining in the third drawer of her dresser was pulled away just a bit in the back. I removed the clothes to the bed and tugged at the paper. Underneath it was Simon's watercolor, which, I had been led to believe, was supposed to have been sent out to be framed.

I turned to Matilda. "Lily did not kill Archibald."

We descended to the kitchen, where I grabbed Prudence and brought her into Mrs Elliott's sitting room. The housekeeper must have known at once something was seriously wrong. She closed the door, crossed her arms, and shook her head at Prudence.

"What have you done now, girl?" she asked.

"I've done nothing but tell the truth," Prudence said.

"That is not quite honest, Prudence," I said. I showed her the watercolor. "Would you care to explain to me how this came to be in your possession?"

The girl's face crumpled. "I was wrong to take it, Lady Emily, I admit that. But it was so beautiful, you see, and I knew I would never have something like it of my own. Lily was lording it over everyone, bragging about how Lord Flyte would do anything for her. She left it on the table in the servants' hall, and I was looking at it there, so lovely, and I just couldn't help it. One of the estate men came to collect it, but I told him Lily had decided she didn't want it framed anymore. I rolled it up and took it to my room."

"You did not remove it from Lily's room?" I asked.

"No, madam, that's God's own truth."

"Mrs Elliott, did Lily tell you the painting was missing?"

"No, Lady Emily, she did not."

"And she did not report her book as missing either?"

"No, as I told you before, she never mentioned receiving it, let alone having lost it."

"Why did Lily leave the painting on the table?" Matilda asked. "I should have thought she'd take better care of it."

"Like I said, she wanted us all to see it so that we'd think she was something more than she is. She doesn't know her place."

"I thought you said someone came to frame it," I said. "Surely that is why Lily had left it on the table. Did you take Lily's book, Prudence?"

"I am not a thief."

"Prudence, if you are lying, you will be in a great deal of trouble," I said.

"I'm telling the truth, madam. I am."

I did not believe her. Matilda and I loitered in the corridor near the servants' hall, below the long row of bells neatly labeled with the names of the rooms upstairs, speaking quietly.

"Prudence was very jealous of Lily," I said.

"That much is evident," Matilda said, "but do you think she killed Archie?"

"I think she may have," I said. "She made advances on Simon, and heaven knows what might have happened if she had tried the same thing on Archibald in the abbey. I am going to ask Davis to keep an eye on her and make sure she does not leave the house. I want to speak to the groom who claimed to be with her the night of the murder."

We went out the back door and crossed to the stables. Most of the grooms had gone with Colin to search for Lily, but Johnny remained, in his room above the horse stalls. I rapped on the door and opened it without waiting to be invited. Johnny leapt to his feet at the sight of me.

"Lady Emily, do you need your horse?"

"No, Johnny, I've come for a little chat," I said. "Prudence stole something of Lily's. Did you know this?"

"Madam, I —"

"You must be honest, Johnny."

"I didn't know she was going to tear it to shreds," he said.

"The book? Prudence took the book?" I asked.

"I told her she should take it. Thought it would be a good joke. Lily was getting so high and mighty, what

334

with her attentions from Lord Flyte. Didn't think it would do any harm. I thought Pru would give it back."

"Prudence took the book," I repeated. Things were becoming much more clear to me. "And she also took the painting."

"I don't know nothing about a painting, madam," Johnny said, "and I promise you I didn't have nothing to do with any of it. I don't go in the house except to eat, you know."

"Did she tell you about the book?"

"She showed it to me," he said. "We hid it under a bale of hay overnight. She was supposed to return it the next day, but Lily hadn't told anyone it was missing, so we weren't sure if she had noticed yet and decided to wait on the returning part of the plan."

"When did she tear it up?"

"Well, you see, madam, she got right scared when you all started asking questions about the murder again, and she was afraid of what would happen if you found out she had taken the book. She came out here after you talked to her in the library. I didn't see her rip the pages. She must have done that upstairs."

"What did she say to you when she came to get it?"

He looked at his boots.

"Johnny, this is extremely important."

"She asked me to help her, madam," he said, "and I did. We didn't go walking the night of the murder. I hadn't taken up with her until after that. I'd been sweet on Alice, you see, but then Pru, well, she came to me and . . . well, madam, I shouldn't say any more."

"I believe we have already discussed the need for you to eliminate those activities from your repertoire," I said. "Why did you tell me you were with Prudence?"

"Like I said, she was afraid. She had been out walking, and she saw Lily, but she knew that if no one else had seen her, Lily might get away with her crime and come after Pru."

"So she asked you to corroborate her story?"

"Yes, madam," he said.

"That was a very terrible, very damaging lie, Johnny."

"I'm sorry, madam."

"Had Prudence other sweethearts before you?" I asked.

"No, madam, just me. She was always setting her sights high, you see. She had a cousin who wound up with a nice settlement after having the baby of her employer's son. I told her it was daft to try to do the same, that things didn't usually work out like that, that her cousin had been lucky. Eventually she started to believe me, I guess, because she started coming around the stables more and more to talk to me."

"After the murder?"

"Yes, madam."

"That's all for now, Johnny," I said. "I want you to go to the house and see Mr Davis. He'll know why I've sent you."

"I suppose I should gather up my things." There was a distinct sound of regret in his voice.

"I am not sending you away, Johnny," I said. "I shall decide what to do about this incident later. For now I need to make sure you do not leave the house."

336

We marched him to the house and deposited him with Davis, who was less than amused to hear Johnny's story. I left them to it and went to see Cook.

"Lady Emily, I'm at my wits' end with the comings and goings in my kitchen," she said. "I need a calm space in which to work if I am to uphold this house's reputation as the greatest culinary center in the country."

This stopped me in my tracks. When had Cook started talking like this? There was no time to inquire now. "I assure you everything will improve as soon as we have settled our investigation. I need to know something of critical importance now, however. Did you have occasion to send Prudence to Montagu Manor in the days before the murder?"

"I did, madam. Lady Matilda's cook was running into a host of problems, what with three of her girls down with the influenza. I told her I could spare Pru during the two mornings before Lady Matilda's party."

Prudence could have met Archibald when she was at Montagu. Given what we knew of his proclivity for other people's servants, he could have seen her, taken a fancy to her, and set up a rendezvous in the ruined abbey.

I turned to Matilda. "We need to find Lily at once."

"If Prudence is the guilty party, why are you so worried about Lily?"

"Can you imagine her frame of mind? I'm afraid she may do harm to herself."

Downstairs

XX

Pru had to actually bite her tongue, bite it until it bled, to keep from laughing when everyone started frantically looking for Lily. It had been disgracefully easy to set a trap for her, Pru thought, and it was just what Lily deserved. What a delight to see that, sometimes, justice could so easily be served, even if it did require a little manipulation here and there. Pru was pleased as punch, like those puppets she had seen once at Covent Garden in London when her mother had taken the children before she got sick. Things had turned bad for her family shortly after that trip, but Pru didn't want to think about that now. Now everything was going her way.

At least it had been until Mr Davis marched into the kitchen and took her firmly by the arm and all but dragged her into his room next to the Pug's Parlor. She had been waiting there for what seemed like an eternity. He hadn't said more than six words to her — five, now that she thought about it, *Do not leave this room* — and then had left her all alone. He had closed the door behind him when he went, and she had heard the lock click, but now there was a great deal of commotion in the corridor. She even thought she heard Lady Emily's voice. Something had happened. Something bad, and she was in a right heap of trouble, that was for sure.

She looked out the window and then really started to worry. Johnny had better keep his rotten mouth shut. Tears smarted in her eyes, and she brushed them away, angry, with the back of her hand. She didn't deserve any of this. She hadn't even wanted to leave her family and had begged her mother to find her a position closer to home, but there was nothing else to be done, not with her mother sick, her father dead, and only two of her siblings old enough to work. Her mother wrote to her every week, but Pru couldn't read the letters. She'd never learned. Once a month on her day off she took them to the smithy's in the village. His daughter would read them to her and take down her reply.

She had never let on how lonely she was. Not to her mother. That would have caused her to worry, and the doctor had said worrying would only make the consumption worse. So she had the smithy's daughter write that she had lots of friends, that she was popular among the staff, and that the girl she shared her room with could read and write and helped her with her letters. It was a small lie, Pru thought, one that didn't hurt nobody. It saved her mother a heap of concern. She had enough of that at home, specially since Pru's brother had been chucked out of Her Majesty's Army.

The sounds coming through the door were becoming more frantic. She heard rushed footsteps in the corridor and banging doors. Ordinarily, banged doors were not tolerated. Then there was a clatter at the door. Mr Davis opened it, his face grim. He was holding Johnny, who looked quite a lot like death, by the collar. Mrs Elliott was right behind them, her sourpuss face worse then ever. Pru knew she was in for it.

"I want to talk to you, Prudence," Mr Davis said. "Johnny is going to join us."

CHAPTER
TWENTY-ONE

Davis had Prudence well in hand. She would not be able to flee as Lily had, and I had absolute confidence he could keep both the kitchen maid and Johnny secure until I was ready to deal with them. Matilda and I went upstairs in a flurry, but I stopped in the great hall and leaned against the wall, my nerves strung tight. "Where could Lily have gone?"

"Could Prudence have done something to her?" Matilda asked.

"She was in the kitchen when Lily left, and hasn't gone out since. I think Lily left of her own volition, but if she was afraid of Prudence — perhaps because she has some evidence against her — she may be trying to protect herself, which is a very different state than running from a murder charge."

"But wouldn't she have come forward with evidence of that sort?"

"Not if Prudence had some means of making her think that would be a dangerous choice." I rubbed my temples and considered everything I knew about Lily. Then, all at once, it came to me.

"Lily is a Roman Catholic," I said.

"Is this relevant?" Matilda asked.

"Very much so. Come." We flew to the stables and asked for a carriage. "She is quite discreet about her faith. Doesn't discuss it much and keeps it to herself. She goes to church in our chapel at Anglemore most of the time, but asks permission once a month to be driven to the nearest Catholic church to hear mass."

"Of course! She's sought sanctuary in the church," Matilda said.

"Not quite," I said. "Champneys, the Nevinsons' estate, is barely a mile from the train station. More importantly, it was owned by Catholic sympathizers during Elizabeth's reign." I ordered the driver to take us to the house.

"Are the Nevinsons Catholic?"

"No, I don't believe so," I said, "but there is a perfect place in the house for her to hide, unnoticed, until she can slip out tomorrow and get to the train. That would be safer than trying to go tonight, when she would know Prudence would be sure to be looking for her."

Champneys loomed above us, a baroque monstrosity. The butler seemed confused at finding us unexpectedly on his master's doorstep, and asked us to wait in the hall while he informed Mr Nevinson of our arrival. A few minutes later, he led us into an oak-paneled library, where the master of the house greeted us.

"Lady Emily," he said. "This is a delightful surprise. You are very wicked to call without warning me. Mrs Nevinson has already gone up to bed, and she will be so disappointed to have missed you." Mr Nevinson was ninety-seven if he was a day, and his wife couldn't have been much younger. They had been a fixture in the

342

neighborhood since they purchased Champneys sixty-odd years ago when its previous owner, a baron of low character who was both financially and morally bankrupt, sold it to keep his gambling habit afloat.

"You must beg her forgiveness for me," I said. "I've come on a matter of urgent business. You know, of course, about the murder of the Marquess of Montagu?"

"Oh yes, quite a dirty business, that," he said.

"I have reason to believe one of the people important to the case is hiding in your house."

"I say! You don't think Mrs Nevinson has murderous tendencies?" He gave me a pat on the arm and grinned.

"Far from it. It is not someone from your family or household."

"We've had no visitors for many weeks, Lady Emily. I think you must be mistaken."

"It is one of my maids, Mr Nevinson. She's not a suspect, but we believe she may have information critical to solving the crime."

He rang for the butler, who confirmed that no one had entered the house that evening.

"She would have been very careful not to be seen," I said. "Would it trouble you for me to look for her? I have a fair idea where she would have gone."

"This is quite more excitement than I am accustomed to. Lead on, dear lady. I shall accompany you, and do anything necessary to protect you from this murderous miscreant."

I looped my arm through his, and we stepped into the corridor. "Will you take us to the priest hole?"

"Blimey, that is of course where you would hide in Champneys, wouldn't you?"

We made our way through corridors and room after room and up stairs until we reached a chamber in the back of the house on the second floor. Red silk hung from its walls, and white pilasters stood in each corner.

"Now then," Mr Nevinson said, "I just have to remember which of these it is." He pulled at one of the pilasters, then shook his head and went to the one opposite. "Here we go." It opened like a door, revealing a small room behind. There, crouched in the corner weeping, was Lily, clutching the small bundle of her possessions.

I stepped through the opening in the wall and went to her, kneeling at her side, and took her gently in my arms. "It's all right, Lily," I said. "You must tell me everything that happened."

"Are the police here yet?"

"No, Lily, we haven't sent for them."

"I can't face it, madam, I can't face what I did."

"Lily, we know about Prudence," I said. "It's going to be all right. We know she destroyed your book and that she took your painting."

"None of that matters, Lady Emily," Lily said, trembling out of control. "I killed him, madam. I killed Lord Montagu, and God will never be able to forgive me."

Mr Nevinson offered us tea, exclaiming he'd never before had occasion to entertain a murderess. I thanked him but offered our regrets. I wanted to get Lily back to

344

Anglemore. Once home, I installed her in the library, sent Matilda to the white drawing room, rang for tea, and asked Lily to tell me exactly what had happened the night of the murder. It took half an hour to get her calm enough to speak. Eventually I called for a glass of brandy, hoping it would steady her nerves. Either it did, or enough time had passed that she was again in control of her senses.

"Please don't accuse Pru of anything worse than she did," Lily said. "We've never got along, and probably never would have, but she's guilty of nothing like my sins."

"Tell me what happened, Lily."

"I should never have gone out that night," she said, "but the moon was so beautiful, and I'd finished up with most of my work. I still needed to do your dressing room, but I knew you'd be up late as I'd heard you arguing with Lady Bromley before dinner. Forgive me, madam, but I've noticed that whenever she upsets you, you stay downstairs until at least midnight. I thought I had time, you see, and I went for a little walk."

"To look at the moon?" I asked.

"Yes," she said. "I didn't want to go too far, but was so taken with it that I kept on walking, on and on, as if I would perhaps reach it. The moon, that is." She drew her eyebrows close together. "Eventually I came to the old abbey and it was the most wonderful thing I'd ever seen. The moon so bright, reflected in the lake and on the crumbling stone walls. I stood there for a little while, and then I realized I wasn't alone. I smelled cigar smoke."

"Did you see anyone?"

"Not at first," she said, "but I thought it would be best to go back to the house. I didn't know who was out there, but I figured it must be a gentleman, given the cigar, and I knew it wouldn't be a good idea to be outside alone with whomever it was. So I turned around and had only taken two or three steps when he grabbed me from behind and pulled me tight against him."

"Who was it, Lily?"

"It was Lord Montagu," she said, the tears flowing again. "He said I looked like I wanted a kiss and I told him I didn't and to please let me go, but he wouldn't. I tried to squirm loose, but I couldn't get away, and it only seemed to amuse him. He said he likes girls with spirit."

"Horrible man."

"He took me real firm then, dragged me into the old abbey, and threw me down on the ground just in front of the ruins of the altar. That made him laugh."

"I am so sorry, Lily," I said.

"I was desperate, madam, desperate," she said. "He was coming towards me again, and I reached around for the first thing I could find to defend myself. I could just get my hands on that piece of stone, and he was back, pushing himself on me. I kicked him as hard as I could and whacked him over the head. I never meant to kill him, I just wanted him to stop. If I had known he would die, I would have just let him do what he wanted."

My heart broke for the girl. "What happened then?"

346

"I was so scared I could hardly think. I went back to the house to finish my work, but my dress was all dusty and torn in one place, so I had to go change my uniform before getting to your dressing room, madam. That's why I was late in finishing."

"Why didn't you tell anyone what happened?"

"Who would've believed me?" She was sobbing now. "I didn't know he was dead. All I could think was that he'd never admit what he tried to do, and that no one would take my word over his. I'm just a maid, madam."

"I would have believed you, Lily."

"When he came into the house, madam, I just about died myself. I knew then God would never forgive me. It was a sign, him dying here."

"It was the nearest place he could go," I said. "There was nothing more to it than that."

"Then I thought maybe I should tell you, but Lord Flyte was so sweet, and I wanted to believe that he really did like talking to me just because he liked me, not because he likes his girls with spirit, if you get my meaning. I thought if he knew what had happened, he wouldn't speak to me again. Not that he will now, anyway."

"But you had to know someone would eventually be blamed for the murder?"

"I could never have stood by and let someone else take the blame for what I did. I can't imagine anything worse than allowing an innocent person to suffer for my hideous misdeed. I know what I've done is unforgivable. I've had nightmares about it ever since. I suppose I just hoped that in the end no one else would be put in harm's way, that the police would decide it was an unsolvable case. They never caught Jack the Ripper, did they? Still, I have behaved disgracefully. I've caused so many problems and made so many people upset. I am more sorry than I will ever be able to say."

"What you did after you returned to the house was very, very bad," I said, "but no one could fault you for what happened at the abbey. You were defending yourself."

"It doesn't matter," she said. "I'm going to hang."

"I will not stand for any histrionics, Lily," I said. "Mr Hargreaves will know what to do."

"I can't accept any help from him."

"I said no histrionics, Lily. Tell me, why did you say you saw someone coming towards the servants' entrance after the murder?"

"I was trying to give myself an alibi," she said, "and I thought by saying it was a man, it would throw suspicion away from me. I know it was a terrible thing to do, but Pru said she saw someone, so I thought I'd just go along with her. It seemed like less of a lie because of that."

There was a sharp knock at the door, and Colin stepped inside. "Davis rode out himself to find me. He's a fine horseman."

"Davis is full of surprises," I said. "I think you should sit down. Lily has quite a story for you."

She managed to get through it without tears this time, and I quite admired her bravery. It was not an easy thing to tell, especially to a gentleman one knew one would have to face again and again. Colin sat

348

across from her, leaning forward, his arms casually crossed, and didn't take his eyes off her for an instant while she talked.

"Why did you run away?" Colin asked. "Why now?"

"I changed back into my uniform after the picnic, and was heading downstairs when Pru came bounding up to me. She told me new evidence had been found and that the police knew who the murderer was. I already thought she suspected me — that's why she was so vicious about Simon, I mean, about Lord Flyte — and I panicked. I couldn't bear to face him, not after that wonderful day, and let him know the awful thing I had done."

"You should have told us at once, Lily," Colin said. "Your case will be much more difficult to defend because you did not. Have you washed and mended the dress you were wearing that night?"

"Yes, sir."

"That's very bad. Did you have any marks or bruises after the altercation with Montagu?"

"I was quite bruised up."

"Are any of the bruises still there?"

"Just one, on my hip, from when he threw me on the ground."

"Emily, send for the doctor immediately. I want him to document the bruise."

I rang the bell and did as he asked. Before long, the doctor had arrived and examined Lily, with me standing by as witness. He wrote up a report at once and told us he was prepared to testify as to what he had seen. Unfortunately, though, he could not make any strong statements about how Lily had got the bruise. He, too, scolded her for not having come forward sooner, but there was an edge in his voice that suggested his opinion of her was lower for what she had suffered.

"Do you think there is any hope for her?" I asked Colin when we were alone again.

"It is going to be very difficult," he said.

"I have an idea. How willing are you to exploit your reputation as an agent of the highest discretion who is particularly skilled in matters concerning the reputations of the aristocracy?"

"My dear, do you not know me at all? I am extraordinarily willing. Tell me your wicked plan."

Downstairs

XXI

Mr Davis's room was set up as a comfortable space to read or smoke or drink or whatever it was men did when they were finished with work. Pru had never spent much time in it, as it would not have been appropriate for the butler to entertain a kitchen maid. Sometimes she heard him and Mrs Elliott having a laugh over a cuppa tea in there, but that was different. Mrs Elliott was the housekeeper. Pru had always thought it was a large room, far bigger than any one person really ought to need all for himself, but then, she would remind herself, every room above stairs would have dwarfed the butler's space. Some people, she thought, were bent on always having more than they deserved.

Now, however, as Mr Davis, Mrs Elliott, and Johnny came into the room, where she had spent heaven knows how long locked in, the place felt cramped and overcrowded. It wasn't the people so much as the anger filling the air. Pru looked at Johnny, who looked away from her, and she felt tears smart in her eyes. He had ratted her out, the ungrateful louse. That was the only explanation, and Pru hated herself for having ever trusted him. She should have known better. She wished she could fling herself to the ground and have a good cry, but that wouldn't get her anywhere. Her life was ruined now, and that wretched Lily was going to come out on top, bright as sunshine, getting everything Pru had ever wanted. Lily didn't deserve a bit of it.

Mr Davis looked at Pru and then at Johnny, his lined face stern and foreboding. "You are both incredibly fortunate to work for such a generous and understanding family as the Hargreaveses," he said. "Johnny, you have lied and revealed yourself to be someone who cannot be trusted. However, the head groom tells us your work is good and has offered to keep a close eye on you. You will not lose your position, but for the next six months will have no days off, and should you show even the slightest hint of misbehavior — you take my meaning — or slacking off you will be gone without a character."

"Thank you, sir," Johnny said. "That is more than I could have ever expected."

"That's quite right," Mr Davis said. "Furthermore, Mr Hargreaves himself is going to be checking up on you and will meet with you once a week when he is in residence to make sure you are not going off the rails."

"Thank you, sir." Johnny had never looked so humble.

"He believes you should have a second chance instead of being flung out with no hope of going anywhere but to the streets. I do hope you do not squander this opportunity."

"I won't, Mr Davis, sir. I promise."

"As for you, Prudence." Pru tried not to squirm as he turned to her. "Your offenses are far more grave than Johnny's. You cannot retain your position in this house. However, Lady Emily has decided to sponsor you at a school for girls of your station, where you will receive an education that she hopes you will put to good use. You will also be taught needlework, a skill that will broaden the scope of jobs for which you may be qualified. She said to tell you it is nearer to your mother."

"Sir! I don't deserve it," Pru said.

"No, you do not, but Lady Emily feels strongly that you will never learn to do good until someone has first done it to you."

Pru didn't know what to say, and she couldn't keep herself from crying any longer. She sobbed, great, wet, heaving sobs.

"Stop that at once," Mrs Elliott said. "Go upstairs and pack your things, you useless girl. You will be leaving before breakfast in the morning."

"I must thank Lady Emily," Pru said.

"She would like you to write her when you have learned to do so," Mr Davis said. "In the meantime she is far too busy to be troubled with you any further."

"Yes, sir," Pru said. "Please do tell her I'm grateful and that I won't let her down. Not again, that is." She gave Johnny a long look, realizing she'd never see him anymore, and went upstairs, wondering how she would explain this news to her mother. She couldn't tell her the truth, not the whole truth anyway. Not the part about how she'd lied. She'd tell her she'd been Lady Emily's favorite and that she'd been treated almost like one of the family and that . . . no. Pru's heart sank. What if her mother wrote to Lady Emily? She'd be caught in even more lies, and Lady Emily wouldn't forgive her again. The truth would have to do.

CHAPTER
TWENTY-TWO

Colin and I spent the bulk of the night setting our plan into motion. Once the search for Fanny Gifford in France had ended, he had redirected his efforts and focused instead on marriage records. That afternoon, with the help of Scotland Yard, he had at last found her, tracking her through a marriage license issued at Gretna Green. Once he knew the name of her groom, she had been easy enough to find in Richmond, where her new husband practiced law.

"Mr Gifford will be pleased about that," I said, "but furious that his sister let him worry for so long."

"She knew he would be angry at the elopement, especially after what had happened with Archibald Scolfield," Colin said. "She decided — against the advice of her husband, I might add — to wait until they had been married a month to send word to her brother. Apparently she felt that was long enough to convince him the marriage was real."

"Was there ever any doubt that it was?"

"No. Her husband should have taken the matter more firmly in hand."

"I did not expect things to have turned out so well for her."

"Nor did I," Colin said. "Apparently she did meet her husband at one of Mrs Chelmsford's dreadful dances. He tried to call on her thereafter, but wasn't allowed."

"Mrs Chelmsford would not have wanted anyone coming in without having given enough notice for her to make the school look less horrendous than normal."

"He thought it rather odd, so he started writing to Miss Gifford. They fell in love, and he proposed, still via letter. He was horrified by what she had told him about the school and arranged to spirit her away in the night. He seems a most decent man. I think she will be happy."

"My ownership of the school becomes official next week. Mrs Chelmsford will be let go the moment the papers are signed. I am very much looking forward to it," I said. "The solicitors have found a building for us, an estate near Hampstead that has fallen into a bit of disrepair — the family ran out of money. We can get it for a good price, and have it ready for the girls by the spring."

"What about a head teacher?"

"Already taken care of," I said. "I've been reading letters of application almost since the day I first met Mrs Chelmsford. The solicitors have been a great help, as has your mother. She had a host of useful suggestions. Now, what about the rest of our plan?"

"The former Miss Gifford will meet us in London tomorrow. Have you heard back from Mrs Tindall and Mr Porter?"

"Yes, they both sent wires in reply to ours. We can count on them. Miss Fitzgerald will travel down with us."

"Very good," Colin said. "This is taking shape nicely. So nicely, in fact, that I believe we need not think about it anymore tonight. It has been a rather trying day, though, don't you think?"

"Quite," I said, thrilling at the way his eyes danced when he asked the question.

"So trying that I find myself in dire need of distraction. Can you think of anything that might work to put the events of the day out of my head? If not, I don't see how I shall be able to sleep for even a moment, and I do need to be sharp in the morning."

"I see," I said. "So if I can't distract you, I would be putting at risk everything we are trying to accomplish?"

"Precisely." He pulled me out of my chair, drew me close to him, and kissed the back of my neck, sending delicious shivers through my entire body.

"It sounds almost as important as Crown business," I said.

"Quite possibly even more important."

I turned and kissed him, very slowly and very deliberately, and then took him by the hand. "Come upstairs, my dear, as I am most concerned. You look in dire need of immediate assistance. For the sake of the Crown, of course."

The next morning, almost before the sun had come up, we went to London by special train, coaching Miss Fitzgerald during the trip. Lily was with us as well, but she sat in a separate compartment with Davis. When we arrived at Park Lane, Davis and Lily went downstairs, while Colin and I went into the library, where Mr Porter and Mrs Tindall were already waiting. We spent over an hour explaining to them what was going to happen and having them practice their testimony so that it would go smoothly when it counted. Soon thereafter, Miss Gifford — now Mrs Ross — and her new husband joined us. We took the two of them aside, into Colin's study, to speak with them privately, wanting to be certain of the precise narrative of their story before continuing. Every detail needed to be right. We were fortunate to be in a circumstance where the truth was all we needed, but clarity was essential to achieve our goal. To ensure that, we wanted our guests — our witnesses — to feel at ease and well prepared.

At one o'clock, Davis brought in Sir James, a gentleman I had never met, but had heard mentioned more times than I could count. So far as I had been able to tell, he was Colin's contact, if that is the right word, when it came to matters that concerned the Palace. Sir James reached out to him when the Crown needed his assistance, and Colin reported back to Sir James. I had, on more than one occasion, suggested that my husband invite his colleague to dinner, but Colin had always refused, saying they preferred not to be linked together unless absolutely necessary. The fact that Sir James was now in our house was indicative of the serious nature of the circumstance before us. He and Colin shook hands, exchanged a few quiet words, and sat down across from our assembled guests.

"You understand how difficult this all is," Colin said. "The Scolfields have suffered a terrible loss, and while of course we all want justice, in this case the publicity that would stem from a public trial would only serve to hurt the family more. As a result, we thought it best to give you a taste of the testimony in private, before you decide how to handle the remainder of this extremely delicate situation. I know we all want to avoid scandal. This is a situation that requires an extraordinary amount of discretion."

"Proceed," Sir James said.

"Mrs Ross, I should like to start with you," Colin said. "Would you please relate to us all that happened between yourself and Mr Archibald Scolfield?"

Mrs Ross shot a pained look at her husband, who nodded to her and squeezed her hand. "I was living near Munich, you see, where my brother runs an inn. We moved there shortly after our parents died. I met Mr Scolfield — he told me to call him Archie — when he and that gentleman" — she pointed at Mr Porter — "were guests in the inn. They stayed with us for quite a while, though I can't tell you the precise number of days. During that time, Mr Scolfield struck up a friendship with me. He told me he was so pleased to see an English rose after having spent so much time on the Continent. I'd never before had a gentleman pay that sort of attention to me, you see. I wouldn't have expected one to." She hesitated and looked at her husband, who squeezed her hand and nodded as if to reassure her. She took a deep breath before continuing. "The long and short of it, Sir James, is that Mr

Scolfield seduced me and used me in a most notorious manner before throwing me over and refusing to have anything further to do with me. It was the worst thing that could ever happen to a young lady."

"I appreciate how difficult this is for you to discuss, Mrs Ross," Sir James said, "but I am afraid I am going to need a few more details. Would you step over here with me? A bit of privacy may make things easier for you." He took her across the room, where no one else would be able to hear what she said, and kept her there for more than half an hour. When she returned to us, we could all see the signs of upset on her stony, pale face. She pressed a handkerchief to her eyes, her cheeks were bright red, and her hands were shaking.

"Mrs Tindall, we will hear from you next," Colin said.

"I, Sir James, am mortified that I ever let Mr Scolfield into my inn. I run a very respectable establishment, you see, and never thought a member of one of our nation's great families would do such evil to a poor maid." She told, in riveting if overdramatic detail, of the seduction and ruin of her employee. When she had finished, Mr Porter spoke, detailing his experience at Oxford and the subsequent falling-out with the man he had considered his closest friend. Then Miss Fitzgerald reported her experience of the decidedly ungentlemanly behavior of Archibald Scolfield. Through it all, Sir James revealed not an iota of emotion. He was the picture of an impartial judge. He was respectful and considerate — he pulled Miss Fitzgerald to the side when he required additional

360

details from her — but gave no indication of what his verdict, if we could call it that, would be. When everyone had finished, an uncomfortable hush fell over the room. I rose from my seat.

"Thank you all for agreeing to come to us today. I know how difficult it is to discuss such private and painful things. Your candor is much appreciated. I do hope this scene does not have to be reproduced in public."

They all dispersed quietly, and we were alone with Sir James.

"It is time you spoke to the girl herself," Colin said. "Come with me."

I had wanted to accompany them, and had argued about it the night before with my husband, but in the end had to agree to whatever would produce the best result for Lily. Much as I wanted to provide her with emotional support during what would be a difficult interview, it was more important that Sir James felt everything had been conducted in the proper way. So I waited for more than three-quarters of an hour while the gentlemen spoke with Lily and Davis below stairs.

It was juvenile, I suppose, but I sat on a chair I had pulled near to the top of the servants' stairs in the great hall. I knew I wouldn't be able to hear the conversation, but I would be aware the instant their boots hit the steps, signaling that they were finished. Once it was evident they were coming, I scrambled to return the chair to its normal location and ducked back into the library. I heard their voices, muffled by the door, then I heard more footsteps, and then I heard the front door of the house open and close. I peeked out the window to see Sir James making his way down Park Lane.

"Devious girl," Colin said, entering the room. "Spying on us, were you?"

"Of course I was," I said. "It was beastly to be left out of the final bits. What happened?"

"Sir James feels strongly that no good could come from smearing the Marquess of Montagu's good name after his terrible death. After hearing how Archibald had behaved with so many other girls, he had no difficulty believing Lily's testimony of what happened before the murder. He agrees she is not guilty by reason of self-defense, and, in the circumstances, the Crown will not file charges against her."

I let out an enormous sigh. "That is a much-welcome relief."

"Indeed."

"You seem less pleased than I," I said.

"Not at all. I'm more pleased than you can imagine to have been able to twist the special favors granted to the upper class to get justice for Lily."

"Yet it still troubles you that there are people who get any special favors?"

"It would trouble me more if I didn't know how to manipulate the system to the benefit of justice," he said. "Right now, however, I want to get back to Anglemore. I need to speak to Flyte."

We left, almost at once, on another special train, this time traveling in the same compartment as Lily and Davis. Three of us were jubilant, but Lily's spirits were low.

"It doesn't feel right," she said. "I killed a man and I'm not being punished."

"Lily, you killed a man to save yourself," Colin said. "That is a very different thing from murder in cold blood."

"I still killed him." She screwed her eyes shut and clenched her fists. "I took a life and will never be able to forgive myself."

"God will forgive you," Davis said, his voice all business. "No doubt he already has. One can only imagine a deity has far more nefarious things with which to concern himself. Now, I cannot have you distracting yourself from your work with this, Lily. The State Rooms need a complete cleaning, and I cannot trust anyone else with the details of that but you. The woodwork is a diabolical mess after one of the footmen tried to polish it. You know how intricate the carving is. It requires an expert hand to keep it in tip-top shape. You will come to Mrs Elliott in the morning and discuss what can be done to improve the condition of the woodwork in the King's Bedroom."

I smiled. Davis was a wise man, knowing exactly how to pull Lily out of a descending spiral of guilt and self-hatred: good, honest work. "Dreadful King never did come to the house, did he?" I asked.

"So much the better for us," Colin said. "Fond as I am of Anglemore, I am not sure I could live happily in any house where Henry VIII had tarried. No, I much prefer things as they are."

"The perfect situation," I said. "Close enough to royalty to need State Rooms in case of a visit, but not so close to have to suffer through the visit itself."

"Precisely," he said, clasping my hand.

"I am afraid, however, nothing perfect can last forever," I said.

"Whatever can you mean by that?" Colin asked.

"The Queen wants to see the boys," I said. "It is all my mother's doing, of course, and she swears it was only because she thought it would do Her Majesty a world of good to get out of Windsor for a short while."

"The Queen is coming to Anglemore?" The look of abject horror on my husband's face was priceless.

"Not until after Christmas," I said. "There is plenty of time to prepare."

"Madam, I —" Davis could hardly form a coherent word.

"Don't worry, Davis," I said. "You've got Lily on your side."

"The Queen?" Lily's eyes looked as if they might pop out from her head.

"After Christmas," I repeated, smiling. No one would be thinking much about Lily's unfortunate experience now.

When we reached Anglemore, Mrs Elliott and the other inside servants were lined up to greet us, along with Johnny. Colin had wired ahead with the good news about Lily, and her colleagues were pleased to see her return. Mrs Elliott went so far as to embrace her. Prudence was already gone, on her way to school, where I hoped she would learn a better way to behave. Johnny could hardly meet Lily's eyes as she walked past him. She stopped and stood directly in front of him.

"I forgive you, Johnny," Lily said, "and I hope you can forgive what I've done."

"You didn't do nothing the rest of us wouldn't had we known what was happening," Johnny said. "You don't need forgiveness, Lily."

She gave him a weak smile and turned to make her way around the side of the house, presumably to the servants' entrance.

"No, Lily." Simon was standing in the shadows. I hadn't noticed him until he spoke. "Come through the front door."

Lily burst into tears and ran. I started after her, but Colin laid a hand on my arm.

"Let Simon go. It's only right."

Downstairs

xxii

Lily appreciated what everyone had done for her. Truly, she did, but that didn't stop her feeling sick the whole train ride back from London, and now, at Anglemore, she only felt worse. She couldn't bear to face Simon, not now that he knew the awful thing she had done. Even if he could forgive her that, she had lied, over and over. If only things had turned out differently at the abbey, if only her blow hadn't been lethal, then she might have had a chance at real happiness. Now, though, she didn't know what to do, so she ran away from everyone gathered at the front of the house and went around the back, past the French doors of the library and through the gardens until she reached the abbey. She hadn't gone there since that awful night, but now she felt she must, and she went straight back into the old church and knelt before its broken altar, praying for a forgiveness she did not feel she deserved.

She heard footsteps but did not turn to see who had followed her. It didn't matter, did it?

"Lily, my dear, please, please, you must let me forgive you." Simon's voice came from the opening in the wall where once there would have been a magnificent door.

Lily did not move to look at him.

"I have done unspeakable things," she said.

"You had no choice," Simon said. "You did what you had to do to save yourself." She could hear his footsteps, moving closer to her, and for the second time, a gentleman approached her from behind, unseen. Her heart pounded.

"I lied. That was a choice, and a bad one at that."

"You were scared."

"That's no excuse," Lily said.

"You're human." With gentle hands, Simon raised her from kneeling and turned her around to face him. "And I love you all the more for it."

"You can't possibly love me." Lily swallowed a sob, and her shoulders started to shake. She loved Simon. She knew that beyond doubt, but she did not deserve his love.

"I do, Lily, in a way I didn't know was possible for me. I love your strength. Most girls would have been too afraid to do anything but succumb to Scolfield's wicked will. You stood up for yourself."

"And murdered him."

"It was not murder, Lily," Simon said, touching her cheek very softly. "He brought it upon himself, and so far as I can tell, it was high time someone whacked him over the head."

"He didn't need to die."

"He wouldn't have if he had behaved like a gentleman. There's no use in dwelling on what happened, Lily. He put you in a diabolical situation and has no one to blame but himself for the outcome."

Lily looked away. "I should never have lied about what happened."

"No, perhaps not, but it is an understandable mistake. You were scared, and rightly so. In the end, no one innocent was charged with the crime, so no further harm was done."

"I despise myself for all of it."

"In time you will learn to forgive. For now, though, I need to know something else. You may despise yourself, but do you love me?" Simon asked.

She looked into his eyes and was overwhelmed by their warmth. "I do," she said. Her heart felt like it was melting.

"That makes this much easier," Simon said. He took her hands. "I cannot imagine a life without you."

"Now you're talking nonsense, Simon. Not only am I a maid, I killed a man. None of your friends would ever accept me, and there is —"

He silenced her with a kiss, and Lily knew in that instant that she would never be able to deny Simon anything he wanted.

"Emily has written to Mrs Hargreaves, her mother-in-law, who has offered to take you on as her companion when she sets up house in London. You won't be a servant any longer, and I shall be able to call on you . . . and court you."

"Court me?"

"How else do you expect me, eventually, to be able to convince you to marry me?"

"Marry you?"

"Surely you do not think me such a cad that I would have less than honorable intentions? The past must stay the past, Lily, and together we can build a future." He kissed her again, and Lily pulled away, unsure of what to do. "Allow yourself this happiness, my dear," Simon said, his voice full of such sincerity that Lily could do nothing but obey. She trembled, with fear and joy and relief and pain all rolled together, knowing she had no right to feel this happy, but unable to stop it all the same.

CHAPTER
TWENTY-THREE

Colin and I let Simon go after Lily. The staff stood agape until Mrs Elliott scolded them fiercely and ordered them back to work. We followed them inside and sought out Matilda and Rodney, who were waiting for us in the music room. Colin had wired them as well. I thought it best Lily not have to face Matilda straightaway, as I was uncertain how my friend would react to Sir James's decision. Happily for us all, she took it better than any of us could have hoped.

"I am disgusted by what Archie did," she said. "I would never have wished him dead — you know how I loved him, Emily — but I was also well aware of at least some of his faults. He was a complicated man, and, sadly, not complicated in a good way. He brought this violent death on himself. I feel more pity for that poor girl he attacked than I do for him. Perhaps that makes me a bad person . . ." Her voice trailed away.

"I won't try to convince you you're a good person," Rodney said, "but the bad in you doesn't stem from how you feel about this situation. Instead, I would suggest we think about some of your other qualities.

You are extremely bossy, Boudica, and I cannot help but notice that your staff live half in terror of you. I think —"

Matilda had gone bright red and looked as if she might explode. I turned to Colin, who nodded to the door. His hearing was sharper than mine. I hoped he had heard footsteps. The next instant Davis opened the door.

"Lord Flyte is in the white drawing room, sir, and would very much like to see you and her ladyship."

"Thank you, Davis," Colin said.

"I am not sure I have ever been more grateful for the opportunity to leave a room," I said as we made our way through the great hall. "They are likely to throttle each other." Davis opened the door to the drawing room, where we found not only Simon, but Lily as well, waiting for us.

"We've some news, Hargreaves," Simon said. He was grinning like a schoolboy, but his face was pale and he was bouncing ever so slightly on his heels. "I do hope you'll take it well." Lily was biting her lip so hard I was afraid it would bleed, and the handkerchief wrenched in her hands was in danger of being rent into pieces.

"Lily is leaving service, is she?" Colin asked, slapping his friend on the back. "Well done, old boy."

"You will accept the position with Mrs Hargreaves?" I asked.

"If she'll really have me, madam," Lily said. "It's too much, really, especially now —"

"You don't worry about any of that," Colin said. "My mother will take excellent care of you and mince anyone who dares bring up this incident."

Unlike my mother, I thought, wondering what she would do at this news.

"I shall be traveling to London on a regular basis now," Simon said, "and may even be forced to do the Season."

"You are happy, aren't you, Lily?" I asked, crossing to her and taking both of her hands in mine.

"Yes, madam, very, very happy," she said, "although I don't think I will ever believe I deserve it."

"This is a wonderful thing. I am delighted for you both, as I am certain the future holds much happiness for you. We ought to celebrate." I rang for Davis. "We need champagne — the Bollinger — and Alice sent up at once. Glasses for you and Alice as well, Davis."

"Madam, I will of course gladly bring the champagne, but I do not know that it would be appropriate —"

"Do not argue with me, Davis. I can be quite fierce, you know."

"I insist, Davis," Colin said. "We both should know by now not to cross my wife."

"Very good, madam, sir." He nodded at each of us.

"And bring in Lady Matilda and Lord Montagu, Davis," I said. I could see Lily tense.

"I don't think Lady Matilda will much want to see me," she said.

"I have already apprised her of the details of what happened," I said. "You have nothing to fear."

Matilda proved the point to Lily at once upon entering the room. She went directly to Lily. "I am so humbly sorry for what you suffered at my cousin's hands," she said. "Please believe I had no inkling as to that side of his character."

"It is I who must apologize to you," Lily said. "I did a terrible thing."

"It is your intent that matters most to me, Lily," Matilda said, "and I do not believe in the slightest that you meant to kill him."

"I didn't." Tears were starting again. Simon passed her a handkerchief to replace the one she had all but shredded before.

"We will have none of that," he said. "This is a celebration."

"What are we celebrating?" Matilda asked.

"Love," I said.

"Rodney, you beast," Matilda said, smacking him soundly on the arm. "I very specifically told you I wanted to speak to Emily myself. This does not bode well in the least for our marriage. We're engaged less than a day and you're already ignoring my wishes?"

"You are engaged, Matilda?" I asked. "To Rodney? How is this possible? You despise each other."

"I always despised him more than he despised me," Matilda said. "Never, ever, forget that."

"I realized that I have never before so enjoyed bickering with someone so much as I do my darling Boudica," Rodney said. "She was dead set on leaving Montagu for London, so I realized the only way to make her stay was to marry her."

"It will be a dreadful bore, of course," Matilda said, "and I don't want to have to spend the rest of my life reminding you my name is not Boudica."

"Whatever you wish." Rodney slipped his arm around her waist and gave her a kiss on the cheek.

"Emily, are you telling me Rodney said nothing to you about our engagement?" Matilda asked.

"Not a word," I said.

"Then how did you know we had occasion to celebrate?"

"We didn't know the two of you required celebrating. Lily is leaving service to become companion to an extremely great lady, which means, of course, that Simon will be able to court her."

"Lily! What a delightful surprise," Matilda said, hesitating for only the barest second before stepping over to kiss both her cheeks. "You deserve happiness, especially after all that happened to you."

"I am delighted for you, Lily," Rodney said. He slapped Simon on the back. "You must be awfully pleased."

Davis returned with Alice and the champagne. Alice wrapped Lily in an embrace and then stood behind her, hanging back from the group, obviously feeling out of place. Colin went to her and started chatting with her about the weather, a topic near and dear — not to mention unthreatening — to the heart of every person in England. Davis had just popped the cork on the first bottle when my mother came into the room.

"This is unexpected," she said. Her eyes fell on Lily, and then on Simon standing in such very close proximity to the girl. "What is going on here?"

374

"Lady Bromley." Colin crossed to her and took her by the arm. "I should like to have a private discussion with you. Would you come with me?"

A nervous silence fell over our happy group during their absence. They returned no more than a quarter of an hour later, but every minute had seemed like an hour.

"I understand you will be leaving service," my mother said, standing directly in front of Lily.

"I am indeed, Lady Bromley," she said.

"I wish you much luck in your next endeavor, and do hope you always remember from whence you came." I scowled at her as she gave Lily a strained smile and shook her hand, but did not address her any further. "I am informed congratulations are in order, Lord Montagu."

"I'm a lucky man to land Boudica," he said and kissed his bride-to-be full on the lips.

"Lord Montagu!" My mother stepped back, horror on her face. "Such behavior does not behoove a peer of the realm. Perhaps you have spent too many years in the New World. I shall have to take you under my wing. You will come to me first thing tomorrow morning and we shall have a little chat."

"Yes, Lady Bromley." Rodney grinned. "I look forward to it."

"And you, dear Matilda." My mother gave her a little hug. "I am so pleased you will not have to leave Montagu. A very wise decision on your part, and a mature one. Affection may come with time." She lowered her voice to a whisper with the last sentence.

Matilda did her best to hide her laughter behind her hand.

Davis poured the champagne, and we toasted. The first bottle was quickly drained. Once he had opened the second bottle, I pulled my husband aside.

"Whatever did you say to make my mother behave so well?" I asked. "She cannot be even remotely prepared to accept Lily as your mother's companion, especially as she must have figured out the girl will eventually marry Simon."

"She was onto that at once," Colin said, "and quite upset until I told her that when the aristocracy proved themselves capable of embracing the social changes sure to come I might — just might — be prepared to reconsider the Queen's offer of a dukedom. Particularly if she made sure that no one — no one — heard about Lily's involvement in Montagu's death."

"You did no such thing!"

"I did."

"And she believed you?" I asked.

"My dear, I have never seen her look happier."

"You're in a spot of trouble now," I said. "You tell her this and the Queen's coming to visit? You'll be a duke before you know it."

"Not at all, my darling girl," he said. "I said *might*. No promise was made."

"My mother has got her way in situations where she had far less than a 'might' going for her. Prepare yourself, Your Grace. I fear your future as a commoner is very much at stake."

"Not to mention our marriage," he said. "I remember once, years ago, your mother was bent on seeing you a duchess, and you told her in no uncertain terms you would never be the wife of a duke."

"Quite right. I remember it well. Now here you are, about to become a duke. I suppose I shall have to divorce you." I sighed. "What a pity. I have grown awfully fond of you, you know."

"If you feel that way, there is only one way for me to proceed," he said.

"What is that?" I asked.

"I cannot allow you to divorce me, so you shall have to brace yourself, my dear, as I am once again on the verge of refusing a generous offer from the Queen. Her visit to Anglemore is bound to be deeply unpleasant for everyone involved."

"Particularly now that we have lost the one member of the household capable of adequately preparing the State Rooms," I said. "I don't suppose we could disappear to the villa in Greece for the foreseeable future and pretend we had forgotten the visit altogether?"

"All we can hope, my dear, is that my work sends us abroad before the Queen is ready to travel."

"Paris," I said. "Paris is lovely this time of the year. Surely, my dear, you can find at least one expat aristocrat there in dire need of your specialty, the sort of assistance that requires more than a modicum of discretion?"

"For you, my darling girl, I will find a hundred." He pulled me close to him and kissed me. I was lost in the deliciousness of the moment when I felt something sharp prodding my back.

"Heavens, Mother," I said, "don't you know it is bad manners to use a parasol in the house? That is something that would never be tolerated at Anglemore Park."

She frowned, but lowered the parasol. It was a small victory, yet one I would gladly take.

WOLF WINTER

Cecilia Ekback

There are six homesteads on Blackåsen Mountain. A day's journey away lies the empty town. It comes to life just once, in winter, when the Church summons her people through the snows. But now it is summer, and new settlers have come. It is their two youngest daughters who find the dead man. Their father is away. And whether stubborn, or stupid, or scared for her girls, their mother will not let it rest. From the wife who's unconcerned when her husband is absent for three days, to the man who laughs when he hears his brother is dead, to the priest who doesn't care, she asks and asks her questions, digging at the secrets of the mountain. They say a wolf made those wounds. But what wild animal cuts a body so clean?

THE WOMAN WHO WALKED
IN SUNSHINE

Alexander McCall Smith

Mma Ramotswe is reluctantly persuaded by Mr J. L. B. Matekoni to take a holiday from her detective work. But she finds it impossible to resist the temptation to interfere with the cases taken on by her co-director — secretly, she intends. This leads her to delve into the past of a famous man whose reputation has been called into question, and to join forces with a new assistant detective, Mr Polopetsi. While "on holiday", Mma Ramotswe also manages to help a young boy in the search for his missing mother; and then of course there is the agency's arch-enemy, Violet Sephotho, scheming to set up a rival secretarial college. In the end, Mma Ramotswe finds that a little trust goes a long way, especially when it comes to having confidence in her dearest friends and colleagues.